BLACKWOOD

Count of Bahvil

H. Sulfwin

TERRASECT

Published by Terrasect

Terrasect
PO BOX 3723
Norwich/NR7 7FA
www.terrasect.net

Book Layout © 2017 BookDesignTemplates.com

Blackwood: Count of Bahvil by H. Sulfwin. -- 1st ed.
ISBN 978-1-83924-101-7
Hardback ISBN 978-1-83924-001-0
eBook ISBN 978-1-83924-102-4

For Grandad,
If I don't see you through the spring, I'll see you through the fiction

875, 3RD Era

It was a rather wet and windy day that changed the direction of things. It came not two weeks since Mazog's sister, Maralin, had come to stay, and all those bar the day she had arrived the weather had been equally poor, even if it did seem to worsen a little each day. The trouble was, as Mazog was half-Orc he could take to the frost and bad weather like a fat man takes cake, forgetting that the rest of us – including his non-Orc sister – do not like to do so, despite our furred clothes; no matter how alluring the wilderness around our home was.

I must admit, we were such an unlikely bunch; an Imperial, a Nord, a half-orc and his half-Nord, half-Imperial sister, and an Agrian. Yes, I know, more people than I've mentioned, but all in good time...you want to know now? Okay fine, if I must.

Mazog, as you know, is a half-orc, who is generally wise beyond his years; he is strong and a fearsome fighter who's wits are as sharp as his sword, and has his mother's radiant blue eyes, and the almost grey skin and large canine teeth of his Orcish father. His sister Maralin was...I mean is a fair haired and pretty lass (who seemed to have the strangest ability to grab my attention at the most inopportune times; often having the effect of causing me to be unable to speak in normal sentences). The Nord, Zaxx, is quite the strapping lad you would expect from the north; tall, rustic-brown hair swept back over the ears, and eyes that seem to pierce through your very being. Tau, our Imperial friend (who has just kindly offered me a steak of wild boar, I might add), is rather...curious; he speaks softly and his mannerisms portray him as the artful type, and admittedly this is true to some extent, however, he is a giant of a man and truly a hunter, one anyone would be glad to have by their side in battle or out in the wilds (I mean, who else would chase after bandits wielding a warhammer, hurling abuse at them?). That just leaves me, the Agrian. "Lizard" as ignorant folk call me. But enough of the introductions; I believe you began reading this for the story, and not general chatter.

So where were we? Oh yes, I remember...

It wasn't as if the day had been unlike any other, but there was a sense of foreboding; it's hard to explain really, but it was something in the air, something not quite noticeable playing on the back of the mind.

We had spent the earlier parts of the day practicing archery indoors (our home had quite a long, if narrow, cellar), whilst

Maralin and Mazog had been out shopping for silks for her sewing; although upon their return, Maralin put us all to shame with her aim.

In the evening we spent time between being in the tavern and harassing the local eijit, Tomm Mcorkell, a drunkard who hurled abuse at nearby people, and was generally disliked by all. I personally found it particularly amusing to throw apples at him; not sure why though.

As we sat at our usual table, with an extra chair for Maralin, we talked about our past adventures.

"...and you fell in that ant mound? Ha-ha, priceless" Maralin laughed heartily.

"Hey! I can't help remembering you pushed me" Zaxx replied.

"Course she did" Tau scoffed "how much mead had you had by then? Five bottles, six?"

"That ain't enough to make me stumble" he boasted as he took a swig from his frothy tankard.

Maralin and Tau just laughed at that.

"Another pitcher Jesel" Mazog called to the barmaid as he drained the last drip from our now emptied one, then turned back to us "You guys remember when we helped Leonard with that missing livestock case?"

"Aye, what a game that was" I replied, giving a small chuckle at the memory "To think a rival farmer would try to frame his brother-in-law."

"Yeah, but it's the *how* of the way he did it that gets me" Zaxx laughed as he shook his head.

"Here you are fellas" Jesel announced as she placed the pitcher in the centre of the table "Maralin, I meant to ask when you came in, how is Norindale?"

"Oh, beautiful as ever Jess" Maralin chimed, eager to tell her friend of home "and there's this new forest city the High King is having built at the base of the Norain Mountains; I saw the caravans of obsidian and granite being shipped when I travelled back to Blackwood."

"A forest city?" Zaxx asked "You left that out when you first arrived."

"No, you were drunk" she turned back to Jesel "And you'll be pleased to know that they solved the crop failures."

"Oh that's a relief to hear" she said, picking up the empty pitcher "I was worried what would become of them when winter struck."

"Aye, we all were" Mazog added.

"So a forest city then?" Jesel asked, mulling the thought over "I like the sound of that, although it must be costing the King a lot of coin to do that right."

"That's Nords for you" Tau said quietly "always eager to spend the coin when times are good."

"Aye" Jesel giggled "Well, give us a shout if you need any more mead" and with that she got back to tending the bar.

It was a few hours later, after Maralin had retired for the night, Mazog having followed after her, or rather staggered out after her (after several failed attempts to walk out of the door), when I was getting the thirteenth...no forte....no wait...the sixteenth tankard of mead for both myself and Tau – whilst Zaxx was out of it, lying unconscious, half on the table and half pirouetting with his chair – that a man, in what looked like a black and grey robe – though my sight was so blurred it could have been pink and green – approached me about Maralin, myself and our little group. It was hard to focus on what he had been saying – was saying I mean – but I managed to gather the words: "...three   of you...Blackwood...assistance...boar...recommended...month minimum...five thousand gold coins...delicate nature..." I shut off after that last bit.

The next thing I recall is waking in front of the fire, with a headache that would cripple a mammoth, to the sight of Maralin sewing, Zaxx vomiting (it later became apparent he had somehow managed to keep drinking) and Mazog sharpening his short-sword, with Tau not being anywhere in sight. Just as I was about to query his whereabouts, I heard cursing and the ever familiar sound of a warhammer, not merely crushing, but destroying bone; I had no doubt that he had found another giant rat.

"Good morrow my friend" called Mazog, noticing my consciousness as he shuffle our pack of cards.

"Good morrow" I replied; I must admit, I was partly sarcastic in my tone, but he didn't seem to notice this.

Zaxx had stopped vomiting long enough to bring me some bread and cheese, as the rest of them had had their fill already. I thanked him as he rushed back to the bowl he had been emptying last night's mead into. As I ate, I could not help but feel troubled, but not know why, only then to get distracted by Maralin.

I watched her hands move as she sewed. How delicate her fingers worked! I could not help my eyes drift up her arms and to her face; and how I paid attention to her expression, one of calm focus and bliss. Her green eyes, how they were illuminated by her green satin and golden silk dress, and how every curl in her hair had its own persona.

My bit of daydreaming was cut short by a quick and sharp rapping on our door.

Having just finished breakfast, I went to open it, and as I did, I was greeted at first by a friendly gesture of hands, which then quickly changed to a scornful look of disgust as the visitor gained full view of me, withdrawing his hand also.

Mazog was quick enough to retort for me.

"You look as though you've had a night with a lustful sow stranger."

The man, who was short and a strange, creepy fellow, replied to this quite well I think, giving him a sneering look before speaking; though it sounded as if he were reciting from a scroll.

"I am Blake"-his voice sounded gruff, as if he had gone ten rounds in the arena-"I have been sent by Count Balford's Aid..."

"Please get to the details." I'll admit it was rather rude, but people like Blake aggravated my just by being there.

"Silence lizard"-normally I would have cut him for that, but I feared his blood would spurt onto Maralin's embroidery and stain it-"my business does not concern you, I am here to collect Tau, Maralin and-"

"What?" Maralin said quizzically, in quite a surprise as she lifted her head from her sewing. I had perked up, remembering scarcely what I had spoken of to that man in the tavern.

"Tell me, Blake, the Count's Aid, does he happen to wear a black and grey robe, with an emerald crest upon it?" I queried, with an essence of satisfaction (although I have no idea as to how I remembered even those details). He gave me a somewhat worried, quizzical look.

"Yes...how did you know?" he had refrained from calling me lizard that time, though that was probably due to an element of dread as to what I would say next.

"I made the...business deal, with him personally"-oh the look on his face was a picture-"and I believe I requested time to discuss with my associates."

I'll admit it, I had no idea what we discussed in the tavern, but guessed this Blake fellow wouldn't know either.

"Very well" he gritted "I shall return with the Count's Aid and coach, soon."

Closing the door as he departed, I turned to the others, and to yet another greeting; this time one of the same uniform expression of 'What have you done *this* time?'

To this I replied, quite apologetically:

"I have absolutely no damn idea."

* * *

It turned out that I had, firstly, somehow managed to convince the Count's Aid that Maralin could teach the Count's niece embroidery – as I say, not sure how I managed that, I didn't know he had a niece at the time – and that he had approached me in order to gain my services, and as such the services of our group in the form of personal guard, to both him and his niece, and to deal with a, quote, "sensitive" investigation.

Our journey to Bahvil had been largely uneventful, although we did get better acquainted with Doncaster – the Count's aid – when we made stops for eating and sleeping; Blake however, stayed quiet and distant (which, to be honest, I was thankful for). Having taken three days, we finally arrived and drove through the main roads towards Bahvil Castle.

As the coach moved across the cobbled streets towards Count Balford's estate, I could not help but notice the inhabitants of Bahvil. I will quickly tell you that Bahvil is thirty leagues from Blackwood, which I guess is why the people look so...quaint. They were dressed more smartly than I was accustomed to, but not so much for us to stand out like a sore thumb. There were many taverns and inns, as well as shops and merchant houses with goods and services ranging from fine jewellery and silk clothes to armorers and apothecaries; the streets themselves decorated with various flowering shrubs and plants that fed Bahvil's famous honey farms.

Maralin had looked somewhat glum for most of the journey; that quickly changed when she noticed the 'culture' (as she put it) that flowed through Bahvil. It was nice to see her smile. Tau had fallen asleep before we even got to Bahvil and wasn't likely to wake even if the coach were to set on fire and crash (though if he caught the scent of succulent meat or fine eggs, however, it would be a different story).

I guess you're wondering about Zaxx and Mazog, right? Well they were with us too; Mazog was sat next to his sister, looking protective (truth is, he was liable to rip the arm off any man who got near her and beat them to death with it) and giving me glances – he did this throughout the journey – that made me feel rather small, but then I guess I deserved it. Zaxx was doing what he did best when traveling: drink mead and sing badly.

As the coach pulled up through the castle's white painted cast-iron gate and across the courtyard, the castle came into full view. I must say, it was not the grey types one sees these days, but a brighter, almost white colour; with strong, solid oak doors and furnishings. It wasn't a large castle, but certainly wasn't small.

As the servants carefully took our belongings to our accommodation, we were led through the – rather grand – main entrance (the oak doors I mentioned), and through the Great Hall (I personally did not find it that great, tasteful with nice tapestries hung from the ceiling yes, but not great) and into the 'guests dining area', as our guide put it.

The Count, we were informed, had gone out hunting and was not expected back 'till the morrow. Needless to say, we had a hearty meal of fresh fish (Bahvil is near inland docks), salted bread and various fruits; which beats Mazog's stew any day.

Now our accommodation…that was interesting. We were in a moderately sized room – situated in the right wing of the castle – with plain green tapestries with oaky-red stitching. The interesting part was that, bar a door to the last quarter of the room, which had a king-sized bed and oak furnishings (by rights it should be classed as another room, but it's not my castle), we would have to sleep in the presence of one another. Needless to say, Maralin had the 'secondary' room to herself;

with the rest of us having screens to put up; not that it made any meaningful difference.

Perhaps I should explain; Zaxx snores, Mazog is prone to eating at the strangest hours (and the strangest things) and Tau is...okay, but I honestly prefer sleeping alone – with the odd exception – and I dislike undressing with others around.

***

Around midmorning we had breakfast with the Count. We were seated around the dark oak table, being served fresh raisin bread and spiced ham, with a choice of soup, waiting for the Count – his place at the table already made up – when he descended the stairs at the back-left of the room. I'll take the time to describe him to you: he wore an expression that was a strange mix of malice and kindness, his hair was mid-length, just that bit shorter than Zaxx's (with flakes of, not white, but almost a lemony colour amongst the brown), stern yet soft eyes, dark as the oak that made the furnishings around him. He was well built, and despite his age, looked quite youthful. Oh yes, he was wearing off-purple and white silks with gold jewellery encrusted with gems (you should have seen Maralin's face; she loved it).

"Good morrow to you all" His voice boomed across the whole room, perhaps the entire castle as well. Either way, we replied with a harmonious "Good morrow".

After a few short moments of awkwardness as he took his seat, we relaxed into conversation with the Count. He told us how his hunt had gone, Maralin inquired about his silk-ware and jewellery and so on. But the question remained, at least in my mind, what else did I agree to? What was this delicate investigation I remember being mention?

"I hear from my Aid that you and Tau are quite the team of hunters; tell me, what is your favourite prey?" The Count asked, turning the conversation more towards why we were here.

Something about how he asked the question troubled me, but I replied all the same; even if Zaxx looked mildly forlorn at the non-mentioning of his name.

"I would have to say...the Blackwood sickleback for sure" (Now for those who don't know, a sickleback is a six-to-seven foot tall, boar-like creature with curled horns pointing away from its face; it moves fast and tastes more like beef than boar).

"Interesting, interesting"-he seemed to be saying it more to himself than anyone else-"so do you think you can uphold your...work? That is serve as both my, and my niece's, personal guard?"

There was a small silence. Thankfully Zaxx started the conversation again.

"Trust me, they can fight as well as I drink."

The Count gave a small chuckle to this; which was good, it showed he had a sense of humour.

"So what of Zaxx and myself, of what work can we expect to be called upon to do?" Mazog, bless him; he was trying hard to 'talk proper'. The Count rubbed his chin thoughtfully before replying.

"The two of you"-as he spoke I could see the thoughts processing in his mind by the way his eyes shifted-"can expect to patrol Bahvil midweek, and to do and act as my Aid instructs."

It was odd. He went from casual to business-minded quite quickly, but moreover, I had the distinct feeling that being his personal guard was not going to be just that.

"Count Balford, may I enquire as to the subject of the delicate matter your aid mentioned when hiring us?" I asked.

The Count was looking down at his plate, cutting up a slice of ham with silver cutlery, taking his time to reply.

"As you say, it is a delicate matter, one that would be improper for us to discuss here" he responded finally "For now, all I shall say is that you shall be acting as an adviser of sorts, but rest assured, you shall find out soon enough" he gave what I assume was meant to be a reassuring smile before taking a bite of the ham.

"Of course" I smiled back, and returned to spooning leek and potato soup into my mouth as sophisticatedly as possible.

"So Maralin will be tutoring your niece the finer points of embroidery?" Mazog asked as Zaxx ripped some raisin-bread in half rather loudly.

"Yes, Doncaster told me your friend here was rather persuasive in the matter, not that it would take much; I have been saying she needs some of the more...feminine skills."

"Oh? How so?" Maralin asked innocently.

"She has always had an interest in the more laborious of skills, despite her delicate nature. It is good for her to do such things of course, but there are certain things they do not teach

which are expected from a noble lady" the Count seemed ruf-
fled by this so slightly it was easy to miss.

I continued to get a measure of him as our conversation continued, looking for subtle hints in his body language and
mannerisms. There was an air about him that gave me a slight
nagging sensation, despite the charisma he projected. It was
something in his eyes when he looked at Maralin, or talk came
close to his niece, something well hidden, a look I could not
quite place.

I really should have listened to that nagging feeling.

***

Nigh on a week had passed since our arrival, the Count had
permitted Maralin to go into the market district of Bahvil and
purchase needlework supplies – so long as she took Mazog with
her as a guard – and Zaxx was drinking with the Counts Aid; it
turns out he is quite a laidback and relaxed fellow – and Tau
was accompanying the Count's niece, who it turns out was also
quite pleasant.

Her name was Carmel, and was a bit younger than Maralin
(nearing her nineteenth year), and quite the sweet little thing;
she had brown, no, mahogany-brown hair with majestic curls
that gave the slightest hint of red in the right light, and vibrant
greeny-blue eyes. She seemed so innocent. It was strange, I had
but glimpsed her, yet something about her had captivated my
innermost thoughts, with the more I tried to think of other
things, the more she seemed to occupy my mind.

As for me, I was with the Count, finally revealing the nature of the 'delicate' situation.

We stood in his Meeting Hall, which doubled as a War Room in times of crisis and war, situated in the middle half of the left wing of the castle, around a large, heavy table ended by two smaller ones. The Count had organised the Captains of the guard, one for each city district, to discuss the 'situation'; the situation being the hunting down of a group of Agrian thieves, and their fences.

I should have known. Why else would a Count hire an Agrian?

Hire an Agrian to catch an Agrian. It's a sad truth, one that is all too commonplace. I could tell that although the various Captains were being polite and well-mannered, some had only a deep disgust for me and my presence. It wasn't personal, it's just my race; there was a lingering prejudice from a long forgotten and ancient conflict. Though few across the land held such a foul sentiment, those that did so held to it strongly, if not unshakably so, and were – to my knowledge – all of aristocratic Imperial decent.

The Count on the other hand, he was hard to read, but as far as I could tell at the time he had a neutral stance; there was no fondness nor hatred, just a mutual respect for me (or at least my skills) but that was it.

"Gentlemen, this here is our new Advisor on Agrian Affairs."

That's how he first introduced me to them.

'Agrian Affairs'.

Lovely.

It was the briefest of introductions before we got down to business. Laid out on the main table was a parchment map of the city, with various flagged pins showing recent places of incident.

"...and so it appears, Sire, that these incidents are the result of co-ordinated attacks by at least two different groups"-that intrigued me; Agrians, whilst respectful of other clans, don't like mixing groups-"and have had witness of Rejik taking known thieves into his home after sundown."

"Rejik?" I queried.

"An Agrian assistant of the merchant Belothor, he has two merchant houses he is caretaker of for him" answered one of the Captains.

"Belothor... yes, that would make sense" the Count mumbled, clearly planning as he rubbed his chin. He turned his head to me.

"What would you suggest?"

"I..."-I wasn't sure what to say at first, but then I had an idea-"I would suggest setting up a stall in the market. A stall with marked gold, placed"-I pointed to an area with the most flags-"here."

"And by what manner of good would that do?" scoffed one of the prejudicial Captains.

"A stall with gold will always be prone to thievery, and if your men have the right information, the gold will turn up in Rejik's place, assuming he is the leader."

"How can you be sure of this?" one of the Captains asked "how do you know they won't run and keep it for themselves?"

"Agrians, even those who are thieves, respect leadership. If you still have doubts, have some guards tail them in plain clothes."

I must admit, I don't follow that sentiment, well, not all the time.

"What would stop Rejik from storing the gold at one of Belothor's merchant houses?" queried the Captain from the Market District "We have had reports of Agrians not affiliated with Belothor going to and from his merchant houses."

"Why would he endanger his work with Belothor? He surely would wait until a point at which people are less likely to recognise the goods" I responded defiantly "And have you searched those buildings for stolen goods, or confirmed any of those particular Agrians as thieves?"

"I'm sure you understand the delicate, racial nature of this? How we cannot be seen to give a search warrant simply because some Agrians were seen near a point of interest?"

It was at this point the Count surprised me.

"Could a man be their leader?" he asked, breaking the conversation indifferently.

"Pardon?" I was taken aback by both the question and implied slight to my race.

"Could a non-Agrian be their leader?"

It was odd; at that moment there was a twinkle in his eye, one of cunning and ill intent.

It was quite unnerving, but still I replied, the Captains around me looking at him much the same way I did, only more confused by his suggestion.

"In theory, if he had earned their trust and partook of Agrian custom, yes"-I began to get that nagging feeling again-"do you not think Rejik to be their leader?"

"As Captain Bough said, there are at least two groups working together, and I've been acquainted with Rejik, he's smart, but not that smart."

The Captains agreed and started advising the Count on likely suspects, and I was excused. Typical. My race being denied even the intelligence to plan crime, although that's not a bad thing.

Is it?

Still, the meeting had left me confused; whilst my advice had indeed been asked, and it had been listened to, it was pretty menial, obvious even. I had yet to bring up the strangeness of two thief-clans working together, and when the real need for my mind arose, I was excused. Odd, to say the least. Though how the Captains agreed to the Count's idea without reliable evidence has to say something.

Not much happened after that, bar Maralin returning with some new silk-ware and more silk string for her embroidery, and Zaxx once again vomiting into a bucket (although this time it was accompanied by Mazog's singing, which would give most people reason to heave like the heavens).

Things were quiet the next couple of days too, as I was personal guard to Carmel. As we walked through the Rose Gardens, near the Plaza District and which ran all the way to the front of the city, it struck me she was quite a capable girl. Or

at least that was how it seemed by the way she talked and carried herself.

"…I even got to forge my own dagger at the smithy"-quite
proud of that she was-"I carry it with me always. Uncle warns
me to be careful though, says such things are too laborious 'for
one so frail'. Sometimes I think he fails to notice I've grown."

"Frail?" I asked, eyebrow raised "You seem strong enough to
me."

She gave a little laugh.

"That is high praise from an adventurer like you" she smiled.

Her voice was sweet and soft, but sometimes I got the feeling she was trying to flirt with me; though that could have just
been my ego.

"What is your full name Prime?" she asked as she picked a
white rose.

"I tend to not give that out to anyone, Lady Carmel."

"Am I just anyone?" she playfully feigned hurt as she wove
the rose into her hair.

As she did I noticed something of a resemblance to the
Count, not physically but in certain traits and mannerisms,
such as sweeping back her hair over her right ear.

It was while I was thinking on this that she threw her arm
around mine and clasped hold of my hand – I have to say, it
made me jump – before twirling around, facing right up
against me.

"May we dance?" her eyes sparkled with joyous energy, like
miniature stars, such that I could hardly refuse.

"If you insist my lady" I smiled.

"But it is only proper that both parties introduce each other before a dance, is it not?"

"Aye" I grinned, amused by this tactic "Aye it is."

With that I took a small step back and gave a little bow as I spoke.

"M'lady, may I, Sylon Primus Blackwood, have this dance?"

She gave a cute smile that wrinkled her nose, amused by my name.

"Why yes fine sir, you may dance with me, Lady Carmel Ur"- she gave a brief curtsy-"consider yourself honoured" she smirked.

So we danced amongst the vibrant blooms, attracting the attention of a wandering minstrel with a lute.

As we danced to his tunes and melodies, I took the time to study Carmel. Her wavy hair swayed smoothly through the air, yet stayed gently near, if not over, her shoulders. Her skin was pale, but only to a point at which her eyes, her green-tinted blue eyes, shone brightly, her darker hair glistening in the sunlight. Oddly enough, she reminded me of Maralin for a moment, especially as she was wearing a green and blue silk dress, its skirt flowing elegantly as she moved. And how she moved effortlessly, with such joy and...fondness? Was that the emotion I could see in her eyes?

But despite all this, I could not seem to read her, much like her uncle. In fact, I got the feeling that she, like the Count, had something...hidden; but something unlike which he was hiding. The thing is, as odd as it may sound, I got the sense that she was hiding a thought, an emotion; something that you could not explain even if you wanted to.

As we finished our dance I realised a small crowd of visitors to the Rose Garden had formed, with a few of them dancing round us, whom gave us a small but sincere applause, to which we gave a little bow, Carmel giggling as we did.

"First time for everything" I muttered.

"Oh? And here I thought you a professional showman" Carmel whispered, mock serious.

I found myself fond of her, for she was friendly and good natured, and she seemed to have taken me as a new friend.

"Shall we continue our walk m'lady?"

"Yes and no" she pulled me by the arm as she led me off "first we need to get some scones and cream from the Garden eatery."

"Will there be jams of some kind?" I asked, suddenly hungry.

"Oh my dear Sylon, more than you could count."

Thus began what was arguably the best luncheon in recorded history, even if all that jam gave me griping pains later on.

As we sat upon the finest chairs on the meadow-like lawn of the eatery, scoffing clotted cream coated scones adorned with all the jam one could reasonably get upon them, we shared a few laughs as I told her of my past adventures, and she shared a few anecdotes from her life growing up as a noble. Somehow she even managed to remain graceful despite getting a blot of jam on her nose, which I found cute.

"...and so that's the story of that" she ended one of her tales, taking a bite of a particularly large scone.

One of the eatery's waiters carried over another fine selection of jams, having spotted we were about to run out imminently.

Carmel thanked her politely, the waitress offering her a kind complement on her dress.

As she walked off I turned back to Carmel.

"The people genuinely care about you don't they?" I asked, reflecting upon all the interactions she'd had over the last few days.

She just gave a little shrug.

"I hope so."

I picked up one on of the pots of jam, attempting to read the tiny label.

"Cider apple jam?" I smirked "Best I don't tell Zaxx about this one"-I put the pot back down-"This how it is with all your guards?"

She shook her head, mouth full of cream and jam.

"No...no, not really" she wiped the corner of her mouth and grabbed her cup of cooled herbal tea "Just the ones that I find interesting."

"Oh, so I'm interesting am I? That'd be a first"-I pasted some of the thick cream onto the last blueberry scone-"So how many others have been interesting then?"

"Well"-she took a sip of tea-"you'd be the first, truth be told"-she paused a moment-"Well, it depends if you count Master Furgus."

"Master Furgus?"

"Right, you've never met have you?"- she gestured for the pot of cream on the far side of our little table as she put her cup down, and I obliged-"When I was younger he helped raise me, which is funny looking back, seeing how he is the castle blacksmith. Master Blacksmith, I should say; makes the best metalwork anywhere in the kingdoms so he says."

"The Count had you raised by a blacksmith?" I found it equal bits novel and amusing.

"It was not quite like that. I had maids and nannies, but Uncle was never really good with children, or had the time, so he had Furgus play the father figure, so to speak." She looked at me somewhat sombrely "See, Furgus is well respected and trusted like no one else in Bahvil, but he... he had lost his daughter, before I was born, and so Uncle knew he would always protect me."

I nodded silently, feeling awkward at having brought up the subject.

Sensing this, she gave me a smile and changed the subject.

"Gosh, would you believe how much we've eaten?"

"I know; feel like I might regret this later" I said holding my stomach "I feel I might just burst."

"Please don't" she asked "I would hate to have to replace you with another boring guard."

"Ha-ha...ouch" I laughed, my stomach feeling stretched by too much food.

"Probably best we take the long way back" Carmel said, getting to her feet "but first I must compliment the cook on such fine scones."

"And jams" I said, hefting myself up with some effort "One cannot forget the jams."

"Oh I won't" she chimed "I'll be dreaming of them tonight, especially that blueberry one."

"Who'd of thought this would be what I'd be doing as a personal guard to a Lady" I said as I caught her up.

"Well it's a good job you're interesting, else you'd have had to have watched me eat those scones all by myself" she mused.

"That's a bit cruel."

"But delicious."

I pondered on that a moment.

"...Yeah, it's hard to argue with that."

*

That night she dominated my thoughts more than Maralin had ever done. Her lustrous eyes had enchanted me, and there was no defence against it.

* * *

The morning after, however, was not so quiet. The band of Agrian thieves had struck – as I had expected they would – and had been followed back to one of Belothor's merchant houses; the one that Rejik lodged in.

The Count had ordered for his most loyal guards to be readied in case of such an event as this, and once the lookouts had reported this observation they descended upon the building like a locust horde with the precision of a longbow user, cutting down the few Agrian thieves that were there, with the exception Rejik. The rumour amongst the castle staff was that Rejik had been shouting his innocence, pleading that he did not know those Agrians; but what else would one do when caught?

What I didn't expect, strangely, was to be summoned by the Count to his court for Rejik's trial.

"Why'd the Count want you there?" Mazog asked as I got myself ready.

"Not sure; but this doesn't sit well with me."

"Oh?"

I turned to face him, looking away from the small mirror in our room.

"He was only apprehended today, and I have yet to even interrogate him."

"Are they going to let you?"

"..."

"Prime?"

I took a deep breath, rubbing my eyes as I did.

"Mazog, I get the distinct feeling that I'm only involved to put a reputable Agrian face on the side of the prosecution."-I took a seat on my bed-"I mean, look, first we have that meeting with the Captains of the Guard, and what? I say the most basic of things – things they should have been doing anyway – and then I'm excused before any further details are discussed. And now I don't even get to interrogate a star suspect to see if the problem runs deeper" I near shouted as my exasperation finally showed itself.

"Prime"-Mazog grabbed my hand-"Perhaps you're right. Perhaps the only reason you were hired was to make the Count look good, maybe that's why you were assigned to guard his niece as well; make people say 'oh, the Count lets a Agrian guard his niece? He cannot be prejudiced against them'-"

"Is this supposed to be helping?" I interrupted him.

"Point is, five thousand gold coins split between us will go a long way, so if it's just a case of the Count looking good you keep going along with it."

"But what if there's more?"

He looked at me dead in the eye, and gave a reassuring smile.

"Then I would tell you to listen to your instinct; it's never failed us yet."

I gave a small nod and got back to adjusting my clothes in the mirror. Mazog stared at me, waiting a moment.

"...is there anything more going on?" he asked eventually.

"Well I don't know that there is" I replied as I buttoned up my collar "But this *investigation*, it stinks of worse, something corrupt. I mean, why not arrest all the thieves they found when they apprehended Rejik?"

"True, they did have them seriously outnumbered" Mazog pondered my assertion.

I brushed down my cloths one final time before making to leave for the trial.

"I think I'll request we catch another thief to interrogate and see how the Count and Captains respond" I said as I opened the door, looking back at Mazog as I did.

"You just let us know if...well you know; we'll have your back."

"I know" I smiled, closing the door behind me.

As I walked down the hallway towards the Court Hall, I pondered the rumour of Belothor making an appearance. Was he to appear as a witness, to bargain for Rejik, or just to spectate? I could not dare to guess.

Just before I entered the hall I caught Captain Bough talking to one of the jail guards.

"Captain Bough" I called "Might I have a word before the trial?"

He hurried off the guard then looked to me.

"Yes, yes of course Prime; but it'll have to be quick."

I should mention that Bough was one of the Captains that was not prejudiced against Agrians, and actually seemed to like or respect me.

"Good, I was wondering if we will be interrogating Rejik at all?"

Bough looked at me puzzled.

"His trial is about to begin."

"Yes, but he could have information on the thief-clans; or rather he should if he's guilty."

Bough mulled it over, before stepping close as to whisper.

"Prime I respect you, I hope you know that. But the other Captains – not all of them – they...take issue with an Agrian interrogating another Agrian."

"And you?"

"Pardon?"

"Do you feel that sentiment also?" I asked sternly.

"Of course not, no sensible person would think like that. I'm just saying it would be difficult."

"May I make a suggestion?"

"Sure" he gestured.

"What if we captured one of the thieves? Could you convince the other Captains that it would be a good idea for me to interrogate one?"

He rubbed his chin thoughtfully.

"Maybe. I give you my word I'll try."

"Thanks Bough...would it help if I brought this up with the Count too?" I asked.

"I wouldn't, not that the Count feels...*that* way, just that the other Captains would start...being awkward."

"Understood" I nodded "Should we go in?"

With that we entered the Court Hall – which was essentially a part the Great Hall separated by architecture – and as we did, one could not help but feel the atmosphere, one of disgust and loathing, yet somehow stricken with fear. Gathered were a number of people, including the Speaker – an official who done everything a judge would do bar the sentencing and final word – who was standing to the left of the Count's throne, subtly reading the scroll of charges. At the sides of the hall stood members of the court, all in their finery, eagerly watching and waiting, like ravenous vultures, muttering to themselves. I chose to think most of them were like this because they hated crime and criminals, and not the fact that they got to punish an Agrian.

I took my place next to Bough and another Captain on the opposite side of where we had come in, catching a glimpse of Belothor as I looked around the room, and as I did the room fell into a respectful silence as the Count entered and walked to his throne.

"This court is now in session" he proclaimed, almost disinterested in tone, as he took his seat.

With this the speaker began reading from his scroll as Rejik was literally dragged by his chains to the steps below the Count's throne.

"Rejik of Dairkwood, you stand charged with making dealings with thieves and organising their group, aiding the corruption that has begun to infect our beloved city. It is here you will be given judgement by our Count before the members of his court. What say you?" the Speaker boomed.

I pitied Rejik. The barbaric way in which he was brought to court had shocked me, and the almost gleeful look in the eyes of some members of the court was deeply unsettling; it was the first time that I had seen them in a truly ill-light, their prejudice openly displayed.

Rejik had clambered to his knees.

"I..."-the poor man struggled to form words-"I ca...I...was..."

He shifted his head back towards the floor and sobbed, shaking his head; I could see tears rolling down his face.

The Count's expression was...terrifying. Cool and collected, yet menacing, anger clearly lying behind his eyes. He did not move his gaze from Rejik; he did not move at all.

"With the accused failing to provide a statement of defence, it is by the power granted by this court and its people, that Count Stanlious Balford shall now pass judgment, which shall be exact and final."

The Count then then rose from his seat, an air of distain emanating from him.

"Scum like you are poison, infecting not just our city, but all the cities in the land"-the distain in his voice, it cannot be described, only experienced-"thus your judgement is this: Execution, which shall take place a fortnight hence, where you shall be hung until you are dead; 'till then you shall spend your last days held in the darkest depths of the castle dungeon so you cannot see the miracle that is daylight."

Rejik burst into uncontrollable tears; though his cries were more like shrieks. What was odd was that Belothor had stood silent, not even changing his expression, which was like that of many other onlookers, of disgust. What was odd about that was, he wasn't looking at Rejik – as one would imagine – but at the Count. As Rejik was dragged off and the court began to disperse (after applauding the Count), I caught something out of the corner of my eye; something that made me question Rejik's guilt.

Count Balford smiled.

***

As I took a stroll around the top floor of Castle Bahvil, thoughts of the previous day's events on my mind I came across Carmel looking out at the city below.

I asked her what she thought of those with a prejudice against Agrians the Count kept around him.

"It makes me uncomfortable, even before I met you" she said "Uncle says it is best to keep such people close, so you can keep an eye on them and stop them from doing something rash, but I don't know. They are so few, and without his attention they would quickly find themselves without power, so I wonder how sound his logic is."

"So not all of Bahvil is against Agrians then?" I asked, half joking, half not.

"Of course not"-she gave me a gentle shove-"the people of Bahvil only care how decent someone is, and not much else. But those sycophants Uncle keeps near him, I dare say they are the last few of that disturbed mind-set in our land."

"Sycophants? I didn't know the aristocratic class were so out of favour with you."

"It's only about twenty of them" she rolled her eyes as she spoke "and they're mostly old anyway."

"Fair enough" I said, gazing back out the arched window she had been looking through when I came across her.

We looked out at the city in a calm silence together, our hands not quite touching.

"When I'm Countess, there will be none of that nonsense I assure you" she smiled "And a lot more feasts of scones in the Rose Gardens too" her voice chimed in a fun, mock serious way at that last bit.

"I'll hold you to those scones."

"I hope you do."

* * *

A week and a day had passed since Rejik's trial, and I found myself once again acting as Carmel's personal guard during the day. She had no studies due to the Solstice Dance being sched-uled for the evening, and no formal appointments either. We had started the day late, but began by seeing the castle Blacksmith, who had recently set up a new smithy, which was to be managed by his old apprentice, in the city's Temple District. As we arrived we could see could see him and his apprentice carrying in a recently delivered order of unrefined ore.

"Master Furgus!" Carmel called to him, picking up her pace as she waved to him.

He turned to face her, holding his arm above his eyes to shield them from the sun, a big smile growing on his face as he saw her.

"M'lady" he called back in greeting, a small chuckle shaking his bristly, curled beard "How many times must I ask you to just call me Furgus?"

"Then what would be the point of having the title of a master blacksmith?" she joked.

"So to what do we owe this pleasure?" he asked as he put down a lump of ore he had been holding.

"Thought we'd see how the new place was coming along, perhaps get a few tips whilst we're here" she replied soothingly as she looked over the lumps of rock, marvelling at the thought of turning them, crafting them, from broken cobles to shining steel.

"If m'lady is offering to do me work for me, who am I to stop her?" Agatha – the apprentice – laughed as she dusted her hands off on a grey rag "This that new soldier boy you spoke of Carmel?" she asked, nodding at me.

Carmel blushed a little.

"Hush you" she said, trying to conceal her mild embarrassment "Besides, you're not really a soldier are you Prime?"

"Soldier, guard, what's the difference?" Furgus asked, helping steer the conversation away from whatever Agatha had let
slip.

"Truthfully I'm not either, sir."

"Oh, how so?" he asked as he hefted a small crate of ore off
the ground "Don't suppose you'd like to help Agatha?"

Agatha rolled her eyes and grabbed the other side of the
crate.

"You're getting old, old man."

"The cheek of this one" he scoffed.

Carmel gave a small giggle, now looking at the unlit forge.

"Well" I began "the Count hired me for my...expertise, as he
put it."

The blacksmiths emptied the ore into a metal bin of sorts
used to sieve out impurities and such (I confess I'm not too sure
what they were, but this is what I understood from what Carmel explained to me).

"I fail to see the difference lad" Furgus exhaled as he wiped
his brow.

"It's to do with the spate of thievery plaguing the city" Carmel chimed nonchalantly "So he's more of an investigator of
sorts."

"Lady Carmel, I have orders not to divulge-"

"You can trust Furgus, Prime...and Agatha, on her good
days."

"Be glad you have noble blood lass, or I'd whip your hide for
that" Agatha laughed, half serious.

"You don't follow etiquette much do you?" I smiled, more of
an observation than a question.

"Only during weddings or funerals mister Prime" Furgus replied "that or when the Count is showing us off to the High King's Generals and the like."

"See, that's why they're some of my favourite friends...well, almost my only real friends" she strode up beside me "See this ore?"

She held in her hand a small, rust coloured rock that held small veins of shining gold.

"This is a form of iron, called pyrite, it's quite common up in the mountains around here"-she handed it to me to feel the weight of it-"Furgus told me that in the old, old past, its colour made people think it was gold."

"Caused a whole lot of trouble when they realised their mistake" Furgus continued, Agatha going inside the main building for some errand or another "but by then it was too late."

"Too late?" I asked handing the ore back to Carmel.

"Aye; see people travelled from all over to here in hopes of gaining enough riches to set their families up for life, and they built up a large town that grew larger every day. A whole way of life, built upon a lie no one even knew wasn't true"-he took the ore from Carmel-"Would you like me to save this for you to forge my dear?"

"If you wouldn't mind Furgus, I have a good feeling about that one."

"I'm sure you do" he chuckled.

"So, what happened in the end, once everyone figured out it was iron, not gold?" I asked, curious of the history.

"Ah, well" he began as he wrapped the piece of ore in cloth and stuck a note to it "by then a whole economy and community had been forged – no pun intended – and the iron did turn out to make particularly high quality steel, so after some...disruption, to put it mildly, the people worked to make the town a trading hub; which was doable thanks to Lake Poyal and the rivers that come and go from it."

"Which is where Bahvil gets its name" Carmel added "Bahvil; it means 'lying steel'."

"I would never have guessed" I said crossing my arms.

"Well, consider that a lesson lad; there's always more to something than how it looks on the surface."

Something about that statement seemed particularly apt to me.

Carmel went inside to see how the new build was looking on the inside, and see what Agatha was working on. I was about to follow her in when Furgus stopped me.

"Hold a minute lad" he said, placing one hand on my shoulder "I care deeply for that girl, as if she were my own. I've seen her grow from a wee bairn to the fine young lady she is today."

"I can see that by how you act around her; your mannerisms betray you" I smiled.

"Ah, I'm sure they do. But listen here, and listen well; I don't know you, although you seem the honourable sort by how you carry yourself, but you come from Blackwood–"

"How did...? Oh, Carmel told you" I interrupted, before remembering Agatha's question.

"You come from Blackwood" he carried on "and I know you folk tend to be...to be...quite promiscuous"-he looked at me sternly, and I could see his soul in his eyes-"if you hurt her, or mess her around–"

"I understand Furgus, you have my word-"

"-I'll put you in the forge."

We stared at each other in silence a moment before Furgus broke it with a bellowing laugh.

"The look on your face lad...priceless."

"Furgus, remind me to never get on your wrong side."

*

We stayed with them for an hour or so, talking about the forge and how Furgus single-handedly forged the swords for the whole castle garrison, before making our way back through the Plaza District to visit its various fountains and statues before we returned to Castle Bahvil.

"Lady Carmel?"

"Please, just call me Carmel, Prime" she chimed.

I felt myself blush, though I'm not sure why.

"Okay; Carmel, if it's not too bold a question to ask, what happened to your birth parents?"

She went silent for a moment, somewhat taken aback by the question, but not offended as far as I could tell.

"It is a sad story Sylon, are you sure you want to hear it?"

"Yes, of course, but do not feel obliged to satisfy my curiosity if it will upset you."

"No, it does not upset me, it is just... so very sad. But thank you for your concern" she smiled, playfully playing off a barely concealed sense of loss, taking a little breath before speaking "My father was killed in a hunting accident, not four days before I was born. Poor Blake had tried to save him, but alas..."

"I'm sorry."

She gave a little laugh.

"Why, were you there?" she chuckled "Sorry if that seems dark; I just figure laughing is better than crying sometimes."

"I get that."

"So, four days after the accident, I'm born, and my mother is all conflicted with sadness and joy, but also even more sadness because of the joy."

"Is she...I mean, I've not seen or heard..."

"No...a week after I was born she threw herself from the southern balcony...or fell due to a loose tile. It's hard to tell, so they tell me."

"I...I don't know what to say" I fumbled.

"Do not worry about what words to say. It is a sad thing that belongs in the past. Nothing we can do about it now." She mused thoughtfully "My handmaid tells me that it is spoken of as 'the tragedy of Lady Amilia' amongst the common folk; perhaps that's why they all treat me so...kindly."

I looked at her, carefully regarding how intelligent and thoughtful she was for one so young. I felt sad for her, never having the love of a mother, or the guiding eye of her father. She had her uncle, and Furgus, looking out for her, but it's not exactly the same is it?

"Hold my hand" she said.

"M'lady?"

"My hand. Hold it."

I obliged, gently wrapping my fingers around her delicate, soft skin.

She gave a smile.

Then a laugh.

"What's so funny?" I asked as I found myself smiling uncontrollably.

"Oh, just thinking how the folk coming to the Solstice Dance would disapprove and gossip at the sight of us" she sighed "We should do this more often."

I stopped and looked at her.

"Should we?"

She gazed back at me, her eyes sparkling brilliantly in the post-noon sun.

"Yes" she said finally "Yes we should."

She began to lead me onward towards the Rose Garden once again.

"Let's see if our favourite lute player is still about."

Her smile is contagious, and I love it.

I love her.

***

Evening had come early that night as clouds came rolling in from the west, and as it had the final preparations for the Solstice Dance were put into place.

As this was a 'high society' event, I was to be stationed in the celebration hall in order to watch as simple security and be on hand should there be any thievery take place; there was to be quite the bit of wealth on display and so made for quite the target.

As easy as it would be for a skilled hand to take extravagant jewellery from someone without notice, I found it highly unlikely that any thief – let alone the highly organised ones I was hired to thwart – would be so bold, or so stupid, as to try to do so in Castle Bahvil, during a function with over a hundred guests and countless security and servants. One could argue that they could slip in, pose as a servant, but the Castle heads of staff would notice someone new; on that I would bet my last gold coin.

What I did expect, however, was for one or two of the aristocratic folk in attendance to have their homes 'visited' whilst they're away, and as such had Captain Bough station a few guards – disguised as beggars – near them to stand watch, but we shall see if it leads to anything of note.

I stood to the western side of the room, against the wall, as each guest arrived and was announced as they entered through the rather decadently decorated grand archway entrance. The furnishings of the whole place were much the same: ancient looking, polished mahogany chairs at the sides of the room adorned with fine pillow fixtures of a velvet red, next to them strong, rounded dark oak tables covered in fine white silk table cloths that gained a brilliant hue and shine when the candlesticks upon them were lit, which were magnificent works of art unto themselves – shimmering brass holders shaped as entwining willow leaves adorned with an ornate enamel base, with the candles themselves delicately carved into the shape of a rose and tinted a near cream pink; it seemed to me quite a waste to see them melt away like that though.

The Count had yet to make his entrance, with Carmel greeting the guests as they got to the base of the expansive stairway.

She seemed both nervous and calm, clearly having rarely done the main greetings. The guest seemed most cordial, perhaps hoping that when the time came for her to become Countess she would remember how they treated her in these early days. Or perhaps they were just being sincere; it's hard to tell really.

All were dressed in their best finery, some bejewelled to the point of impracticality, others wearing more sedate, but imposing, attire.

It was nice to see all the types of dresses I must say, especially the ones worn by the visiting nobles from the Orc Isles; such strange finery, hues of pale, creamy... no, pinkish browns and faintest greens, the tough yet flexible fabric swirled tightly around the torso, with purposeful thick folds spiralling the skirt-like lower half.

Blake was there too, dressed in drab, once-fine dark felt, skulking and scuttling up to people with more power than he, clearly after some political favour or other; I'm sure he was tolerated only because he had the Count's ear, so to speak.

Soon enough, once all the guests had arrived and mostly taken to the sides of the room – though not yet sitting – talking amongst themselves, that the announcer proclaimed the arrival of Count Balford himself. As he walked down the steps he carried himself with an air of nobility, wearing a vibrant violet felt outfit, with white plumage at the cuffs and trim, a large, heavy gold amulet hung around his neck, its encrusted rubies oddly dull.

I gave a small grin as I watched them – the guests – move towards him, each trying so hard not to seem over eager, each clearly wanting to win favour in the local politics, with the exception of the Orcish nobles; they seemed far more interested in the canapés being served by the servants, whom stood silently waiting to be called over by any guest with an appetite for more than political favour.

As I watched I found my eyes drifting from them to Carmel as she played alongside the castle's harpist, as was custom for young ladies of Bahvil's nobility (although I doubt any were as good or gracious as Carmel). Her delicate fingers were covered by a glove made of the finest and thinnest silk, allowing her to play without her soft skin being damaged by the harps harsh string. As she played a few guests sat and watched, a few danced gently, others talked amongst themselves in hushed whispers, and I continued to watch her, captivated by her melody. She was wearing a bright, deep blue dress with long arm-hugging sleeves; there was no embroidery upon it, instead the dress boasted a thin flowing skirt made of a few delicate layers of pale blue and ghost white that formed a teardrop shape when she walked. Her mahogany brown hair almost shimmered in the candlelight, with that which would have been her fringe and top layer was woven into strong, thick plaits that encircled her head like a crown, which flowed down her back alongside her naturally curled, un-plaited hair.

I was rather lost in the sight of her.

At one point, between songs and as she gave a bow to the applauding guests, she glanced at me, and I detected a small, hidden smile.

Have you ever had that emotion, or feeling, of yourself melting? Like, as if there is a surge of some other thing flowing through you, empowering you, through nothing more than a look?

It... it was a strange feeling, but a nice one.

A couple of hours into the festivities and the main band of musicians were playing, situated in the far corner, as fine wines were being handed out on silver platters with fine cheeses. Dances were being performed in the centre of the hall now too, with all but the most competitive of guests now seated or standing at the side in little groups.

The Count approached me, casually standing to my side.

"Enjoying the music are we Prime?" he smiled, though not sincerely.

"Indeed I am sir" I replied politely.

"Not distracting you from your duties is it?"

"My eyes are as sharp and focused as ever sir" I paused "Has there been an incident to which I must attend?"

He took a sup of wine from the goblet in his right hand.

"Captain Bough sent this message via waiter to me"-he handed me a small folded piece of parchment-"When you depart the hall, do so discretely."

"Yes, of course sir" I replied as I unfolded the note.

"Very good" he nodded, before returning to Carmel's side.

I waited a few minutes before leaving via the servant's entrance, as to prevent panic or gossip.

As I hurriedly made my way through the narrow hallways to the holding cells, I re-read the note:

Stopped attempt of theft at attendee's house. One captured, two escaped.

'Who was 'B'?' I thought to myself, as I reached the door to the holding cell, before figuring it must mean Blake.

The soldier guarding the door opened it for me, Captain Bough waving me in as he gained view of me.

"Ah, Prime" he greeted me "you have my note?"

I held up the piece of parchment.

"Right, then let's get straight to it" he gestured towards the captured thief, seated on an old stool, his hands and feet chained.

"Mylous here was apprehended as he tried to escape the scene."

Mylous looked at me with an air of disgust; perhaps he felt I had sold out my 'kind' by working for the Count, not that it mattered.

"Which house was he escaping from?" I asked Bough.

"We're not sure, but I'm sure our guest will tell us all about it" he smiled, gesturing to Mylous, who remained silent "No? Don't want to share, huh?" he turned back to me "Facts are this: our men saw three thieves leaving the properties of Lady Edi and of Mister Blake."

"Two of whom escaped" I muttered "How was this one caught?"

"Daft berk tripped over his own feet, luckily for us."

I contemplated how best to approach this interrogation; do I try trickery? Play the 'you make us Agrians look bad' card? Bribery? Torture?...No, not torture, that rarely, if ever works; and is not worth the dirtying of my conscience.

"Right" I said as a pulled up a chair in front of Mylous "Let me make this simple for you Mylous"- I looked at him square in the eyes -"we have witnesses – guards – who caught you in the act. You were seen, as were your two accomplices. You answer my questions, things will be far more favourable for you; don't, and I dare say the Count will make *you* the example, understood?"

He just stared back at me, defiant.

"Right." I said clasping my hands together "You see Bough here?"- He glanced quickly up at him then back to me -"he would probably beat you into submission, whether you told him what he wanted or not. Now I don't like that, but if you won't talk to me, I may have to leave the room, think for a while and that, and Bough, he'll be here, with you. Alone."

Mylous nodded ever so slightly.

I could almost feel Bough grin.

"So, first question: who is ordering these thefts?"

Mylous stayed silent, but was visibly shocked by the question.

"Okay, okay, let's go for an easier one: what were you after? What was your mark, your target?"

I could see Mylous weighing up the pros and cons of answering.

"Papers" he said, reluctantly.

"Papers?" exclaimed Bough in disbelief. I waved him silent.

"Just papers? Not jewellery or coin?"

He gave a slight nod.

"Right, papers. What kind of papers?"

Silence once again.

"Mylous, you're making it hard for me to help you here" I said in a friendly, but warning tone "Was your group looking for something to forge? Blackmail perhaps?"

He shook his head.

"So information then?"

Another slight nod.

I looked back at Bough.

"Not much of a talker is he?"

Bough just laughed.

"So you were sent to steal papers, or rather information. From both houses?"

"No" Mylous grumbled.

"Now you said you were only ordered to get papers-"

"Not two houses"-Mylous cut me off, before looking between myself and Bough-"How favourable will I be looked upon for this?"

"I'll put it this way, you won't have to worry about never seeing the sun again" Bough said dryly.

"Right" Mylous licked his lips in thought.

"So whose house was the targeted one?" I asked, one eyebrow raised.

"Dunno *who's*, know it was the one on the right."

"Blake's" Bough whispered into my ear as he leant down.

"And the information, what was it?"

Mylous shrugged.

"Mylous" I warned.

"I swear, one Agrian to another, I know not of what the papers detailed."

"On your oath?" I asked.

"Yes, on my oath I do not know. Rejik never told us why-"

"Rejik?" Bough asked.

Mylous realised what he had just said.

"Hold that thought Mylous. Bough, a word outside?"

"Well?" Bough asked once we were out of earshot of the cells.

"Rejik is in the dungeon cells."

"So?"

"He's been there for a week."

"Still could have had it all planned out before we arrested him at Belothor's warehouse" Bough shrugged thoughtfully.

"I just...there's something more, something we're missing" I had a nagging feeling I just couldn't shake.

"You think Mylous is holding out on us?"

"No...but I think there is one more thing he could answer" I said as I moved to walk back into the holding cell.

"Mylous" I called "just one last question."

He just looked up at me, half hopeful, half very worried about what he let slip.

"Who is organising your group?"

"We-we don't have a leader-"

"Really Mylous? You're lying." I got up close to him, but not too close "Agrian thieves do not work together like this. Two clans, working together? With no leader?"

"Y-you misunderstand..."

"Do I?"

"We're hired" he spluttered "Hired."

I stepped back.

Bough looked at me.

"What is it?" he asked.

"Mylous...you and all the Agrian thieves were *hired*?" I asked, my mind racing.

"Yes...well, me and my group-"

"How many in your gang?" Bough interrupted.

"Bough, wait." I said firmly "Carry on Mylous."

"Me and mine were hired by Rejik, but the rest, that so-called clan?" he paused hesitant "They say they were hired to just thieve, and leave some in merchant houses owned by Rejik's boss."

"Belothor" Bough muttered.

I gave Bough a quick glance.

"Your clan of thieves, none of them are the ones going in and out of the merchant houses?"

"No, no, we were hired for *specific* things. And discretion. It's why we had talks with the other clan; they were drawing too much attention."

I could sense Bough was getting restless, eager to get his hands on the thieves that had been polluting his district; Mylous was lucky I was in charge of this investigation, other-wise...well, it would be most unpleasant for him.

"Who hired the other clan?" I asked calmly.

"I do not know."

"Tell us damn you!" Bough shouted, visibly putting the fear in Mylous.

"I do not know, I swear"-Mylous looked at me almost pleaful-ly-"on my oath."

I looked at Bough then back at Mylous.

"We're done here...for now."

Bough went to the door and called for the guard to take him to his own cell.

"Why you work for Bahvil types?" Mylous asked me in a hushed voice "You know they hate our kind, don't you?"

I thought on that a moment as I helped him off the chair, his chains rattling as he stood.

"Only the aristocrats." I replied in a whisper as Bough came back in with the guard "And how else do you show you're better?"

He seemed to like that idea, though clearly doubting it.

As he was about to exit, he seemed to remember something.

"Wait, wait!" he exclaimed "It's not much but there is somthin' else."

"And what might that be?" Bough asked.

"When we told Rejik that it wasn't us who were doing the other thefts, he acted all angry and frightened."

"Frightened?"

"Yes, said no matter what we get them papers and leave them at the dead drop."

"A place to leave stolen items to be collected." I explained to Bough before he could ask "You have its location?"

He shook his head.

"Only clan leader and Rejik."

"You've done good Mylous" I said as I gestured for the guard to continue taking him to his cell.

*

"So" Bough began as he wrote down notes at his desk in the interrogation room "I guess we talk to Rejik next; good thing his execution isn't due for a few more days, ay?"

"Quite" I said absently as I contemplated upon my troubling thoughts "Bough, if I were to say there was something more to this, how would you go about things?"

He looked at me puzzled.

"What do you mean?"

"What would you do, if this goes deeper than it seems?"

"Deeper?"

"Who would you tell?"

He threw his arms in the air, exasperated.

"By the divines Prime, what is it you're getting at?"

"Who would you tell?"

"The other Captains, the Count, the head of the night watch" he shrugged "So what is it? Because to me it seems simple enough."

"How so? I asked as I picked up a spare quill to fidget with as I went over my theory in my head.

Bough stood up straight, putting his quill back in the ink pot.

"Rejik hires one clan to thieve information to extort and blackmail, Belothor hires another to thieve goods he can sell in other cities for a pricey sum" he answered as he absently ordered his desk.

I stared back at him nodding silently for a moment.

"Yes that would be the simplest answer."

"...What is it Prime?"

"Tell me, Rejik and Belothor, what is their relationship?"

"Rejik is Belothor's right-hand-man, assistant, accountant-"

"And?" I interrupted.

"And what?...Oh." The penny finally dropped.

"So, with that in mind, do you really think that either would not know what the other is planning? Even so, why would Belothor, one of if not the wealthiest merchant around these parts hire Agrian thieves to steal things he could buy without a second thought?"

"You're suggesting a conspiracy? A frame job?" he asked in a tired, if not totally disbelieving tone.

"What I'm saying is that one thief being not-so-subtle about where they're leaving their loot is one thing, but a whole clan?"- I put the quill back down on the desk-"I have to look into some things, Bough, and none of us may like what we find."

"So, you have a plan I presume? And what of Rejik?"

"Let me talk to Rejik; he may be more trusting of an outsider such as I"-I lightly stretched my arms in thought-"As for a 'plan', all I'll ask is you wait on this information."

"Prime I must inform the Count, it is my duty" he said firmly.

"Then tell him about Rejik hiring the clan of thieves, and make it ambiguous."

Bough was clearly not pleased with these demands, his brow a deep frown.

"Prime, I am not comfortable with this, and I answer to the Count." He grabbed the parchment he was writing on and hurriedly rolled it up "And if you're suggesting that what I think you're suggesting-"

"I suggest nothing. I merely ask you give me a few days to make enquiries."

We stood in silence a moment as he wrestled with his morals.

"You have one day" he said, pointing at me with the rolled parchment "and I cannot officially sanction you talking to Rejik; but if you have something by evenings end tomorrow...just make sure it's concrete."

"That's all I ask."

"Right" he huffed "You be careful now."

And with that we parted ways for the evening, and I made my way back to the festivities in the celebration hall, all the while thinking.

That's my problem you know, always thinking.

***

I had lain in my bed not even an hour before my restlessness drove me to get out of bed, that deep, nagging thought yelling at me to speak to Rejik sooner rather than later.

It was some ungodly hour of the morning, the sounds of the evening's celebrations now long gone. It was a funny thing, standing watch over the wealthy elite of Bahvil, knowing many of them saw me – at best – as something of a novelty, a thing to gossip about and comment upon. Not that it was most mind you, nor any of the visiting nobles. It would be wrong of me to say it was solely a Bahvil thing, but there was some leftover sentiment from some now ancient war or another amongst its people; not that the common folk held such a stance, Bahvil being something of a trading city. Still, there was always that thief stereotype (not that it didn't have something of a strong foundation, all things considered).

As I slipped into the dungeon and descended into its depths I began to hear talking between two voices; one was unmistakeably Rejik, but the other I had not heard before, or at least couldn't recognise, and was a gruff, sympathetic murmur.

I hugged the side of the wall as I came to the corner around which lay Rejik's cell, cautious not to cast a shadow in the light of the lone torch sconce, taking careful, delicate footsteps as I did.

"...I cannot let this happen to you Rejik" the gruff voice begged.

"No, do not fret my dearest" Rejik coughed, audibly tearful "you are surely suspected, why else has he had me framed and locked in here?"

I dared to peer around the corner; there stood the second voice, Belothor, concealed beneath a simple unassuming cloak, its hood pulled down.

"That vile creature" Belothor spat, choked by an obvious sadness "he is less than living, how dare he..."

"Belothor, please listen. If you confront him now he'll set upon you as he did me, or worse."

"I cannot stand back and watch you die" Belothor's voice elevated a little, a lone tear glistening in the torchlight as it rolled down his cheek.

"But if you do not all we have worked to do would be for nothing" he grasped tightly on Belothor's hand through the bars "Please...I beg of you to flee to Hamurfel with what we have gathered, so that this might not be all in vein."

"It...it's not fair Rejik. All of our plans, our retirement..."

"I know. I know. But think of Lady Amilia" Rejik's eyes were pleaful and desperate "Think of her. Think of Rufus. They need justice."

There was an uneasy, emotional silence between the two soulmates.

"I...I don't know what to do without you."

"It'll be okay my love, it'll be okay" I could see the tears welling up in his eyes; I felt such pity for them, for the sorrow they felt.

Perhaps that was what drove me to make my presence known to them, or perhaps just my own desire to quench my own troubling questions.

I walked into the open, immediately catching Rejik's attention, causing Belothor to turn on the spot, his hand reaching for something on his hip.

I raised my hands.

"I have but one question" I began, not giving them a proper chance to react to my sudden appearance "didn't Lady Amilia die from an accident, or by her own hand?"

They both stared at me warily.

"I get it. I got you put in there Rejik; only I didn't did I?" I asked as I slowly moved towards them.

Belothor's hand twitched on his hip; probably a concealed dagger I thought.

"I know you were after information."-I turned to Belothor-"and I can guess you didn't hire those other thieves."

The pair of them stayed silent.

"Who was it Rejik? Belothor, who is it?"

"You expect us to trust you, when you work for him?"

"The Count?"

"The Count."

"Balford?"

"Yes" Rejik replied.

"That...fits" I lowered my arms "So I guess Blake keeps a record the Count is otherwise unaware of?"

"How did-?"

"One of your men tripped up, and I got him to talk."

A look of fear and shock ran over the both of them.

"Belothor, the Count, he'll be coming for you" Rejik said, panicked.

"You...you did this to us!" Belothor shouted angrily, making a move towards me.

"Hey now, we've got time...well, 'till end of evening tomorrow" I said as I stepped back defensively.

Belothor gave a quick glance back at Rejik, who gave a weak shrug.

"What can you do?" he asked.

"Truthfully I'm not sure. What I need is to know what you have on the Count."

"He is no Count" Belothor spat.

"In my desk, at the warehouse office, there are Blake's off-the-books records" Rejik responded "hopefully."

"Assuming the thieves completed their job" Belothor added.

"Okay, I can work with that. But what exactly did Balford do to Lady Amilia?"

"Her husband's death was no accident" Belothor winced as he remembered old pain "and Amilia, hers was not her doing either."

I nodded silently.

It was most unfortunate, as I had really began to like it here, and now...now I had to try and take down a Count. You know, as you do.

* * *

During the morning I resolved to tell Mazog what I had learned; after all, despite the impression he exudes, he does give good advice.

"So they said nothing else?" He was leant back on his chair looking at the ceiling, as he normally does when weighing up the facts and options before him.

"Not a word more." I shrugged my shoulders.

"The thing is..."-he paused for a moment-"the thing is, if the Count had done something, he most assuredly would have destroyed any evidence."

"But he wouldn't have known about Blake's secret records"-the thought suddenly coming to me-"wait, wasn't he on Rufus's hunt?"

"No...actually yes, yes I think I heard that. But he's a seedy creature, you may not get anything out of him, and even if you did, he would surely inform the Count – then you would be the one being executed."

It was true. Even if I had solid evidence, a direct witness, Balford would be quick to silence me.

Unless...

"I wonder, could we get Zaxx to have a look through Rejik's desk?" I queried "See if he can get hold of those papers?"

"The whole place is on lock down, but I don't see why not; Doncaster should be able to get him a warrant so the guards let him in, especially if we 'suspect' evidence of other cohorts to be on the premise."

I loved his thinking. Doncaster, being laid back and trusting, held Zaxx and Mazog in high regard, so there shouldn't be a problem there.

I gave a brief smile.

"Sounds like a plan."

***

As we hatched our plan, Maralin was doing some sleuthing of her own, albeit inadvertently.

As she was walking down one of the tapestry clad hallways, she came upon a maid, curled up and crying.

"Whatever is the matter?" she asked, speaking softly, in a sympathetic manner, as she crouched down, putting a hand on the maid's shoulder.

The maid looked up, her eyes laden with tears.

"He...he killed her..." she sobbed in disbelief.

Maralin was taken aback by this, and decided it best that they spoke in her chamber, so that none could interrupt, or more importantly, overhear.

Meanwhile; Zaxx, having produced the warrant from Doncaster, was busy rummaging through Rejik's office. Now he isn't the gentlest person when it comes to searching for things, but he certainly had a knack for finding them. After (presumably) demolishing half of the living area searching for the right desk – for what must have been along the lines of three hours – Zaxx came to what he described as a typical clerk's desk, the one Rejik used for accounting.

Here's how Zaxx told it:

> As I examined the desk I found nothing unusual, just the standard clerk items really. But just as I went to move on, I noticed something; the desk was made of light maple wood, but there was a small square section, made of a cheaper, ever so slightly lighter wood at the back. I pressed it just to see, and I was proved right. A thin, half-inch thick compartment emerged, filled with various papers. Most of these were 'off-the-books' transactions, but eight of them were written by a different hand, thus I presumed they were Blake's. Now as the stationed guards were waiting for me to come out, and would probably frisk me case I took something – which they did – I had to scroll them together with the warrant in order to smuggle them out, which unfortunately has crinkled some of the words up a bit.

Trouble was, unbeknownst to us, that slimy creature, Blake, was paying attention to Zaxx's movements, and had observed him leaving Rejik's office.

* * * *

Maralin had sat the maid down on her bed and tried to comfort her, but she stayed tearful.

"After all he said..." she sobbed into a handkerchief Maralin had given her.

"Just take a few deep breaths then speak" Maralin held the poor maid's hand and rubbed her shoulder comfortingly. The maid then wiped the tears from her face, took those deep breaths and composed herself.

"'Tis the Count m'lady"-according to Maralin the maid seemed to be in disbelief at her own words-"I've just overheard him and that merchant, Belothor. I wasn't eavesdropping ma'am, it's just they were shouting with such force, I couldn't help but listen."

"Arguing you say, what was it about?" Maralin spoke in a gentle, soft tone, as she always would when talking to a troubled soul in need of reassurance.

"It was about the Count's sister, the Lady Amilia, about her..."-she paused a moment, hesitant, her lip quivering-"...her accident."

Maralin, not having known about the Count's sister – or the events that happened around her – at the time, chose the pretence of knowing; concealing her worry.

"What about it?"

"She didn't jump, nor did she fall"-each stared into the other's eyes with the same fear-"she was pushed."

* * *

Dusk had been and settled, and all of us bar Tau had retired early for the night, Tau being on duty 'till the first signs of dawn. Mazog and I were looking over the notes Zaxx had liberated, with Zaxx himself uncorking a bottle of the local mead. Maralin, wearing her 'comfy' night gown, was practicing her footwork of a local dance she had been shown. Had I of been paying attention to her expression, I would have seen her troubled, but alas I was focusing on Blake's now crinkled words, searching through the secrets he'd compiled; time quickly running out before Bough would hand Balford our findings.

"Mazog, how long do you think this will take?"

"A lot quicker if we took it to Rejik" he murmured, writing any noteworthy text onto a blank piece of parchment.

I just rolled my eyes.

"We don't have the time to sneak in and out of the dungeon; there's too many guards stationed by him now anyway."

Maralin, now dancing with a slightly sober Zaxx, began to take notice of our conversation.

"Why would guards be a problem?" she asked in a quizzical tone.

Not wanting his sister to get involved, Mazog rebuked the question.

"Nothing you should worry about, just focus on your dancing."

She pulled a disapproving frown.

"Charming."

It was at this point Zaxx dropped us in it.

"There just diggin' dirt on Balford" he blurted. He needs to stop drinking so much. Seriously.

She stopped dancing and looked from Zaxx to Mazog, and then to me.

"You mean the Count?"

This time Mazog looked disapprovingly at Zaxx.

"Yes"-he turned to Maralin-"the Count."

A little under an hour later and a darker image had come through.

First was what we could get out of Blake's now crinkled handwriting; that Rufus's 'accident' was indeed no accident, and that Blake – on the orders of the Count – had fired that so-called stray arrow that mortally wounded him. Second was what Joahana – the maid Maralin had comforted, who just so happened to be Carmel's handmaid – had overheard; that Lady Amilia had been thrown from her balcony, having tried to escape the castle. But the complete story was much darker than we could imagine, though the last piece of the puzzle I would not find until a while later.

"So presumably, the Count had Rufus killed – either out of jealousy, spite or some other reason – and Amilia found out one way or t'other" Zaxx spoke as he pondered the facts, still in that limbo state between sober and drunk.

"Obviously she was distraught and tried to leave, probably to tell Rufus's father, the Count of Hamurfel"-Maralin wavered for a moment before continuing-"To think he killed his own sister...how could anyone do that..." Her voice teetered off, saddened, obviously discomforted by it all.

"But what of Belothor and Rejik?"-Mazog leaned forward, clasping his hands together-"Rejik would have been told by Belothor, but who would tell Belothor...Zaxx put more wood on the fire..."-he paused for a moment-"we're missing something."

I nodded, taking a sip of mead as I went over everything in my head, pondering each and every detail.

"Dangerous thing, killing the son of another Count" Zaxx sighed, leaning on the back of Mazog's chair.

"We need to have a 'chat' with Blake" I said at last.

"Why, we have Joahana, and Blake's letters?" Maralin asked.

"Motive, Maralin" Mazog replied as he swatted Zaxx off the back of his chair "We don't have a motive, the *why*."

"But Prime, surely we have enough to convince Bough?"

"Perhaps, well, hopefully" I said as I rose from my seat "I'm going to take what we have to him now."

As I gathered up Blake's papers Maralin bid us all goodnight, wishing me luck as she did.

I sincerely hoped I wouldn't need it.

***

I rushed through the halls, passing from the fancy, decoration-clad walls of the sleeping quarters to the plain ones of the holding cells and Captains offices, holding tight to Blake's papers.

Just as I entered the hallway heading to Bough's quarters I bumped into him; clearly I had arrived just in time.

"Prime!" he exclaimed as I almost knocked him off his feet.

"Sorry Bough, but I have something you need to look at" I waved the papers at him.

He took a deep breath.

"The Count is expecting my report in a few minutes."

"Bough, please" I leant in close as to whisper into his ear "These are Blake's personal notes."

Bough looked at me quizzically.

"Why would that...? Never mind, let's make this quick."

Once inside his office he began to go through each paper, carefully studying each one, his hand placed upon his chin thoughtfully as he leant on it.

Finally he spoke, putting down the last page as he did.

"I don't believe this" he said in a tone I couldn't quite read.

"But...it's right there, you just read it."

"I still don't believe it" he exhaled heavily "syphoning of city funds, political backhands, and...this!" he hit the last page with the back of his hand, before getting to his feet.

"Bough, I understand it is a difficult thing to come to terms with but-"

"The man unleashed thieves amongst his own people, trying to frame Belothor, this...this is madness!"-he put his head in his hands-"Ordering the assassination of his own son-in-law..."

"There's more Bough."

"More?!" he seemed almost incredulous at the prospect.

"We have a witness, so to speak, who overheard Balford and Belothor arguing"-Bough looked at me expectantly, nervously-

"an argument that would indicate that the Count's sister, Lady Amilia, was killed by-"

"Don't." he begged "Don't say it." He slumped back into his chair.

A moment passed as he tried to decompress the information he had learned, tried to make sense of it.

"You know it's not enough, don't you Prime?" he said at last "The other Captains...the fact you're Agrian, he could use that against you."

"I do; it would make it easy for the Count to pay someone to say these papers are forged, or simply frame Blake and place me as under his employ."

"We need to take him in"-I gave him a worried look-"Blake, Prime, we need him to testify to the other Captains."

"What of Belothor?" I asked.

"Belothor can wait, first we-"

It was at that moment that Tau burst into the office like a mad bull.

"Prime! There you are!"

"Tau what is the meaning of-" Bough began, before Tau cut him off.

"The prisoner – Rejik – just tried to escape."

"What?"

"He nailed Doncaster's assistant."

"Blake?" I asked, a wash of fear coming over me.

"Yes, Blake. When I got back to the room and told Mazog he told me to come straight to you."

Bough and I looked at each other silently, each of us knowing, but unable to act.

***

According to Tau, the Jailer had come across Rejik standing over Blake, who was speared through the chest with a broken chair leg. Because of this, the Jailer had cut Rejik down in an instant, deeming him too high a risk to keep in the cells; though he protested his innocence over Blake's death, shouting that he'd found Blake that way.

It was upsetting to say the least. Maralin excused herself from breakfast that morning; I fear she was more upset than she was letting on over these events. What's more, not long after dawn had come, I was once again summoned to Balford's Meeting Hall, and I could not help but feel apprehensive over it.

When I entered, the Count (how could I bear to call him that honoured title?) was leaning over the oak table, once again with a map strewn across it, with a few other bits of parchment, along with five Captains standing to attention around the table; Bough was noticeably uneasy, but he played it off as being up so long after little sleep.

"The thieves have struck again"-he spoke without lifting his head, staring intently at the information before him-"yet the man thought to be their leader is dead."

"Sir..." I began (it felt disgusting to be cordial), but he stopped me there.

"We suspect Belothor. Does the idea of him being their leader make sense to you?"

By now I was at the table, looking over the map and other pieces of parchment. Many of the thefts were not what one would expect, such as those that didn't match their location or make reasonable sense. I slowly began to realise that most of these 'unusual' thefts followed the same pattern as my patrols, including the ones I've had with Carmel.

My hand was being forced, and I could do nothing about it.

"It is reasonable to suspect him?" He repeated sternly.

I had to keep calm.

"Yes, it is reasonable."

"Reasonable."-he gave a menacing smile-"How quaint. Tell me, how would you trap this kind of prey?"

He was toying with me, I could feel it; he was aware I knew something, and I could not protect Belothor and myself at the same time.

"To trap such a man, you would need to tempt him with something, something rare, something he desired."

I felt a pit in my stomach as I gave as vague an answer as I could possibly get away with, my mind racing to find a way out of this situation that didn't result in my head in a noose, or relieved from my shoulders.

He gave a foul laugh.

"Lure him in for the slaughter."-his eyes twinkling with some unknown emotion-"I like your style."

I felt a shiver go through my spine.

"What evidence have you obtained, or will it be an interrogation?" I asked in as plain a voice I could.

"What more evidence does one need? We have known thieves visiting his merchant houses, consorting with his assistant, and you want more?" Balford laughed.

"The Count is right; besides, we can get a confession out of him quite easily" added one of the prejudiced Captains with a sneer.

I looked around the room, person to person, Bough giving me an apologetic glance, unable to help me.

"It looks like the matter is settled then" I shrugged, feigning disinterest.

"Indeed" said Balford, waving me away, as one might do a fly "You may go."

As I walked back to our room, I quickened my thoughts, knowing it was only a matter of time before Belothor found himself in chains, being dragged before Balford's court to receive his 'judgement'.

I had to think fast; and so, as wise or foolish as it was, I took a little detour to Carmel's chamber.

***

I just caught Maralin, still shaken by the state of things, as she finished her early morning session with Carmel. I told her to warn Belothor, and to tell Mazog of what I had learned.

Before I could continue with my plan I had to see Carmel; Maralin commented that she had been asking her about me a fair bit recently. She was wearing a silky-white satin dress braided with sparkling strands of a silvery-blue, greater than that of a sapphire, that went well with her complexion and made her eyes shine; I could not help but be captivated. Time was of the essence, but she was worth the risk; if things went wrong, this may be the last chance I'd get to see her.

* * *

By nightfall our small group had formed a plan; a risky one, but the only one that was open to us.

As the others stayed at the castle – Maralin making a note to visit Bough – I visited Belothor, who was dead, as far as Balford was concerned anyway. I should explain:

After my visit to Carmel, I had discovered that Mazog had 'encouraged' Doncaster to issue a warrant for Belothor's arrest; however, he had also engineered it so that he and Zaxx would be the ones to apprehend him. Having informed Belothor of the plan beforehand, the three staged a public fight and a chase that led them to an unfenced bridge which Belothor was shoved off, falling to his death; only in reality he was caught by a patient Tau, who coated Belothor's head with fresh goat's blood from the market (it was quite the convincing sight, so I was told; so much so Zaxx had thought they had actually killed him).

After presenting his 'corpse' to Doncaster, Tau and Mazog took Belothor to Joahana's small room to hide in for the time being, with Zaxx distracting any potential witnesses as they moved him (Joahana didn't mind thankfully, but did ask to be kept out of our plan as much as possible, and she was to stay with a friend in the meantime).

As I took a seat in Joahana's room, Belothor offered me a tankard of wine, but I politely refused, and he could tell what I was thinking.

"I'll presume you want some answers." He poured some mead into the tankard he had offered me as he spoke, his voice slightly choked.

"Why did Balford have Rufus killed? How did...how do you know all this?" although he would have told me regardless of whether I asked, I needed to ask all the same.

"I know because I was the one who was getting Amilia, and her daughter, out of the city. I was to take her to the coast with one of my trading ships, and from there to Hamurfel."

He took a sip from his tankard.

"As for why he killed Rufus..."-his voice deepened slightly, as if bracing for what was to come next; as if he could not speak the next few words without seething hate and unending pain of the sickening truth that he was to reveal to me...and nothing could have prepared me for what it was-"...he killed him because Rufus found out that Carmel was Balford's daughter."

My mouth opened slightly, my eyes widened. I could not speak.

Belothor continued.

"Balford had raped Amilia, his own sister"-I could see Belothor still could not believe how such a horror was possible, even after all this time-"Rufus found out months later, when he found Amilia curled up and sobbing in the corner of her room, worn out from months of stress, fear and undeserved shame."

Belothor emptied his tankard in a single mouthful.

"Rufus had asked me to get her out of the city, as we are...were close friends..."

He leaned his head back on the wall behind him, still holding the empty tankard, tears rolling from his eyes silently.

I gave him a moment to gather himself.

"He had Blake make it look like an accident with Rufus, but Amilia...she knew. I dread to think how much terror she must have been in. If only I had got to the castle sooner..."

More tears fell from his eyes, despite his efforts, rolling down the contours of his face. I could feel my own running down mine.

"How...Why now, why after all these years have you tried to take him down?" I tried not to sound accusing, and I wasn't doing so, I assure you.

"What hope had I against the word of a Count?" he snuffled "But then Rejik...my poor Rejik..."-he pulled out a small, smart handkerchief and dabbed his eyes with it-"One of his old thief clan mentioned they would be doing business in Bahvil, and so took the opportunity to ask them for a favour."

"To look for evidence?"

"Exactly, exactly."-He began to pour another tankardful of mead-"They said they'd look into old rumours for us, for old times' sake; anything after that would have to be paid for."

"And they led you to Blake and his secret records?"

"Yes, but not before Balford took notice of the reports of snooping questions and oddly specific thefts and trespasses."

As I digested the information Belothor had freely given, I had but one thought:

Carmel, did she know...did she know any of this?

I had to find out.

***

That night I found myself unable to sleep, the events of the last few days plaguing me. I spent seemingly countless hours thinking them over, each event, each fact, going over them again and again, wrestling with the sheer speed which they had preceded one another. As I finally began to drift off, I found myself plagued by something else, other than Zaxx's snoring. I began thinking, almost fantasising about her. I longed to be with her, holding her close, her soft warm skin against mine; her majestic curls flowing over her pillow and down her side.

Just to gaze into her star-lit eyes...

***

As the morrow dawned, I awoke to the sound of many, heavy footsteps getting closer. The others had noticed it too, but before we could speak a word the castle guard burst into the room, surrounding me. The Captain stepped forward.

"Prime of Blackwood, you are under arrest for theft against the Count, a crime equal to treason."

The others stared helplessly towards me.

As I was pulled from my bed, I hid my smile, my desire to laugh.

Sure, Balford had caught me in his bigoted, malicious trap, but he hadn't beaten me.

I had a trap all of my own.

Before long I was in chains, the guards dragging me through the Court Hall, just like Rejik before me. And once again, a small crowd had gathered to witness the so-called Count deliver his 'judgement'.

"Prime of Blackwood, you are charged with aiding thieves, theft against..."-the Speakers words fell deaf on my ears; I was focused on the plan ahead-"...and with high treason against the Count of Bahvil. What say you?"

I looked up, and spoke loudly, not quite able to maintain my calm.

"Count...How can anyone here call *that* a Count? You are a wretch Balford, a vile spawn of corruption who entertains bigots and prejudice."

"Such pitiful attempts to distract the court from you, and by projecting your qualities onto me"-he turned his gaze to the gathered crowd in his court-"Not only is this creature treasonous, it attempts to slander me, I who have raised Bahvil high upon my shoulders and governed with benevolence and-"

"You. Are. A. MONSTER!" I shouted, interrupting him, unable to listen to him much longer.

"So says you, *lizard*" he seethed.

"Hehe" I grinned with a small laugh "You shouldn't have said that; after all, your daughter seems most fond of me."

"Wha...What did you say?" I caught him off-guard, and for the first time, I could see the shade of fear in his eyes; now was my moment to strike.

"Carmel – your daughter" I proclaimed loudly, the once whispering crowd now in a tense silence "I'm sorry, don't your sycophants know?"

"Silence him before he can spread anymore hateful lies!" he shouted, rising from his throne in anger as he did. But before his men could react and give Balford the opportunity to smooth everything over with deceit, I broke him with words.

"Balford raped his sister Amilia, her child is his; he killed first her husband Rufus, then her to cover up his vile crime."

The number of horrified faces seemed almost countless, the accompanying silence deafening and enveloping their muted gasps, their voices stifled by shocked disbelief.

"Such evil lies! They show just how disgusting you and your kind really are!" he spat through gritted teeth, his eyes filled with hate as he tried to worm his way out; something I would not allow.

"Your daughter disagrees with you."

His expression of anger turned to confusion, then swiftly into fear, as a hooded figure emerged from the crowd, revealing itself to be Carmel, throwing her hood back as she spoke.

"You monster!" her voice shaking with anger, hate and a rage fuelled by sadness and a sense of violation to her very being.

I caught sight of several small tears as they ran down her face, my heart breaking to see her in such pain.

"Carmel, this deplorable creature lies to protect itself!" he was beginning to crack, attempting to save himself; stress evident in his voice.

"He does not lie" said a third, slightly gruff voice.

Balford turned to see Belothor, accompanied by Mazog and Tau.

The Count shattered.

Belothor's still being alive pushed him beyond his breaking point; with his eyes widening, he drew his sword and charged at Belothor.

"Guards! Kill them, kill them ALL!" screaming wildly with darkest fury, he lunged toward him.

As the present guards drew their swords the gathered crowd began to flee from the hall, wailing in disorientated confusion.

Balford failed to strike down Belothor as Mazog and Tau defended him, and so attempted to flee, but was blocked from getting to the garrison by Maralin and Zaxx, whom had been hidden at the back of the crowd until this point. Tau had leapt into battle, crushing attacking guards like insects with his mighty warhammer, as Mazog slew those foolish enough to try and take him.

Zaxx and Maralin fought tirelessly to keep the fiendish 'Count' from escaping. I assisted where I could, choking nearby guards with my chains, punishing those who attempted to get to Balford.

A break appeared in their ranks, and after a dash towards me, Tau smashed my chains with a single blow as Belothor threw me a sword from a fallen guard; quickly dispatching an oncoming guard behind Tau as he did.

Try as I might, I could not find Carmel in the confusion.

More guards poured into the hall, responding to the commotion, escalating the risks of fighting in such a confined space.

Tau was taking several out with each blow, whilst Mazog and Belothor dispatched those attempting to strike him mid-swing, taking the brunt of them. I had picked up another sword and fought several guards at once, each trying to pass by me. Whilst we held the guards back, preventing them from aiding Balford, it became apparent that these guards were of Balford's choosing; those that would fight mindlessly for him and not Bahvil or its people, and were part of that contemptuously bigoted crowd of sycophants he kept around him.

As I blocked an oncoming blow I was staggered back, just long enough to see Balford ram his sword through Zaxx's hide, running him through. I swung back at my attacker, decapitating him, and attempted to get to Balford, but we were being surrounded.

I spotted terror in Mazog's eyes as he frantically fought his way towards Maralin and Balford, whom were locked in battle.

We were cut off, forced to watch helplessly as Balford threw Maralin to the ground. We made a push to get to them but the few guards left kept us back.

Zaxx was bleeding out on the floor, unmoving.

Balford stood over a disarmed Maralin, preparing to strike her a fatal blow.

"No one can take this from me! You hear?! No one, not even a wretch like you can take this away!" he screamed manically, revealing his terrifying madness.

Before he could strike her, Carmel, like an avenging angel, appeared from the garrison steps behind them and thrust her self-forged dagger into him, plunging it deep into his dark heart.

His body fell backwards onto the cold floor, the dagger still in him, as guards descended the stairs from the garrison, led by Doncaster and Bough, and under the command of Carmel. They swiftly dealt with the remaining guards, taking those who surrendered to the dungeons whilst the others moved the bodies that littered the hall.

Carmel stooped down over the evil creature, whispering something into its ear before wrenching her dagger from its body.

Mazog was now holding Maralin close, tending to her, whilst Tau had scooped up Zaxx, and with a company of guards and Doncaster, set off to find the castle physician.

Carmel was now sobbing into Belothor's shoulder; he too was in tears.

Despite the on-going noise, my mind had gone silent, blocking all but the tears. I looked upon the monster's face, its expression just; one of fear and pain. I could only hope it would come as some comfort to its victims. Carmel. Belothor. Rufus and Lady Amilia. The framed Rejik. I hope they find peace.

I hope they have found peace.

＊

I wandered the halls that night, unable to sleep. I wondered, and still wonder, if more could have been done on my part. Zaxx was stable according to the physician, but we all worried nonetheless; Tau staying at his bedside almost the whole time he was confined to it. Maralin slept huddled against her brother, each needing the comfort and safety of the other's presence.

And as for Balford's loyalist guards (what few of them remained), they had all been detained and stripped of their position – along with the prejudiced Captains thanks to Bough, and Carmel – and were now awaiting trial in the castle dungeon.

As I wandered, I encountered Carmel looking out of the great arched windows into the horizon.

"How strange life is" her voice was softer than usual; she turned her head to look at me, teary-eyed. "Tell me Prime, do you think me a monster?"

I was taken aback by this.

"How could you be a monster?" I enquired, my tone soft.

"I killed my uncl-"-she caught herself-"...my father"-she turned back to the horizon-"I came from that monster..."

"You slayed a monster"-I put an arm around her shoulders-"but you are no monster. If anything you are an angel."

She turned her head back to face mine, and looked into my eyes. I could not help but get lost in her now bright blue eyes, with their green tint glistening in the window's moonlight.

"See, it is not the circumstances of one's birth that matters" I continued "But rather what one does with the gift that is life."

She gave a smile, turning herself to face me completely, and put her arms around me.

"You're an honourable man Sylon."

She rested her head on my shoulder, and together we looked upon the silvered landscape a while.

"'Tell me Sylon Prime, is it me you want or Maralin?"

She is a surprisingly forward person, all things considered. But alas, it was time I accepted the truth and embraced it.

"Who I want is who my heart desires..." I began, my voice and words far feebler than my heart.

We stood a while in the moonlight.

It was odd. Almost all my life I had cared and longed for Maralin's affection, but I had not truly loved her, not in *that* way. Carmel on the other hand, had sparked something in me I had never felt before.

"Carmel...would you like to have a dance in the Rose Garden?"

A brief moment of silence passed in the midnight air.

"Sorry...it's an inappropriate time, but I do-"

"No, no, I would like that" she interrupted gently.

She looked at me, and I at her.

We had found what we had been looking for.

And we're never letting go.

CHAPTER TWO

877, 3RD Era

Standing at the balcony, I reflected upon what I had just done, taking careful note of what was around me. Pink flowers from the wilds hung down from the railing, to my right stands Maralin, a blue rose. Softly she put her hand round mine. I could not gaze her in the eyes, despite my wanting, though she did not shift hers from mine.

In the street bellow people passed, unaware of our presence, some familiar neighbours and shop-keeps, others new faces. This wasn't what I was used too, and whilst we were still in Blackwood, this new home was...it was something I wasn't prepared for, perhaps the only thing I hadn't. Perhaps I should explain a few things: the relatively new city of Blackwood – situated nigh on a mile from my...our old home – whilst small and mild when compared to other cities, left me lost within its vastness. I may have managed well in the past, but that was back when I knew I could go home, away from the confined spaces of the city walls. Yet it was not this that concerned me now, as something far more insidious was occurring; for, unbeknownst to Maralin, in our cellar lay a man daggered through, a dark liquid coating the stone floor. And what was worse was who he was: Leonard Diamando, Captain of the guard.

* * *

Let us backtrack to two weeks ago, when Leonard had asked me for some advice on a missing persons case he had been working on.

"I'm not sure what to say Leonard, this is a pretty strange case" I said as I read the reports he had handed me.

"I know; it's why I asked for your opinion" he said as he cut into an apple.

"All poor and desperate, all gone at the same time, in the same way, for the last few months; how have I not heard this in the old rumour mill?"

"I told the Count's assistant and he told me to inform the men that if a single word got out it'd be on their neck."

"Charming. Why is it when they want to stop panic they do so through fear?" I muttered as I putt the papers on the desk beside me "Any leads?"

"Just that a hooded man in a blue tunic was seen each of the nights one of them went missing, usually driving a horse and cart, but that's about it."

"Hmm"-I folded my arms-"It's a pity we can't predict who'll go missing; any distinctive markings on the tunic or cart?"

"Just a sickle on the tunic's sleeve; but only one witness saw that, and he might have been drunk at the time."

"A sickle...right" I shifted in my chair, uneasy.

"That mean something to you?"

"No, no...just adding it all up in my head and thinking out loud" I smiled, politely dismissing his question and my previous thought "But as I said, this is one strange case."

He quietly chewed a couple of apple slices, looking out of the second-floor window at the midday sun.

"Am I missing a connection between these men Prime? Other than the fact they're poor, that is."

I looked back at the papers, thinking on it a moment, before picking them back up, skimming through the details of each person again.

"Huh." I uttered automatically.

"What is it?"

"These men...almost all of them are ex-guardsmen."

"Already looked into that; each were dishonourably discharged, but not in any connecting way" he sighed, cutting off another chunk of apple.

"No...there's something else, I'm sure of it" I held my chin in my hands, searching deep into my memory to see what my intuition was begging me to remember.

Leonard stared at me expectantly.

"Well?"

"I could swear I know...oh my, they...at least a few of them are, Leonard, I think they were guardsmen for Eizekiel."

He sat upright in his chair.

"Eizekiel...where do I know that name from?"

"He was a nobleman; the one who had his keep decommissioned years back."

"The one whose son-"

"Yes. That one." I cut him off quickly "So perhaps someone is looking to settle old scores against them now they're vulnerable."

"This could change things" he said after a moment, having put his apple half down "But why now, after all these years?"

"That I don't have any idea on" I shrugged apologetically "But, unless this is a spate of truly random abductions, it's the best lead you've got."

He got up out of his chair, fastening his short-sword and dagger sheath to his belt.

"Prime, thank you for your help here, but I have to go ask questions in the dark corners of the city."

"No problem" I replied as I got to my feet "But if you need any help, you know where to find me."

***

Fast forward two weeks to the morning of that day, where Maralin and I had been out to a jeweller to commission a gemmed tiara for mine and Carmel's day of marriage – Maralin was helping me make arrangements as Carmel had been detained by her official duties in Bahvil and wouldn't arrive for the next few days or so – having set the date of the ceremony for the height of spring the following year, and had bumped into Leonard as we browsed the market for that evenings meal, just as Maralin enquired about a joint of mutton. We had only been in the new home three months, but had already got to know and make friends with a few people, including Leonard, who was widely respected by all who met him; I should note that we had met before – during our past exploits – and thus he valued my opinion. We talked a while about our plans before he made his excuses to leave, but not before asking if we could talk in private in an hour or so.

"So how was Leonard?" Maralin had not talked to him, bar her initial 'Hello' and 'how are you?' greeting, as she was bartering with Flax the butcher.

"Just the same as usual, complaining 'bout petty thefts but otherwise fine. Oh, and he'll be popping round sometime after noon; he needs my advice on those missing persons cases I told you about."

As we strolled back home, the daylight blossoming over the walls of white-washed stone, we talked carelessly, waving at the odd acquaintance as we passed them.

"It's a shame about his wife" Maralin sighed, turning her thoughts back to Leonard "has his son talked to him yet?"

Leonard's son, I should mention, blames his father for his mother's passing despite the fact that nothing could be done for her; she had contracted a disease called 'sickle fever', it is not always fatal but she had been weakened after a long journey from Hamurfel.

"No. It eats away at him though; it's why he throws himself into his work the way he does. I tried talking to Falkner but you know what he's like, won't listen to a word."

As we approached home the subject changed to the wedding once more, though this time it was as to who would be invited, bar the obvious few.

"What about Belothor? Whilst we are not close as such, he was a friend of Carmel's mother; and it would give Joahana someone else she knew to talk to, other than us."

Maralin gave me a teasing look.

"You're not doing this for her, even if she is a maid of honour." she chuckled; I just gave her a comical look "And besides, the only person she'll be thinking about talking to is Tau...and by talking I mean getting intimate with-"

"Maralin!"

She chuckled loudly with laughter.

"Anyways, Zaxx and Mazog are her friends too" she sighed as she caught her breath.

"I know, it's just...Carmel's been through a lot, and I want the day to be perfect for her."

"And what about it being perfect for you?"

"So long as she's there and goes through with the ceremony I'll be happy" I gave a little smile "But I just can't help but worry about every little detail, you know?"

She gave me that look; the one that tells you 'you're being a fool'.

"Stop fretting, it's not like we have a deadline to meet is it"-She put her free arm around mine-"besides, I already sent Belothor an invitation."

I looked at her and she gave me a smug grin.

"You know how to wind me up, you know that?"

"Yes, yes I do."

***

It was just after lunch that Leonard came around, announc-ing himself by his trademark rapping on the door before entering. It was when I greeted him that I noticed that he looked tired; as if some deep sadness had drained the life out of him, his eyes slightly bloodshot. It was true he pushed himself hard at work, but this was something else, something more.

"Is there somewhere we can talk in private?" he queried; obviously he did not want Maralin to overhear us.

"We can talk in the cellar my friend; I need to select a bottle of wine anyways" I smiled, and whilst he gave a smile back it was faint, and I could sense it was only out of politeness that he did.

I closed the cellar door behind me, Leonard having already descended the steps, and browsing over the wine rack.

"I thought you were more of a mead person" he remarked in a dry tone.

"Indeed I am, but Maralin prefers wine with her meals"-I pulled out a bottle from the top shelf, dusting it down-"she particularly likes this one, it's dark in colour and tastes quite divine when warmed slightly in the sun or by fire."

He nodded agreeingly, placing a hand on his waist-belt.

"So what troubles you Leonard?"

"There has been a...situation. A development you could say, in the missing persons case; I was hoping you could help me with it."

I turned to face him completely.

"Anything you need old friend" I smiled once more; though it quickly faded. The look in his face was of sadness, immense sadness.

"I've always respected you, you know, even on that first case you and your friends worked on."

"The missing livestock?"

"Aye; how you solved that was a work of art."

"Thanks" I smiled, as I looked back at the bottle, checking the label a second time; Maralin is rather particular about her wine, so it was worth a double check.

"I'm sorry friend" he muttered, a tear rolling down his eye as I looked back at him.

My expression turned to confused, but before I had chance to respond, he pulled his hand from his belt, revealing he was holding a dagger, and tried to strike me down.

Luckily my reflexes were fast enough that I could grasp hold of his hand before he could land a mortal blow. We struggled, the wine I had been holding crashing to the floor, the dark red liquid within smothering the stone beneath it. I tried to speak, trying to reason with him, but he held my throat with his other hand, attempting to choke me. My left hand held back his dagger, my free hand attempting to push him away. His strength was immense, despite both his age and appearance. Eventually my back was forced against the wine rack, his dagger getting ever closer to me; I made a split-second decision to stop pushing back, and instead pulled him by his dagger hand into the bottles behind me, just avoiding the blade, and, with all my force, hammered him on the head with a handy bottle of wine.

All was suddenly silent.

I stood looking down upon him, the neck of the wine bottle still in my grasp, disbelieving as to what had just occurred. He lay motionless; I turned him onto his back to see his dagger had pierced him in the chest, near the collarbone, a few shards of glass in his face. It was hard to tell how heavily he was bleeding; the dark wine had stained him, and coated most of the surrounding floor. Not surprising when over dozen bottles have been smashed, not including the one I had hit him with. I crouched beside him to check his breathing, and whilst it was faint, it was there.

Shaken and disturbed by such a sudden turn by a well trusted acquaintance, and unsure of what to do, I walked up the cellar stairs and left, locking the door behind me, before proceeding to get a clean set of clothes and look for Maralin. I found her, as you know, on the balcony, gazing at passers-by and the deep blue sky. I did not want to get her involved, as difficult as that would be to do. Mazog and Zaxx were a few days ride out too, and so I ultimately resolved to investigate by myself.

* * *

Dusk had begun to fall, the cellar was sealed shut, and I had just finished writing letters to my companions. Maralin was reading a book Mazog had sent her a week ago, something about historic moments in Blackwood, blissfully unaware of the trouble I was in. I made my excuses to go out and began to wander the street. It was still pleasantly warm despite the darkening sky, for it was the height of summer, and as I journeyed without a destination I watched the people around me; a few wandered to and from the market, and the odd person visiting the apothecary, each and all wrapped up in their own lives and stories. I pondered on how many of them would even be able to guess what the other was going through or experiencing, or how many would believe my tale if I were to tell it.

I was attempting to clear my head, but to no apparent avail; I even walked past the White Dragon Inn, its window alight with candles and shadows of honey-mead filled tankards, without a thought, which says something.

It was on my way back, on what must have been my second hour since I started, that I bumped into Falkner quite literally.

"Have you seen my father? I...I need to speak with him." He said awkwardly, the hint of rage unnervingly in the corner of his eyes.

"Erm..."-I panicked a little-"I saw him in the market around late morning time."

What can I say, I wasn't lying.

"So you haven't seen him since then?" he queried.

"No, not at all"-Okay, that was a lie-"Say, what's that on your neck?" I asked, seeing some kind of recent wound just below his collar.

"Oh that, I dropped my razor when shaving is all" he smiled, before wandering off.

I felt guilty, but I couldn't tell him the truth...could I?

I headed home more swiftly now, my trauma having morphed into determination to find out why Leonard had attacked me; and if I couldn't wake him, move his unconscious body to somewhere else, preferably far away where I could do so and ask questions without fear of discovery by Maralin.

As I entered I found Maralin still in the sitting room, asleep next to the fire, still holding the book she had been reading. I crept over to the cellar, gently opened the door and slowly descended the steps. When I looked up from where I was putting my feet I got a shock that sent me backwards onto the floor; Leonard's body had gone, vanished, disappeared.

****

Astounded. Gobsmacked. Perplexed. All good words for the utter confusion going through my mind. Where had Leonard gone? More importantly, how had he gotten past Maralin, through the locked cellar and front doors?

Feeling defeated by all this, my determination drained, I walked back up the cellar steps, locking the door behind me more out of instinct than anything else. I entered the sitting room, carefully prising the book from Maralin's hands, placing her bookmark between the pages and setting it down on the table beside her chair. Carefully I put my arms under her, lifting her slowly as to not wake her, and carried her up the stairs to her room. I lay her atop her bedsheets, which were a soft layering of green and white fabric, making sure her head lay comfortably to the side as I rested it upon her puffy pillow.

I stood and watched a moment, watching her chest rise and fall with each breath, and the contentment upon her face as she dreamed, before leaving for my own bed, hoping I would get as good a sleep as she was having.

I spent the best part of the next day combing the red-stained floor for signs of movement, though it was damn near impossible, all that wine had turned into a congealed carpet overnight, one that made my search something of a wasted effort. As I took my time to examine the cellar walls, I pondered the events that had led to this, examining every detail; Leonard's expression, his mannerisms, the way he had said what he said. As for Maralin, she had – thankfully – gone to the Temple to organise some traditional Blackwood flower arrangements and other fanciful decor for the wedding; which was to be held in Bahvil due to Carmel being its Countess, in case you were wondering.

Aggravated, I revaluated the situation, and began smashing more wine bottles against the floor (perhaps not the best approach, but hey, it's good therapy); there was, as usual, method in my madness, for should there be any secret hatch in the floor, the wine should run to it. Evidently I was wrong though; as I watched the wine run across the floor it revealed nothing, though perhaps this is just as well, because if it hadn't I probably would not have leant against the old torch sconce behind me. For as I did, the fixture moved back into the wall, and a small, well concealed tunnel was revealed. It was small enough for someone to crawl through, but only just, and what's more, it was part-way off the ground, situated on the left-hand wall as you enter the cellar. You would have thought I would have noticed such a thing before, but no, somehow that had avoided discovery until now. Which kinda' begs the question of how Leonard knew about it. As I went to climb inside the thing shut like a trap; thankfully just before I had put my hands in its way, giving me a short burst of relief that they were still attached.

So the picture, as I saw it, was that a wounded Leonard had pushed back the fixture – which was quite stiff – ran and crawled into the tunnel before it shut; he must have moved fast, for I counted only thirteen seconds from pushing the trigger to the thing snapping shut (and trust me, the thing could quite easily take an arm, or leg, off like a leaf from a tree).

Taking the time to write Maralin a note saying I had gone for a stroll and not to wait up for me, I hefted the wine rack over and next to where the tunnel was, leaning it against the wall. I pushed the sconce back as far as it would go, darted over to the opening and wedged the now broken wine rack into it, sprinted back to the torch-scone, pushed it back once again, and dived into the tunnel, pulling myself forward as quickly as possible; just as well seeing as it snapped the rack almost as if it were a bundle of twigs. Thus I began a rather awkward crawl towards my unknown destination, hoping it would not lead to the sewers; there's far too many people down there who know me.

***

After about an hour of travel in the pitch dark, my body aching from the many confined movements I had made, I came to what felt like a stone wall. There were no turn-offs, no vertical climbs or descents, just the wall. I felt around, patting the rock for some kind of fixture. Nothing. A sense of panic was brewing within, and I had no time or desire for it. I glided my hands down the sides of the tunnel; nothing but rough surfaces. I pushed against the wall; it did not give. I was stuck in a hole with no exits, and claustrophobia was beginning to rear its ugly head. At least, I thought, it wasn't being flooded.

Then, after leaning on what must have been a small pressure-plate, water began to surge into the confined crawlspace, causing me to shudder at both the sudden coldness of its liquid embrace hitting me, and out of fear.

But this sword of fate had two edges; on the one hand I could drown, on the other I could see (well, feel) that the water was coming from the top-right corner, on the side of the tunnel. Thankfully this re-instilled my usual sense of calm, as I figured that if the water had a way in, I had a way out. Through feeling slowly and carefully this area of the 'dead end', pushing my hands through the stream of water, I found it was hinged so that it may be pushed upward, but worked out it would only do so when the tunnel was completely filled with water.

At this point the water was up to my waist height (bear in mind I am on my hands and knees at this time); I closed my eyes for a second, began to breathe slowly, with each breath being a bit longer and slower. I opened my eyes when I felt the water start to cover my face; I took my last few breaths, then the water took me under.

I pushed at the hinged corner, still blind in the dark. It was slow to open, obviously rusted enough to hinder its opening, but not enough to become brittle. I clambered through, catching myself on the narrow exit, only to find the tunnel was less than a foot wider, and every yard or so there was another hinged opening. I had counted two minutes, and still there was

no light, no sign of reprieve. My lungs had begun to recycle the
air within me, my head starting to ache, my heart beating heavily and slowly; I did not go frantic with my movement though,
for I knew this would make it worse. Fifteen openings later and
a slight glimmer began to form in front of me, like that through
a grating. I pulled myself upward, half swimming, half climbing up the narrow tunnel. My body had grown desperate for
new air, my lungs constricted with pain, my brain felt shriv-
elled, my muscles making their last bid for the surface, feeling
taut and twisted. Mere seconds away from taking a fatal breath,
I manage to pull my face above water, though only by an inch, a
grating blocking my path; though in all honesty I was just glad
for the respite, and the luxury of breathing. It must have been
ten minutes I stayed there, recovering my lungs and organs
from their ordeal.

Thank the Divines there wasn't a lock on that grating.

Seriously.

***

Having climbed out onto the dry stone floor of wherever I
was, I contemplated closing the grating as I rung out my shirt.
Deciding it was best left the way I found it, I began walking
down an ill-lit hallway. The light was coming from a strange
mix of fading sunlight (through purposeful holes in the ceiling,
not unlike where the grating was) and dying torches; probably
lit by Leonard. There was nothing of note about this place, dull
grey rock and stone made all parts of it, a few weeds growing in
patches of sunlight, the odd side path to other floor gratings

filled with water; obviously this was some kind of hub connecting multiple buildings. The only two questions I had as I strolled cautiously though what can only loosely be called a hallway, was why such a system was built, and how Leonard had managed to get through the tunnel, and its traps – especially with his wound; I mean, I near enough drowned, so he should of...shouldn't he?

Two hours since entering the tunnel, I had come to what first appeared to be another dead-end, but upon further inspection was a subtly hidden door. I looked at the unlit sconce to my left, instinctive pushed it, though it did not give, and so I gave it a pull; as it arched down it triggered the stone door to swing open slowly, and only just barely. Figuring this too would be on some sort of timed mechanism, I held the sconce down for as far as I could get away from it, before swiftly edging around and through the opening it had presented. I looked around the old stone room I found myself in as the stone door closed behind me, realising quickly it was some kind of cellar, and made for its steps; I looked back from whence I came in curiosity, finding the hidden door was well and truly that. As I reached the top of the steps I came to a door, a new door, out of place in this...place. I put my ear to it, listening for any sounds I need be worried about.

Nothing.

Slowly pushing the door open, I edged into the room. As I looked about the room I realised I knew it; it was Falkner's. As I wandered through I spied a wounded Leonard unconscious on a make-shift bedroll upon a two-seated lounger. He had evidently tried to bandage his wound himself, though he had made a poor job of it. I inspected the room, locked from the inside, keeping a cautious eye on him. An open journal page indicated Falkner was out on some errand or another, inadvertently giving Leonard a place to hide.

No indication of why Leonard tried to kill me though.

I drew his sword from its sheath and poked him with it.

"Wake up Leonard."

He stirred, beginning to wearily open his eyes; shock and fear followed, suddenly etching itself upon his face.

"I think we need a little chat" I spoke calmly, although I'm sure my tone betrayed my anger.

His lips quivered, trying to grasp how I had found him.

"P-Prime!"

I rested the tip of the sword on his chest.

"I believe you owe me an explanation, my dear chum."

"I-I...I-It, it's not what you think...I, err, I needed to, to..."

"Why do I get the feeling I'm not going to get much sense out of you?"

"Prime, l-listen to me I-"

I leaned a bit harder on the sword.

"Prime please! I did it for my son! My son!"

I eased up on the sword, but only a little.

"Why does he want me dead? I have not wronged him, have I?" My eyes searched his for honesty.

"He doesn't, he was taken, ransomed for your death" he pleaded.

I pulled the sword off him, holding it not an inch away from his chest.

"The missing persons case..." I muttered "Do you know by who?"

"No..."-He paused for a fleeting second-"I know his messenger, his name that is...what do you...what are you going-"

"To do?"-I leaned closer, raising the sword up to above his neck-"that depends."

He rushed his words.

"He's called Brayth, an Agrian, you'll find him-"

"At the Leather Back tavern." I interrupted.

He looked at me confused.

"You know this creature?"

I leaned in close, bringing the sword down, and pulling him to his feet.

"That creature is my brother" I hissed angrily.

His eyes widened, shocked to his core.

"Why didn't you tell me Leonard?" I asked, having dropped the sword, both my hand holding him up by the collar "You should have said something, instead of going straight to kill me!"

"I-I'm sorry Prime...I panicked and they have my son..." he sobbed "I can't lose him too..."

I put him down, pitying him.

"How...What happened? How did they get Falkner?" I asked, searchingly looking into his tear-filled eyes.

"I...I asked questions down at the Leather Back, probing some contacts for information on the missing persons, and their link to Ezekiel" he sat back down on his bed-roll, wiping his eyes "I offered coin if they asked 'the right people', and a week and a half later Brayth turns up at my door holding a package, says he has to see me open it" he gave a shudder.

"What was in it?"

"Grisly stuff. What was left of those asking questions, so I was told."-he looked up at me-"I was going to arrest Brayth there and then, but he then handed me Falkner's armlet, the one his mother gave him..."

"Damn" I sighed heavily, dismayed.

"So Brayth is your brother?" he asked, his voice still cracked by the tears.

"Adoptive brother." I corrected him "He was my uncles son, but was left orphaned after a harsh winter, back when we were both too young to remember"-I had no idea why I was telling him this, but perhaps it was some instinctive response to distance myself from Brayth-"You should have said something in the cellar."

"I know...I know...I was, I am so very frightened of what they would do to him."

I then remembered something obviously wrong with what he was telling me.

"Leonard...I saw Falkner yesterday, not long after our...skirmish." I said as it dawned on me.

His face was that of disbelief; a good sign he hadn't been lying to me.

"That's not possible" he shook his head, his eyes the most serious I had ever seen "That's just not possible!"

"Calm yourself Leonard, we need to focus."

"Calm? I tried to kill you, almost got *myself* killed – twice, counting that damned tunnel – for my kidnapped son, who is walking around free? How is this something to be calm about?!" he exclaimed, holding his head in his hand, trying to hold onto his sanity.

"Because we need to work out who is behind this, and that needs thought and reason, not panic and rage."

He took a deep breath.

"You're right...you're right."

"You should stay here; I'm going to get my short-sword and have a word with my brother."

"Prime, I should come, I-"

"You are a liability at the moment" I interrupted "And we both know you won't be able to control yourself."

"But-"

"Do I need to remind you, you tried to stab me to death instead of asking for my help?"

"...no" he said sheepishly and ashamed "I'm so sorry."

I gave a weary sigh.

"I'm doing this for your wife, Leonard; think yourself lucky I was there to ease her passing when she died, else this might have ended differently."

He just gave a weak nod.

As I went to leave through the front door, I turned back to him.

"By the way, what the hell is that passageway?"

"Old escape routes the assassins used back in the day of the Dred King."

"I thought this city was only recently built?"

"It is, but it was constructed over the ruins of the ancient one that once stood here" he blew his nose on a handkerchief

"And before you ask, I didn't know for sure that the tunnel hadn't – or wouldn't – collapse when I went in; I only knew it existed from the old city maps in the castle archive."

I stood silently in the doorway a moment.

"By the divines Leonard, you're a goddamned idiot!"

I slammed the door behind me, realising just how lucky I had been these last few days.

***

Having fetched my sword, I had made my way to the Leather Back, grabbing a bite to eat on the move from the market. Dusk had fallen near an hour when I reached my brother's humble abode.

I kicked the door open; there he was, collecting empty pitchers and tankards from the tables. He looked dead at me and went for a broadsword hung on the western wall. I ran and tackled him just before he could get it. We fought, punching each other as best we could as we rolled across the tavern floor, half emptied pitchers falling to the ground, spilling their contents. At last we scrambled to our feet, throwing anything remotely like a weapon at each other, until finally I had him cornered. I picked up a nearby pitcher, and after taking a sip, broke it over his head, throwing him across the table to our left, breaking a chair at the other end. As he tried to get to his feet, I smashed another jug of ale over his head. Lifting him off the floor, I rammed him into the wall and held him by the throat.

"Why the hell do you want me dead?!"

"Ack! Kaghg!" I was holding his throat a little too tight. Shame that. I loosened my grip and allowed his feet to fall to the floor.

He took a deep gasp for air, his throat sore.

"How do brother..." he croaked.

I slapped him with my free hand.

"Tell me. Now."

"Tell you what–"

SMACK. I backhanded him this time, so hard it actually echoed through the empty tavern; a bit harder than I meant to.

His eyes turned to me, distrustful and bitter – angry even. Kind of made me feel a bit guilty for that backhand; only a bit though, he did pass on orders to have me killed after all.

"Well?"

"Hit me once more brother, and I swear...I swear I'll–"

"ENOUGH! Do you not think I have better things to do than smack you about, huh? Do you not realise I'm planning my wedding? That I'm finally finding happiness? Why in the Divines name are you doing this?!" I felt the rage in my voice, the little patience I had now totally lost.

His eyes softened slightly, though still bitter.

"His son is safe."

"Not what I asked" I seethed calmly "And his son walks free about this city, so yes I know he's safe."

He regarded me silently for a moment.

"Brother, do not take it personally. Much coin was offered"-I bit my lip, holding back the urge to backhand him again-"And I did not know his son is free; I swear on oath I was told he was held captive."

"So what can you tell me?"

"What coin can you offer me? Or perhaps a turn with your woman?"

That did it.

CRACK.

With an almighty thud he landed on the stone floor, bleeding, the table I had just smashed him through no more than a strewn mess of splinters now.

Grabbing him by his collar I pulled his head off the ground.

"YOU. WILL. EXPLAIN. EVERYTHING!"

He stared at me disbelieving.

"NOW!"

Fear had swallowed his mind, his eyes, and loosened his bladder.

He could see the emotions writhing within me, unsure of what I might do next.

"B-brother...I-I, I needed the c-coin...'"

"Not an excuse, nor an explanation." I spoke coldly, not even the slightest bit of humanity in my voice; no one talks about my love like that – not even my brother – especially after they played a part in my attempted murder "Talk. Now."

"H-he calls h-himself B-Balford..." his voice faded as he began to cry.

I stood up, letting his head bounce off the floor, recoiling from this...this news.

Balford...Carmel had struck him down herself...I saw it. I saw his blood pump out of him, his body go limp.

Someone was playing with me, tricking me; well, attempting to.

I do not like being played with. But...this was something *else*, something nearer revenge, but why? And about what and whom? To my recollection I had not wronged anyone.

And Balford was dead, so he was, of that I was sure.

It made no sense.

My brother was pitifully crying as he attempted to crawl away.

I put my foot on his back and leaned close to his ear.

"Where is Balford?"

He tilted his head just enough to glimpse me out the corner of his eye, all red and puffy from tears.

"U-up s-stairs" he whimpered.

"Great." I mumbled; he would have heard all of that, whomever he was "I guess he'd be expecting me then" I said to myself as I drew my sword and made for the stairs.

*

I moved slowly, tiptoeing up the stairs, attempting to hear any subtle sounds of movement. Some of the room doors were ajar, others seemed tightly shut. I edged round the first door: nothing; just a bed and a desk. Slowly I progressed to the next room, one of those with a shut door. As I moved towards it I realised something, a question I should have asked downstairs: the inn-keeper, and his wife, where were they? I frowned at myself as I contemplated their involvement; Marry and John, if anything they would be hostages, not likely to be after my blood.

It was just as I was about to open the door that I stepped, stupidly, on a loose floorboard. Its creaking bounced off the walls in the otherwise silent hallway. I froze, my nerves on tenterhooks, holding my breath in silence as I awaited the sound of an inevitable attack now my position was known.

Then, I heard someone knock into the door behind the one I was facing.

I spun around to see a hooded figure come at me with a wood axe, just managing to duck under it as its metal head smashed into the wood of the door.

I stumbled in the confusion, attempting to regain my footing when another hooded figure bust out of another closed door further down the hall, knocking me to the ground with his hammer, despite my blocking it. I managed to open my legs as the axe the other one had split the floor open; any higher and my voice would have gone up an octave or two.

Stabbing the one with the hammer in the shin, I managed to roll onto my knees, just in time to block a death blow from that axe, just as a third hooded figure joined the fray.

'How my luck never changes' I thought to myself as I pushed myself back as hard and as fast as I could, my sword raised defensively.

Then suddenly – and unexpectedly – my brother, blood-soaked and splintered, rammed the broadsword from earlier through the chest of the axe wielder, before swinging it in a wide arc at the bemused third would-be assassin, cleaving the head clean off. He gave me a wink before being belted by the hammer of the one I had injured, collapsing to the floor like crumpled parchment. I lunged from my kneeling position, severing the man's hand, causing him to squeal in pain as his hammer dropped, the hand still tightly grasping it. I held my sword against his throat, the blade just cutting the surface.

"Where. Is. Balford?" I spoke calmly, clearly and so very coldly, through gritted teeth.

I imagine his eyes would have been full of terror, though they were concealed by his hood

"I-I...Falkner, h-he..."

I comforted the man with words.

"Tell me and I shall ensure you do not suffer" I said, giving him a forced and weary smile.

The hooded man nodded, shaking with shock. I figured he wasn't going to last long like that.

"Falkner, he p-promised m-much coin, h-h-he, h-he"-the man was starting to go into a deeper state of shock-"h-he s-said y-y-you s-stole h-his b-b-bride..."

I raised an eyebrow questioningly.

"A-a-a g-g-girl c-c-called c-c-c-car-m-m-m-m-"

"Carmel?"

He nodded, shaking furiously now; I had removed my sword from his throat, and having sheathed it, I held the man by his shoulders.

"Where is he?" I spoke softly with false warmth.

The man grasped my left arm, trying to steady himself.

"P-p-p-please, m-m-my f-f-fa-family, th-they kn-know n-n-n-nothing."

I nodded at him, a silent reassurance I would not seek them out.

"C-c-crove-s-s-shaw…"

He was shaking uncontrollably, no matter how much I tried to keep him still.

"Croveshaw?"

He nodded as best he could.

He had lost a lot of blood. Too much. And the shock…Ordinarily I would allow such a man to live, one who has confessed and seems truly sorry – clearly doing what he must to sustain his family – but this man…he was suffering…dying…slowly.

I could not let him suffer.

A faint crack echoed down the hallway, the man slumping to the floor, no longer shaking. As I got to my feet to check on my brother – who was still breathing – I noticed that all the hoods were a pale blue. As I went to check the sleeves for that distinctive mark, I heard some muffled voices; 'Marry and John' I thought. I approached the door the sound was coming from and kicked it open, and there they were, bound and gagged.

As I removed their gags they each gave a sigh of relief, thanking me as I untied them.

"'Fraid I've made a bit of a mess John" I apologised as I removed the last of their bindings.

"A mess can be cleaned" he said rubbing his wrists.

"True, but"-I turned to Marry-"I wouldn't take a look out there if I were you."

She nodded, still a bit traumatised. I turned back to John.

"You need to call the city guard…just brace yourself John, not all of those men are in one piece."

Marry winced at that.

"Sure. Can't be worse than Zaxx's mess though ay?" he joked. He was like that, always trying to lift the mood, even if he was deeply shaken.

(Just a point of clarity; it was not so much that the Leather Back is one of Zaxx's favourite Inns, so much as *all* Inns are; least when he isn't vomiting up their ale that is.)

I gave him a nod, and was about to leave when I turned back to them.

"Oh, by the way, can you look after my brother? Just...chain him up as soon as he is able to move...actually, probably best to do that before then."

***

Croveshaw, a place inhabited by the ghosts of the dishonoured, if Blackwood folk law is to be believed. Though I regard it as more of a fort that was poorly built and even more poorly defended in its time.

I had informed Maralin of what she needed to know, and had rode out to where I could meet up with Mazog and Zaxx, as I thankfully knew which road they were taking to Blackwood.

As I met them traveling north up the Southern Road, I found that Tau was with them too, which was another thing to be thankful for; in no small part because of that warhammer of his. As I rode my trusty steed, I could not help but ask myself why Falkner would seek such a complicated and bloody revenge. Why did the hooded aggressor say it was about my marriage to Carmel, which had yet to even happen?

It didn't make sense.

I pulled another frown.

'No' I thought 'this is something else, something worse; he's put all these distracting, irrelevant bits of information out there to throw me off balance.'

I also thought on how Carmel was traveling via the longer, scenic route from Bahvil to Blackwood, and hoped that would keep her away from this madness.

And then, in the back of my mind, it hit me.

That symbol, the black sickle...was it him?

But it couldn't be that...could it?

No, that was not, should not, be possible; or so I thought at the time.

Either way, I was going to get answers.

****

Having met up with my friends I explained to them the events that had befallen me as we rode towards Croveshaw. Mazog gave a loud curse once he had heard it all, disbelieving at my brother's part in it all; Zaxx questioned his motive behind saving me, and I reasoned that he most likely realised he had a better chance of staying alive with me around than dealing with whoever had hired him.

Night had fallen swiftly that day, and with little visible to guide us in the moonless sky, we settled around a clump of saplings growing out from a group of cracked boulders. There was enough of a breeze to warrant a fire to keep us warm as we huddled against the side of the clump opposite its direction. Mazog passed me some half stale bread whilst Zaxx made a toast to the Leather Back and proceeded to down a bottle of priory mead. Probably best I didn't know how he had managed to get that, seeing as the only priory he would of past would have been an all-female one.

I contemplated our plan of action, taking a sip of mead as I did.

"So what's the plan?" Tau asked as he pulled up the top of his bedroll.

"Honestly I'm not sure" I shrugged "After the last two days my mind feels shot to hell."

"Can't say I'm surprised" Zaxx slurred "You survived two murder attemptsss, a bar brawl and nearly drowned; it's enough to drive a man mad, happenin' all in the space of two days."

"I dunno, sounds like a typical weekend for you" Mazog joked dryly.

"Perhaps we just kill everyone?" Zaxx added, ignoring the joke.

"I would prefer asking Falkner why he's done all of this" I looked deep into the fire, a quiet worry itching the back of my mind.

"So how about this" Mazog said, as he ripped off another chunk of bread "we sneak in, see if we can get Falkner by himself, but failing that cut down all those that stand in our way; I mean, it's not like they're going to be good people."

"You mean because of the attempted murder and abductions?" I smiled with somewhat forced humour "Why would a little thing like that make someone bad?"

Zaxx gave a hiccupy chuckle.

"But does that sound like a plan?" Mazog asked.

"It'll do" I whispered, lying back into my bedroll "It'll do."

***

We approached the fort from the east side, hoping the glaring light from the rising Sun would help obscure us from view. We had dismounted two-hundred yards back, amongst a nestle of leafy trees. Our advance was slow and methodical, interrupted by silent bounds between areas of cover. As we got within twenty yards from a scalable section of wall, Mazog unslung his trusty viewing-glass and studied the walls of the fort, the rest of us waiting expectantly, Zaxx readying his bow in anticipation.

"Not a soul to be seen" I could tell by his tone he found that to be suspicious.

"A trap?" whispered Zaxx, his hand still ready to draw his bowstring.

"Probably."

"We walking into it?" Tau asked, the others looking at me.

"Yeah" I shrugged, mock serious "it'd be a shame for them to go to all that effort for nothing."

*

We scaled the faded and damaged orange wall swiftly, being careful not to let our weapons scrape against the rough stone. As we entered the bastion, I noticed the lack of guards; not one could be seen. And that was worrying, even by trap standards.

"A place like this should be fortified to the hilt" grumbled Zaxx, his voice gruff with the smell of alcohol.

"Yeah...best we stick close to the battlements. This just stinks of a dirty trap" Mazog spoke with a whisper.

We nodded silently.

As we crept towards what I assumed was a garrison door on the far side of the wall I pondered the whys of what was happening once more. What had I done to wrong Falkner? And why was it so important to him that he was willing to send his own father to kill me? What else could someone so desperate be willing to do?

As you can imagine, that last thought was the one that concerned me most.

Zaxx edged the door open, his short-sword drawn and readied to be thrust into a potential foe, his bow now slung over his shoulder; Tau towered behind him, his warhammer raised. But the room was empty. I mean there were beds, candlesticks, clothes, but the only hint this place was recently inhabited was a long dead fire, its ash staining the floor.

Though none of us spoke, we each knew what the other thought, and so we slowly made our way further in, towards the heart of the bastion.

We knew it was a trap.

We knew we would most likely be outnumbered.

And whilst we knew they would probably think I was alone, we thought it safe to assume they knew what tricks we might pull.

We didn't expect them to have her.

*

As we entered the once great hall of this forgotten bastion, our eyes met with Falkner, sitting upon the throne of a long forgotten noble.

His face was smug; aggravatingly so. He held a sword, still in its sheath across his lap; it was odd, even at this distance it looked...familiar.

We marched towards him, weapons drawn and ready for an ambush.

He rose from his false throne, still smirking.

"Friends, I do hope finding this place was no trouble"-his voice was bold and condescending-"I presume you are ready to beg for forgiveness, no?"

We did not halt our march, nor respond to him. No, our fury – my fury – was too great for mere talking.

But then he started to laugh.

"You wish to kill me then?" he chucked psychotically "Fine. But first let me show you your wedding present oh *honourable* and *noble* Prime. Consider it a thank you for all your hard work."

We stopped abruptly as his men entered the room; not because of them, but because of who they brought with them: Carmel.

"Let her go Falkner" I seethed in panic.

She was crying, her mouth bound so she could not speak.

"Let her go? Ha!"

He unsheathed the sword.

"Do you recognise it Prime? Does this not tell you how this will end?"

"What's he talking about?" Mazog asked, his eyes now sternly looking at me.

I didn't look back at him, though I could feel the others almost begging me to.

That sword...it just couldn't be. I could have sworn I destroyed it.

"That sword...it is – was – mine..." I tried not to show emotion, but I feel that my voice may have betrayed me; I could not fathom how he had obtained Soulbreaker, and it disturbed me greatly.

Falkner just nodded.

Mazog's gaze did not drift from me, though he stayed silent.

"So what if he has an old sword? What don't we know Prime?" Zaxx tried to whisper, though I don't think he has any idea how to.

"The importance of this sword" Falkner replied mockingly "is that it is the one that slew my mother."

I could feel my friend's confusion behind me, lowering their weapons, if only ever so slightly. I could see Carmel's shock, and though she could not speak, I could hear her ask the question.

"Prime?" Tau bellowed the question using only my name, and I hesitated to answer.

Falkner was walking slowly towards us, his men mimicking his movements.

"Well Prime? Do tell your friends what you did."-his voice was becoming slightly hysterical, but somehow still controlled-"Tell them how you killed my mother!"

"Your mother died from sickle fever" my voice was sympathetic, even after all he had done; he was still just a boy who had lost his mother after all.

"Liar!" he screeched with fury.

He marched back towards Carmel, his men readying their swords.

"Do you think me stupid Prime? Did you *really* think I would not find out?"

He grabbed Carmel by her hair.

Tau jolted forwards, and Falkner's men did the same.

"Tau wait" I yelled, a tad franticly, before focusing my attention on Falkner once more "What do you want Falkner? What does hurting Carmel have to do with us? Hmm? It's me you have the problem with."

Falkner released his grasp on Carmel.

"Problem?"-his face began to twitch-"Problem? My mother's death, a mere problem?!"

His sword hand twitched, as if enacting his vengeful thoughts.

I moved towards him. Slowly.

"Your father...he begged me"-I was nervous, but thankfully it did not seem to show-"your mother too; her pain was great...there was nothing that could be done."

He was allowing me to get close to him, and I had lowered my weapon. An action I would soon regret.

"You mean to tell me that my father, the man who was meant to protect my mother, begged you to, what, mercy kill her?"-I could see tears forming in his eyes being held back by sheer fury-"And that my mother agreed to such an end?"

"She did not feel it, she was asleep; had they had poison it would have been different...there was no other option. She felt it best she left this world on her own terms."

We were but three feet from one another. I could have easily dispatched him from there, but...I...I thought I could get him to stop, to let Carmel leave with the others...I could have ended it there and then, but then wouldn't his men have killed Carmel as retribution?

I could feel the tension from my friends.

I could see the plea for help from Carmel.

I could feel Falkner's hate, his desire to kill me.

But I didn't strike him down.

"So, what you're saying...is that it was a kindness?" Falkner had lowered my old sword somewhat, luring me closer, raising my confidence.

"In a sad, sad and unfortunate way, yes" my voice was soft, my sword lowered further still.

Falkner nodded, seemingly understanding. He beckoned two of his men behind him to walk forward.

It was there I noticed something I failed to see before.

One of the men, his hands were bound, and was being held by the other hooded minion.

Just as I was about to speak, the second pulled the hood off the unknown captive.

I froze in shock.

The man was Leonard, his mouth bound, his face clearly having taken a beating.

Falkner walked back to them, pointing at his father as he spoke.

"Do you not think I'd gotten this same sob story from him?" he laughed almost manically, and not out of humour.

"Sob story-?" he cut me off before I could continue.

"How you and my *precious* father ended my mother's misery. HA."

He was now out of reach, and would most likely have set his men on us then if I tried to close the gap.

"Falkner, listen-"

"IM DONE LISTENING" as he screamed he swung my old sword, the sword that had ended his mother's life, cleaving his father's head from his shoulders.

In split seconds he gestured to his men to attack, making his way to the bound Carmel, who was struggling against her bindings.

This was it.
My friends or the woman I loved.
This was the choice.
Hesitation wasn't an option.

I hesitated.

*

Swords were flailing through the once great hall, some striking metal, others rending flesh.

Tau was just managing to hold off five of Falkner's men with his mighty warhammer – which had already crushed three of our foes – though it was becoming more difficult for him to do so. No one man can handle foes at all angles, no matter how strong.

Zaxx and Mazog were back-to-back, parrying blows more often than they delivered them.

Falkner had made it to within a few feet of Carmel, and I knew full well what he planned to do; he wanted me to feel the pain he felt, and I wasn't about to let that happen.

I pulled myself together, mentally cursing my moment of indecision.

With innate fury I hacked my way through the few men between us, pushing through their ranks with a skill I have never had, and never shown since.

Sensing my approach, Falkner drew that accursed sword to Carmel's throat.

My heart stopped.

Everything stopped.

But I would not stop my approach; no, I needed to strike down this...this demon spawn, this vile corruption of a man, needed to keep him from hurting her.

"Falkner!"

He turned his head, smiling at his own triumph.

He began to pull the sword across her flawless skin.

And within that moment I threw my trusty short-sword.

Blood was gushing, though I could not tell whom it belonged to.

I ran with all my might.

I had to know.

Falkner collapsed to the floor, unmoving.

Carmel too, her throat now bleeding, was unmoving upon the broken stone floor.

*

All I could see was the blood on her neck.

I tore a line of cloth from the skirt of her dress, attempting to bandage her apparent wound.

And it was there, in that thankful moment, as I pressed the makeshift bandage onto her neck that I felt her pulse.

Euphoria does not begin to describe how I felt in that moment.

As I pulled back the now blood-stained bandage, I felt her wound, discovering it to be just a flesh wound, like a deep papercut, one which it would be easy to recover from. I felt the luck of it rush through me, realising that had I hesitated even half a second longer I would have lost her. As for her being unconscious, I would later find that she had fainted in that moment Falkner went to cut her throat, which is quite understandable to say the least.

At this point I turned to check on my companions; they were locked in the heat of battle. And whilst they fought with their signature strength and speed, they were encircled by equally skilled foes. Falkner had always been good and spotting military potential in people, much like his now deceased father, but these men seemed different, more ferocious; then I noticed the symbol upon their shoulders.

Just as I turned back to scoop Carmel off the floor, I felt numb. It was like someone had severed feeling to my lower half, though it was a fleeting second before pain flowed through me.

I looked down to see the tip of Falkner's sword – my sword – poking out from below the right side of my ribs, blood dripping down me.

I felt sick and weak.

Instinctively I grasped the end of the sword; I'd be dammed if I was going to let him strike me again.

I could feel his breath against my ear.

"I guess if I couldn't take your bride"-he sneered-"then I shall have to take you instead."

Noting I would not release my grasp on the sword as he pulled back on its hilt, my hands covered in their own blood, he wrenched my short-sword out from his shoulder, and prepared to sever my head, mocking me as he did.

"Say hi to father for me, won't you?"

With than he swung for me, and I braced for it, too weak to evade the oncoming strike.

But the strike did not land.

And what I heard was the most terrifying scream.

I turned my head, and saw that Falkner's right hand had been severed.

Mazog had thrown his only weapon, his trusted sword – his father's sword – to save my life. He had given up his only means of defending himself for me, the fool who led us into this trap knowingly.

And having done so, one of our foes spotted his chance to weaken our defence, landing a debilitating blow into Mazog's left shoulder.

Zaxx quickly dispatched the man, striking him in the centre of his face, before kicking him off his sword.

There were few men left, but not so few they could afford to give up their defensive stance to aid Mazog, who was crumpled on the floor, attempting to fight off the unending agony and stand, raising the sword that had struck him with his other hand.

Tau had taken but a scratch (or at least it was for him, any lesser man would have been slain by now), but he was growing weary, the speed of his strikes waning.

Falkner, grasping his severed stump, blood oozing from it, began his retreat, cursing me as he went.

"I'll get you Prime! I will have my VENGENCE!" he screamed.

I tried to rise to my feet, but my wound made it difficult and cumbersome.

I looked at Mazog.

He looked at me.

"Finish it!" he shouted; though I did not need convincing, his words empowered me with the strength to give chase.

As I finally stood on my own two feet, I pulled my old blade from out of my body and strode after Falkner, my pace ever quickening with my fury.

Now wielding the very blade that had started this series of events, I ended up in a sprint towards my quarry, and though he had a head start, and a lesser wound, he would not escape me.

No, he would pay for what he had tried to do to Carmel. And I wanted him to suffer for it.

He had taken the back passage to the outer courtyard, knocking over cupboards and desks to slow me down, but it was to no avail.

I was gaining on him.

Thirty feet.

Twenty feet.

Fifteen feet.

He had made it to the courtyard door, and I had closed much of the gap.

Desperate, he made for one of the tethered horses, leaving the door partially open as he fled.

Slamming through it, I moved towards him with dark fervour, as he haplessly tried to untether his horse with his one hand.

Noticing me getting ever closer, he panickedly tried to undo the knot that blocked his escape.

As I got to within four yards of him he began to back away, facing towards me.

"Prime, leave me be!" he cowered.

I stayed silent.

"After all you have done to me, you owe me Prime! You own ME!"

His yelling was becoming more and more hysterical.

I continued towards him, maintaining my silence.

"Speak dam you! SPEAK!"

It was more like screeching now.

And he was almost within striking distance. Almost.

"Fine! We're even! Happy?! YOU get to live! YOU get to walk away!"

He had nowhere left to run, with no more space between us.

"GO Prime! LEAVE! YOU CAN GO!"

I kicked him to the ground, his twisted face looking at me, though I could not tell the emotion upon it.

"You CAN'T kill me Prime! You're not like me! You have your *precious* honour!" he spat, seething from his very soul.

"You're right, I'm not like you" I said calmly as I placed a boot upon his chest to hold him down "I actually get my vengeance when I go looking for it."

His eyes widened.

"You should have just talked to me" I sighed apologetically "Recognise this sword?"

I plunged my hated blade into his skull; it went so deep it got stuck in the ground he was lying on.

As I pushed myself up off the sword's hilt, I saw the sickle shaped mark branded upon his collar line.

I took a few steps back, a feeling of nausea sweeping over me before falling to my knees.

It was there, at that moment, that I realised the enormity of what had happened, and how it could have been prevented if Falkner had just talked to me, instead of diving into blind revenge; though I questioned whether he went there of his own accord, or if he was manipulated by our oldest foe.

And it was at that moment I blacked out, succumbing to my blood loss.

***

Whilst I do not fully remember the details of when I regained my consciousness, I do recall it was four days after, in my Blackwood home; Soulbreaker resting on the cabinet across from me

I presume you wish to know what happened to my companions, and I shall gladly tell you: Zaxx had, managing a rare feat of sobriety, fought back Falkner's men to a point at which he could get to Carmel, scoop her up, and make his way out the same way me and Falkner had. Thankfully Tau had managed to throw Mazog over his shoulder and follow suit. But Mazog's wounds were great, and there was a real fear he would lose his arm.

I owed my friends an explanation about Falkner's mother, and so I told them the story, and how it had been Falkner's mother's idea, her choice, and her decision. It did not make it feel any better, even though she was not going to survive her illness, despite it ending what would have otherwise been a painful, undignified departure.

They seemed understanding, if a little distant; I fear my keeping it a secret is what gave them the doubts they still held. Carmel asked if there was anything else I hadn't told her, and I said I had only kept it secret in case it changed her view of me.

"But is there anything else?" she asked sternly, her eyes uncharacteristically piercing.

"Carmel my love, I swear to you I have no secrets bar this."

She looked at me lovingly, if highly displeased.

"So no more ambushes and kidnappings?" she asked.

I paused, that nagging feeling welling up inside me.

"Prime?"

"There is something, not a secret mind you, but something."

"What?"

"Falkner...his neck had been branded with the mark of a black sickle."

She looked at me expectantly.

"It's the symbol of the noble family an old friend belonged to...well, he was a friend once."

"How worried should I be?" she came over and sat next to me.

"I don't know"-I looked at her with all the love I had-"But...does this change things? Do...do you still love me?"

She tilted her head, a sympathetic, caring smile upon her face.

"Oh you silly thing"-she wrapped her arms around me-"I'll never stop loving you; your heart is pure good, no matter how much of an idiot you can be."

I held her tightly, burying my head into her shoulder.

"I thought I was going to lose you Carm" I croaked as I felt tears fall from my eyes.

"Hush now"-she patted me on the back-"Neither of us will lose the other, you hear?"-she gave a soft kiss to my left cheek-"And we have a wedding to plan."

I wiped the tears from my right eye as I pulled back to look at her.

"I love you so much...I just don't know how I'd ever cope..."

"Well just be thankful this cut isn't scarring" she said absently as she felt the line across her neck.

"Please don't joke about that; I'm far too delicate to cope with having gotten you into that situation."

"You didn't put me in that situation"-she held me by the hands, her eyes looking into my soul softly-"Falkner did; there were a million ways he could have handled the truth, and most were not...well, not whatever *that* was."

I nodded silently, still feeling rather traumatised by it all.

She stood up, and began to push her dress off her shoulders.

"Come on; I think we both need a little fun" she smiled sweetly.

By the divines I love her.

CHAPTER THREE

879, 3RD Era

At last our wedding day began to approach, only one and a half months away, and I felt myself getting giddier as each day passed.

I even found myself rewriting my 'Declaration of Intent' – yet another Blackwood tradition – where the groom proclaims his emotions and intentions towards his wife to be. My first draft went like this:

Oh, by what manner of luck have I earned the love of this perfect, angelic, personified beauty that causes my heart to beat in excited rhythm, for whom my mind would melt into thoughts of love and astounded awe whenever I bask in her glorious presence; the majesty of her curled hair, the effortlessness and grace of her each and every movement, the deep unending kindness and purity of heart that has made all that meet her bow in respect and admiration for this most perfect of being.

It was from the heart to be sure, but perhaps too strong and too keen a thing for a noble wedding. Speaking of, there was to be a fair bit more formality because of this, which I would have to endure, however uncomfortable. There were also to be guests from courts of Hamurfel and Blackwood; a political thing to be sure, but a sign of friendship between the regions and cities. Norain was not sending anyone to attend, but had sent a gift of ice-glass from the High King, as is custom, in the form of a snow wolf.

It had taken us a while after the incident with Falkner for us to get everything back on track I must admit, going so far as to delay our marriage by a year, which was understandable I think; to call the events traumatic would be a gross understatement. But we had healed and moved on; the Blackwood city dwelling now being rented out, the secret tunnel blocked and filled in (I figured it would be best that aspect stayed forgotten).

And as for now I was staying at our old home in Blackwood Village with Zaxx and Mazog; Carmel and Maralin being at Bahvil at the moment, preparing her dress – which Zaxx informs me will leave me speechless, in a good way – and other fanciful and traditional Bahvil aspects of the ceremony.

I must say, I do find it most amusing how certain 'higher class' individuals squirm to think that a *'lizard'* like me is marrying a noble like Carmel. I do so love to wind them up, although

Carmel isn't so pleased when I do – namely because she likes to do it instead.

I don't know what I would do without her, she makes me smile so much.

I should mention that Joahana – Ana to her friends – is now engaged to Tau, and is to be a bridesmaid along with Maralin, and that Furgus shall be giving Carmel away, being the closest thing to family she has left.

Zaxx insisted on being responsible for the wines (I shall come to regret that decision, but, if I am being honest, he does become rather entertaining when drunk off his wit's).

Tau is organising the 'Honour Guard'; basically a group of ceremonial soldiers who form an arch with engraved ceremonial swords for the bride and groom to walk under after the ceremony (one of those formal 'Bahvil noble' things I was talking about).

As for Mazog's arm, it had been saved, and after months of agony and physiotherapy his condition began to improve, and slowly he regained most of the movement in it. Most would not be able to tell, but I could see he was not quite the same; the wound had cut deep, and even now made certain tasks both difficult and painful. It doesn't stop him though, and he trains with it nearly every day, attempting to work off the damage.

Our friendship was tested that day, and even now I wonder if he still holds me in the same light as before, but I know that is due to my inner guilt, and not how he behaves towards me.

I have yet to make it up to him in a way that feels just, but I shall, and it will be glorious; but first, I shall need to ask him an important question.

After all, I do need a best man.

CHAPTER FOUR

879, 3RD Era one and a half months later

Our wedding was held just after noon in the great Rose Gardens of Bahvil, Carmel's favourite place, and mine for that matter; it was where we first danced after all. The sun, being just past its peak, gave a slightly angled light that lit up the blue sky, highlighting wisps of cloud that did not dare come together. The roses were in bloom, a mixed aroma softening and intensifying with the varying but gentle breeze that softly caressed the skin.

I stood beneath an arch woven with ornate blooms of exotic aromas, its white frame barely showing through the collage of petals. To my back-right stood Bahvil's High Priest, a somewhat elderly man who was more open to our marriage and my Blackwood customs than I had expected.

Seated upon rows of handcrafted chairs of fine, pale oak, each with its own individual engraving symbolising a purity, or a virtue, were friends, family and various nobles and figureheads. Zaxx sat in the front row on the left side, two chairs in and next to Tau.

Mazog stood at my side, holding a delicate ebony tray, engraved with the Bahvil Arms, which itself held an amulet and bracelet of marriage, nestled on an inlay of white velvet.

On the outer sides of rows were the honour guard, dressed in fine procession-style military clothes of deep navy blue with gold trim, with a ceremonial helm topped with a plume of peacock tail feathers, their ceremonial swords sheathed for the moment.

My nerves threatened to run away with me, my stomach churning with excitement and anxiety. I looked to Mazog and he gave me a comforting nod and smile.

Just then, the court minstrels and harpist, who were situated behind the back row of guests, began to play a gentle, yet beckoning melody, signalling the oncoming bride.

As with tradition, the bridal procession proceeded with the bridesmaids at the front, one holding flowers of the groom, one holding flowers of the bride, with the bride at the back.

First came Maralin, in a stunning off-white dress, lightly frilled at the bottom, with woven silks of green, carrying a Blackwood tulip, its deep red a distinct contrast. She gave me a smile, speaking to me without words. Next was Joahana, whom had a similar off-white dress, only with red silks, and carrying a Bahvil rose, its colour both cream and pink at the same time, one colour fading into the other and back in a random but purposeful manner.

And then, arm in arm with Furgus, who was wearing a bejewelled waistcoat handed down through his family, came Carmel. 'Wow' I felt myself whisper, although words alone cannot adequately describe her beauty in that dress; if I had tried to speak at that moment I would have failed, so in awe of her was I. Her dress was that of a silk-white, woven with faint golden threads, gently matching the curves of her body, complimenting her flawless pale skin, a lighter, near see-through silk covering her arms, and a delicate, ornate bow around her waist. The skirt of her dress was frilled like a frozen waterfall, the near polished silk radiating a glow of perfection; it was neither too large, nor too tight, matching her pace, and moved as if it were part of her soul. Indeed, if one could wear one's soul, she did so that marvellous day. Her veil was a gentle thing; a white gold circlet, delicately rested upon her softly curled, mahogany-brown hair, with the fine-woven silk strands resting upon it, flowing back with her gorgeous locks.

A she walked towards me I felt true happiness, the likes of which we mortals only ever dream of experiencing.

When she was at the arch, Furgus handed her hands over to mine, showing the intrusting of care, and the duty to look after her was being handed over to me. After doing so, Furgus sat in his seat in the opposite row to Zaxx, and next to Belothor and Agatha; who had made an effort with her attire, wearing a formal grey tartan overcoat – the kind that has the buttons come diagonally across the chest – with a matt-red tartan collar that drew out the red flecks in her rustic brown hair.

We turned to face each other fully as the High Priest began to read from the scriptures. She gave me that child-like smile, that innocent grin that had put me under her spell. I smiled back with a grin too large for my face. I could not help it; she is just so lovely. I looked into her green-tinted blue eyes, which glimmered with that joyousness of our first meeting, and fell even more in love with her. It was in this moment, this perfect part of time, that I realised my life was contented...no, perfected...no, I simply cannot explain it, but I think it is accurate enough to say that I realised she is why I live, why I breathe, and it may sound cliché, but it is true.

As the ceremony progressed, and after I had placed the amulet around her neck and she fastened the bracelet around my wrist, and we read our vows my nerves were replaced with a warmth of emotion, and whilst I did not take my eyes off Carmel for even a second, I could swear I could see Zaxx welling up and shedding a few tears (though he protests this is not the case, albeit not convincingly).

As we neared the end of the official ceremony, I had to make my 'Declaration of Intent' (or as I had taken to calling it, the declaration of love).

And my-oh-my was I nervous.

"...And now Prime shall read his Declaration of Intent" said the High Priest in his soft yet booming voice.

Carmel gave me a subtle, encouraging nod, sensing my nervousness, not knowing I had not managed to prepare anything (least nothing I thought suitable).

And so, I gave the following speech adlib, looking deep into Carmel's eyes as I did.

"Carmel..."-I began, momentarily letting my nerves show through my voice-"Carmel, when I first met you I could sense that you were different. You found joy and pleasure in things that others would have overlooked, and not once have I seen your station cloud or stop you from doing so. When we first danced, in this very spot"-I gave a small gesture with my right arm before returning to hold her hand-"it was here that I first felt what I would find out to be love for you. When I look into your eyes...I am lost, yet found. When I look into them I am home and I...I feel as if the weight of the world is lifted from me..."

Small tears began to form in her eyes, gentle squeezing my hand as I spoke.

"...If I had never met you, I would have never known true happiness. I would not know what it was like to live with true purpose, what it is like to be so wholly and completely content with the world. For without you I cannot be me; without you, I cannot exist"-I began fighting my urge to let my tears flow-"I love you Carmel. I wish I could say it more, say it better, but there are not enough words in existence to tell you the true extent of my love. I could speak for a thousand years, until the earth itself reaches an end, and not even scratch the surface of how much I care for you."

I took a small breath, fragments of a tear rolling down my left cheek.

"I will always love you like this, if not more, and promise...I swear upon solemn oath I shall be by your side to the day we leave this world together, and even after that. I love you Carmel, I always will."

"I love you to" she whispered, just about holding her tears back enough to speak.

"With the Declaration of Intent complete, and with the sacred powers intrusted in me, I pronounce you Prime of Blackwood, and you Countess Carmel of Bahvil, man and wife" bellowed the High Priest, in a somewhat triumphant and celebratory manner.

As the guests cheered, and some applauded (and Zaxx cried emotionally), I put my hands around Carmel's waist, she put her hands around my shoulders, the pair of us taking a brief moment to gaze into the others eyes for a moment longer, before finally, in a moment of pure unrivalled ecstasy, we embraced each other in a kiss so simple yet so divine it would make the Gods jealous and green with envy.

After the ceremony we returned to Castle Bahvil to celebrate with a mighty feast, which was held in the grand ball room; the one the Solstice Dance was held in each year. There were dishes of eggs – poached, scrambled, hard boiled and mayonnaised in vol-au-vent casings – in such glorious abundance speckled amongst platters of pies and pastries, spiced fish fried in butter, cauldrons of soup and broth, and of course, dozens upon dozens of scones with clotted cream and jam. The tables had been set up around the edges of the room, leaving a large space in the centre for the dancing that was to follow as the finest musicians in Bahvil played their songs for us; and at one point Carmel played a song or two on her harp, which made everyone's heart melt with its softness and emotion. I shall not lie, Carmel and I mostly ate the scones, sometimes feeding each other ones we found particularly tasty. Maralin on the other hand must have put away a punnet of strawberries or two, even after all the vol-au-vents she'd eaten.

As the mistrals began to play the classic song we had first danced to, Camel and I had the first dance; which as tradition had it, was the waltz. I could not help but smile as we danced, my hand holding her side affectionately, and she smiled back with the same thought.

"Feels strange to dance in front of so many people" I whispered to her as we moved with synchronised grace.

"You should try playing the harp in front of them" she laughed gently and quietly.

"Think I'll leave that to you" I smiled.

As the song came to a close and we took our bows, our guests began to take to the dance floor as the minstrels readied another song. We took our seats for a moment as they danced, saying a quick hello to Tau and Joahana as they got up to join in; they spent most of the evening dancing together, sporadically stopping to drink the fine wine Zaxx had acquired (and pinch all the pheasant legs I should add). Zaxx, predictable as ever, was off his face with wine, and trying to get some of the noble women to dance with him, until Maralin subdued him with the promise of a dance if he behaved. Even the representatives from the other cities and provinces seemed to be enjoying themselves most heartily as the evening went on, some even commenting on how it was the most joyous celebration they had been to; not that they would say otherwise I'm sure.

Belothor was seated for most of the night, only dancing when Carmel insisted he had some fun. Mazog joined in the merriment for as long as he could, until his injury played him up and forced him to take a seat for the remainder of the evening; though this did gain him the attention of some of the nobles' daughters.

"Looks like Mazog will be having company tonight" Carmel giggled as she sipped some spiced wine.

"Lucky berk" Zaxx slurred slightly as he walked up behind us, goblet in hand.

"Why don't you try using some of that charm of yours, see if you can find yourself a girl?" she smiled at our inebriated friend.

"I tried using my charm; all it got me was a telling off from Maralin" he sighed wistfully.

"Oh dear" Carmel patted him on the back "Well, there's still some vol-au-vents left, why don't you go have some of them instead?"

"That...is a good idea" he agreed as he stumbled off towards the food tables.

Maralin shook her head in amusement as she walked over.

"I don't know how he can stand after drinking so much, let alone eat."

"Must be a gift."

Maralin sat down next to Carmel, turning her seat to face her.

"Let's have a look at that beautiful amulet" she smiled, Carmel obliging her gladly "My, it is just perfect for you Carm, so beautiful and delicate."

"Why thank you" Carmel blushed "And I should thank you for organising all the flowers, and my dress; I still don't know how you managed to make it."

"It's just what I do" Maralin chimed playfully "but there's no need to thank me, I was glad to do it."-She took a sip of wine-"So, what happens now, with the whole Countess thing? I never thought to ask before."

"Well, I'm still Countess, obviously" Carmel began "and our marriage doesn't change the fact that I'm in charge, just that Sylon will be the new Count."

"So...Prime will have to answer to you, effectively?"

"Yes, yes he will" she smirked.

Maralin thought on that a moment, before letting out one of her signature laughs, Carmel joining her.

"Sorry, it's just...he's so used to being the leader."

"Oh I know, but it's what he loves about me I think; always doing my own thing and that."

"Aye, I think that's so" Maralin smiled.

The two of them looked on at the guests a moment, watching them dance and talk with grand smiles, Zaxx now flirting with a waitress as she brought what I presumed to be the last platter of vol-au-vents out to the food tables.

"Will you be staying around Bahvil once all our celebrations are done?" Carmel asked, turning her attention back to Maralin.

"For a little while" Maralin nodded "But I will be leaving for Norain by or just after the new year."

"What of Blackwood?"

"I'll be staying there a while with Mazog – in our old house – for a little bit before I make my journey north; it'll be nice to have some brother-sister time, you know?"

"I do believe I do" Carmel smiled "We'll miss you when you go though."

Maralin gave a little laugh.

"Well I'm not going quite yet"-she gave a small sigh-"But I shall miss you too. You must visit sometime; I could show you the Crown, the forest city at the base of the Norain Mountains."

"I would like that" Carmel smiled "If nothing else it would be a chance to test my metal against that famous Norain steel."

"Speaking of steel, how is Furgus? I haven't had chance to see him since the ceremony."

"Oh he is quite well. The smithies are running smoothly and producing a tidy profit, and Agatha is being a real asset to him; won't be long before she is a master blacksmith I'm sure."

"That's quite the achievement, to say the least. I bet your duties keep you from spending much time at the forge though?"

"Too true" she sighed "but I do get the good excuse every now and then; have to inspect the smithies, make sure they're all up to standard and that."

"Don't you have officials for that?"

"I should" she smirked "But I keep 'forgetting' to appoint someone."

"Now *that's* why Prime loves you."

Carmel, took a sip of wine, before setting her goblet down on the table beside her, rising to her feet as she did.

"So, you up for a dance then Maralin?" Carmel beamed excitedly, her cheeks now a rosy colour thanks to the wine.

"Why I'd be honoured to" Maralin replied with an honest grin, gently taking Carmel's outstretched hand.

I watched them dance a while, whilst I chatted with Belothor about various odds and ends. It was whilst this was going on that my left arm and hand gave a sudden twitch, to which Belothor raised a questioning eyebrow.

"Just a shiver going through me; must be a draft somewhere" I replied to his unasked question, brushing it off.

"Right" Belothor nodded, before then turning his gaze at the still dancing Carmel and Maralin "Those two get along like sisters so they do."

"Aye, and I am very glad of it; I don't know what I'd have done if they'd have disliked each other."

"Quite"-he looked back to me-"Speaking of things; where's Furgus? Haven't seen the fellow since the ceremony."

"You know, I'm not quite sure"-I gave a quick glance around the room-"I see Agatha over there – talking to the emissaries from Hamurfel – perhaps she would know; though I would guess he was called back to one of the smithies if he's not here."

"Perhaps; I just wanted to commend him on being there for Carmel through, well, through everything."

"I hear you there my friend" I nodded "I'll just go and ask if she's seen him."

"Right you are" he smiled as I walked off towards her.

As I walked across the polished floor I could not help but smile as I caught the sight of Mazog absconding with a noble-woman he had been talking to; one that was most certainly married.

"...that way you get the best out of your ore" Agatha was talking about metalwork to the Hamurfelions as I walked up beside her.

"Sorry to interrupt" I said, politely bowing my head a little at the emissaries "Agatha, have you seen Furgus about, he seems to have disappeared."

"Oh, he was called back to the Castle Forge; one of the novice smiths has had an incident with the smelter."

"Nothing serious I hope?"

"Nothing a good scolding won't sort out I'd say" she smiled "Anyhow, Syla here was enquiring about our steel."

"Indeed I was" Syla responded "It is a far lighter metal than what our smiths in Hamurfel can forge, and with no of loss strength; we are most impressed."

"And may we once again offer our congratulations to you and Countess Carmel on your marriage" Kyrex, the other emissary from Hamurfel, added.

"Thank you" I smiled "it is comforting to know our friends in Hamurfel care for us in Bahvil."

"The Count of Hamurfel still thinks of the Countess as family, so caring comes naturally" Syla smiled.

"Of course" I replied softly "Tell me, how are things in Hamurfel these days? It has been a fair while since I last visited."

"All is quite well" Kyrex replied "Although the sandstorms have come quite heavily this year; we nearly lost a whole set of villages in the southeast."

"Oh my!" Agatha said, a tad worried for the people who lived there "What of the villagers, what became of them?"

"We lost more than a few good people I'm afraid. But we have sent them what aid we could."

"We would move the settlements" Syla added, going sombre for a brief moment "But they are mining villages, and ore is too precious to leave in the ground."

"Aye" I nodded "But at least they know their leaders care for them."

"Indeed; though we fear that is of little comfort at times."

Sensing that the conversation needed a bit of a lightening up, Agatha started to retell a story about a comically inept leatherworker she once knew, to which they gave a controlled, dignified laugh. As they continued to chat I made my excuses and walked off to find Carmel, who had stopped dancing long enough to pinch the last vol-au-vent off Zaxx.

The night continued smoothly and jovially, dancing and merriment continuing on until close to midnight, and much food and drink consumed, until the guests began to bid their goodnights and goodbyes.

Zaxx, finally defeated by the insurmountable amount of food and wine he had consumed, was carried off by Maralin and Belothor as they bid us goodnight; though whether or not they would throw him into his room or onto the first out of the way lounger they came across was up for debate. Tau and Ana had departed earlier – about the same time as the emissaries from Hamurfel and Blackwood left – and I had no doubt they had more private celebrations to attend to, if you follow my meaning. As for Mazog, I would later find him hastily exiting one of the guest rooms of a noblewoman, his clothes in shambles and put on haphazardly; I guess that wound of his bought him more than sympathy.

As the last of the warming fires began to die down, the last of the guests having either left or retired for the night, Carmel and I had one last dance as the servants cleared and tidied the otherwise empty room.

The evening – and the whole day for that matter – had been full of joyous fervour, and the celebration had gone without a hitch or even the mildest issue; indeed the day had been most perfect, and I do not think we could have asked for more. Finally we were wed, our love now etched in stone before the world, and all seemed right. As we finished that last dance we thanked our servants and cooks most sincerely for their efforts, then retired for the night to our new, soft bed that Furgus had gifted to us for our wedding, its sheets a smooth, silk like fabric.

As for what we did next...well, I'm not telling you that.

CHAPTER FIVE

883, 3RD Era

In the years following our marriage, our time was spent between Castle Bahvil and visiting other cities on state duty; though we always stopped at Blackwood when we had the chance. Tau spent most of this time accompanying us; although this was due to Joahana being Carmel's personal maid more than anything else. Maralin would often visit us when we were at Bahvil, with Mazog only looking in on us when we were in Blackwood for the most part; he usually insisted on Zaxx going with her to make sure she was safe on her journey. As for good old Belothor, we had made him...what's the word...regent, that's it, we had made him Regent of Bahvil, with powers to oversee the cities activities when we were away; we had offered this position to Furgus, but he had politely turned it down, saying his place was at the forge.

Not much, for the most part, happened; bar the rather quaint and simplistic marriage between Tau and Joahana (probably should have mentioned that earlier) two years after ours, and a few good birthday celebrations. I should note that I had made a position specifically for Tau – that of Vanguard – that I organised to give him quite the reasonably sum of gold coin. For the most part things between all of us stayed the way it had always been, only they were a little more distant from me, due to the nature of being married to the Countess and all that brought with it.

I like to think we were making good progress with Bahvil, having encouraged the bigoted members of the 'higher class' to vacate the city as we favoured the hardworking and sincere members of our court and city folk.

It was in the fourth year after our marriage that we heard the joyous news of Joahana expecting her firstborn, and that she was due to give birth the following spring. Needless to say I organised a night out to celebrate, Blackwood style.

Me, Tau, Mazog and Zaxx went to our old tavern (thankfully without my personal guard; they could be such irritating folk at times), and began ordering in the mead.

"Whatever happened to Jessel?" I asked as we took our seats at what was once our regular table.

"Did Maralin not say?" Mazog replied "She moved to Norain, into the first district of that forest city they're still building."

"How on earth did she manage to afford that?" Zaxx asked, somewhat jealous.

"Some cousin on Maralin's side knew of a tavern owner who was setting up shop there, and put in a good word for her."

"Well good for her!" I toasted "Once again proving that knowing Maralin is well worth her showing us up at archery."

"Showing you up more like."

"Still, Norain, that's a long way to travel" Tau added softly "What you suppose they'll call the new city?"

"Maralin says rumour is it'll be called The Crown" Mazog smiled "Sounds about right from what I hear of it too; heck, folk already call what's been built by that name, why make it otherwise?"

"Now this is a tankard of mead!" I proclaimed as the barmaid brought our drinks over "Not like Bahvil with its tiny glasses and *wine.*"

Tau gave a little chuckle.

"Least you get it for free" laughed Zaxx "If I had access to that-"

"You'd be dead man!" scoffed Mazog "Or at least very, very pickled."

"Don't you mean smashed off his face?"

"Hey!"

"To be fair, Zaxx wouldn't be smashed off his face-" said Tau, patting Zaxx on the shoulder.

"You see? Least I got one friend in my corner" Zaxx interrupted.

"Nah, you'd probably be vomiting up half the cellar! Haha" Tau finished, shouting out his laughter.

"Bloody heck man" Zaxx mumbled before downing his mead, slamming the empty tankard onto the table.

"Another round" he shouted to the barkeep.

"Zaxx, we were only messin'" I said, mockingly apologetic.

"Don't matter; I'll hold more mead than any of you."

We looked at each other, a mischievous smirk on all our faces.

"All right" boomed Tau "The last man standing wins, the first to fall must entertain the other three."

"Entertain?" Mazog queried, one eyebrow raised questioningly.

"I know" I interjected "How about...the man who falls first must wrestle a chicken into..."

"Into Tomm the ejit's home!" shouted Zaxx, finishing my sentence with a mouthful of mead.

"Why not a goat?" suggested Mazog.

"Alright" nodded Tau.

"We all agreed?" I asked gesturing with my tankard.

"Yep."

"Sounds good to me."

The three of us looked at Zaxx.

"Oh ruddy hell, let's do this!" he roared.

And with that, we clinked our tankards together and proceeded to exhaust the taverns supply of mead.

Funnily enough, that might have had something to do with Tomm being charged with stealing a cow from a local farm. Can't say for sure; everything past the eighteenth pitcher was an absolute blur.

***

Skipping ahead five months, and we were at Bahvil Castle. Well, most of us were; Mazog was otherwise detained in Hamurfel for some hunting business, if I remember rightly, but said he would make it back for Joahana's...giving birth (is that how you say it?) in four months' time. Speaking of Joahana, Carmel had the castle maids doting on her, whilst Maralin sewn her fitted gowns and stretchable baby clothes. Such good hearts those two.

As for Tau, he seemed to spend most of his time bothering the castle doctor on what to expect, what to look out for, and so on. I tell you, I think he near well drove the man to drink, if not madness.

I had the tedious job of holding court, dealing with crimes (I like that bit actually) and organising the city guard; I got Zaxx to train them on how to spot the more skilled thieves. Some of the Captains wanted to know what experience he had, and I told them not to ask.

It was during this time that we received news that there had been an attack on Blackwood; not the main city itself, but the old hub of the area; our home, the original village of Blackwood (though it is more like a small town in size nowadays).

I leaned back against the throne, hand over my mouth in shock and thought.

"...So as you can tell by this sire, I thought you would wish to know" the messenger finished.

"What of the Count of Blackwood, is he asking for our aid?" Carmel queried as she rubbed the back of my free hand soothingly.

The messenger fumbled with the hat he held in his hands.

"The Count has stated that we have not the men to spare to protect every small village" he was being as careful as he could with his words, and his voice betrayed that.

"But he has not asked for assistance?" Carmel asked again.

"Countess Carmel...the Count has not requested assistance, but..."

"The people have, haven't they?" I interrupted, taking a deep breath as I did.

The messenger nodded silently.

"We must help them Prime" Carmel said, looking at me "Even if it means intruding upon Blackwood jurisdiction."

"I know" I sighed "They are *my* people, my friends, the people I grew up with"-I looked at the messenger-"The Count, he would not interfere with us aiding his people would he?"

"No. Not so long as he is given credit."

We rolled our eyes in unison.

"That damned Decon"-I hefted myself from my throne-"Messenger, go tell your people Prime of Blackwood is coming to their aid" I put out my arm for Carmel as she rose to her feet.

"Thank you sire" the messenger bowed.

"And tell them the Countess of Bahvil sends her best men with him" Carmel added.

He gave a smile of thanks, before turning and hastily going on his way.

"Bough"-Bough had been standing silently by our side during the conversation-"Bring me your best guardsmen; we meet in the Court room" Carmel asked politely but urgently.

"And I'll gather Zaxx and Maralin; they should be with us" I added

"Of course" Bough nodded "Shall I inform Belothor also?"

"Yes, thank you Bough" Carmel smiled.

As he hurried off, she turned to look at me with that knowing expression.

"...You're going over there yourself, aren't you?"

I paused a moment, taking both her hands in mine.

"Yes."

"There's no way to make you stay?"

"No; the people – my village – I cannot stand back whilst others defend my home of old."

"What of this home, of me?"

"I'll always come back" I smiled "Always."

She bit her lip in thought.

"It's the jam isn't it?"

"Yes Carm" I laughed "It's the jam."

After a tense and sombre discussion we decided that Zaxx, Maralin and I would investigate, with plans to send word to Tau if we needed his help; Mazog, being in Hamurfel at the time, was too far away to aid us even if we sent the fastest messenger. With us we took a personal guard of five: Captain Bough, his tactical skill and sharp eye being of more use to us than if he stayed in Bahvil, guardsman James Yates – Yates for short – who was an impressively skilled swordsman despite his older age, Siegfried Monro, the most agile longsword user across the land, though his true prowess was with a dagger, Kyle Sulfwin and Samu the Orc (a rough diamond if ever there was one), who was our heavy hitter – literally, the man duel-wielded a pair of heavy war-axes. Kyle was the youngest of our group, a guardsman whom had risen fast amongst their ranks thanks to his skill and willingness to follow orders to the letter. I had not been convinced of taking someone so young and un-experienced, no matter how skilled, until Maralin pointed out how we were doing tougher things than this when we were his age.

And so, having readied and armed ourselves, taking light provisions with us, we made our way to Blackwood, riding at a near continuous gallop, with Zaxx mumbling every so often how they had better of left the tavern unharmed.

What can I say, the man loves his drink.

***

As we rode into the outskirts of Blackwood Village, we could not help but feel an eerie, all too quiet atmosphere. The sight of smoke towers had been in our view for over a mile, and now that we were up close we could see the devastation in its sicken-ing detail; burnt out buildings, with those unscathed by flame ransacked, doors broken in two, shattered glass crumbling un-derfoot. We decided to dismount, tethering the horses to a still standing stable post, figuring that it would be best to sneak in as inconspicuously as possible.

As we made our way through the streets we came across bodies of the residents, and the marauders that had besieged them, scattered like dead flies, their wounds clearly shown and not quite fresh.

What was evident, thankfully, was that not all the inhabitants of our home had been slain; there were too few bodies for that to be the case; not that it made the sight any better.

We checked the houses that still stood, checking for weary survivors, but all we found was evidence of robbery and struggle.

"Who in the hell did this?" Kyle asked disbelievingly, his inner-city naivety showing.

"Not sure" answered Zaxx as he examined another marauder's corpse for a sign of who they were "none of them have any tattoos, no insignias...nothing" he stood back up, puzzled.

"We should check our home, see if it's still standing" whispered Maralin, with a hint of worry.

"Indeed" I nodded, keenly aware that it would most likely be a ruined shell now.

As we walked past yet more destruction and death, we began to near the tavern, and from a distance it seemed relatively unscathed, even with a small pillar of smoke creeping out from its roof. As we got nearer still, Zaxx began to pick up the pace; at first I thought it due to his mead-loving, but I, along with the others, quickly realised he had spotted movement. With that, we all began to rush hurriedly towards some kind of flailing mass, just behind where the tavern door once was; though we could not tell if it were friend or foe due to the residual amounts of smoke.

At twenty feet from the tavern we realised there was a small group of marauders, five or six of them, fighting over the barmaid, Ysolder.

Zaxx was first on the scene, crashing into one of the marauders, weapon drawn, lopping the head off the fellow he was arguing with. By the time we had piled in it was already a close combat brawl, with Zaxx holding one marauder in a headlock with one arm as he tried to strike the others with his other. Maralin raced over to Ysolder, cutting her binding and rushing her out of the tavern ruins. Bough and Samu had quickly cut down three of the marauders, with Kyle struggling with a fourth. Monro and Yates were trying to corner the one Zaxx had been holding in a headlock until he had to dodge someone's thrown sword. While this was happening I noticed a seventh marauder come out the back to see what was going on. Taking a single look at the ongoing brawl, he ran and dived out of the nearest window – which had been the last unbroken one left – obviously not liking his chances. I gave chase, noting to laugh at what I had seen latter, managing to tackle the man only thirty feet from the tavern. After a short struggle I persuaded him to stay where he was, ramming my sword through his leg, pinning him to the ground.

Zaxx emerged with one of the marauders, now very beaten with his hands tied behind his back, and a bottle of mead. As he marched the man towards me he tried to drink the mead, but brought the bottle back down from his lips, sighing as he did.

"Empty" he proclaimed angrily, smashing the bottle on his captive's head.

The man collapsed to the floor, unmoving.

Bough looked down at the broken thing.

"I think you just killed him" he said plainly.

"Meh" Zaxx shrugged, continuing towards me.

As the remaining marauders were brought out, I quizzed my one as to where his group were stationed.

"So, you going to tell me now, or after some serious pain?" I asked, in a mockingly polite tone, on hand on my sword.

He just spat at me.

"Fair enough" I said, proceeding to punch him in the face repeatedly, twisting my sword with my other hand.

I stopped after about ten seconds or so, just as the others were being lined up by Monro and Yates.

"How about now?" I smiled.

The man just nodded.

"Great!" I turned to call Zaxx "Zaxx...oh, you're right behind me"-I turned back to my captive-"You tell my friend here everything, okay?"

As I marched over to our other captives I could hear the man blubber out everything he knew, and watched Maralin console Ysolda, gently asking her about what happened.

"What should we do with our captives sir?" asked Bough.

I looked them over, pondering on what they had done to my beloved village, to my favourite tavern, what they were going to do to Ysolder.

"Find out what they know" I replied calmly, turning to face Bough fully, dropping to a whisper "then kill them; no mercy, make them know the suffering they have caused."

Bough nodded, the hint of a smile etching itself onto his face for a fleeting second.

* * *

Having gained all the information we could from our captives – and disposing of them – we had made our way to the old chapel to find forty or so survivors that the marauders had locked within. From what we had learned we knew a few useful things: first was that the marauders were a group calling themselves 'Wolfhounds', led, unsurprisingly, by a man called Wolf. Second was the fact that the Wolfhounds we had stopped had been waiting for their comrades to return with prison wagons to take the remaining villagers back to their camp; which leads us to perhaps the most important bit of information, where their camp was. The camp, we were told, was in the north-east direction, on the sloping base of the Järl Mountains, not ten miles from our location, nestled between Dragon Rock and The Great Tear (a large waterfall in the shape of, well, a tear).

The bad news was that this meant we would be hard-pressed if we were to launch an assault, despite the tree cover, as they would have the higher ground. The good news, however, was that we had the element of surprise. It would take at least a day's ride to get to the mountains from here, so we would have time to send for reinforcements from Blackwood City, and send the survivors there for safety whilst we were at it.

As we had entered the chapel we found that the villagers were locked in the chapel's crypt, the door barred with chains. Samu pried open the door with his war axes, with the other men grappling with the stone door to help add tension to the chains, leaving me to attempt to smash them apart with a granite statue of some honoured saint or another, breaking its head off on the first strike. I struck again. And again. And again... and again.

Finally, on the sixth strike, the chain lock snapped in two, allowing us to open the crypt door fully, revealing the forty-something women and children cowering in the dusty darkness. I could not spot one man over sixteen amongst them, even as we lead them out of the chapel. Mothers were cradling babies, children clinging to anyone who looked familiar, some coughing from the crypt dust, others were emotionless, blocking out the reality of what had happened for the sake of their sanity.

Whilst Maralin consoled those poor souls, and Zaxx helped Bough to identify the victims, I took Kyle and Yates to one side.

"I need you two to escort these people to Blackwood City, and after you arrive go straight to Blackwood Castle and tell the Count what's happened, that we need reinforcements sent to The Great Tear. Understood?"

"Yes sir" they replied.

"Sir, how many men should we ask for?" asked Yates.

I pondered a moment, thinking on what the now dead Wolfhounds had told us. According to them they were at least a hundred in number. The fact they were probably in a fortified camp, on higher ground, meant we would need either over-

whelming numbers ourselves or a few small strike teams sup-
ported by heavy archers. Not to mention the odds of them
underselling their numbers. Decisions, decisions.

"Tell him at least forty swordsmen, twenty light archers and
twenty heavy archers."

"Sir, would it not be better to have forty heavy archers?"
questioned Kyle, Yates giving him the evil-eye as he did.

I waved Yates unsaid comment away.

"I thought that at first too, but light archers are less encum-
bered, so they can respond to enemy archers much quicker, and
that could give us the edge, especially if their archers take aim
at our heavy archers, you see?" there was no point in scolding
the man for questioning my decisions; they would ultimately
decide how many casualties we would suffer after all.

Kyle just nodded, reassured by my response.

With that they marched off with the villagers, giving their
horses to those too weary to walk the distance. Maralin had left
with them, insisting – quite rightly – that she could be more
persuasive with Decon than Yates could, and assured me she
would make him willing to lend us more men than was reasonable to ask for. The rest of us steeled ourselves for the oncoming
fight; not the one that would take place on the Järl Mountains,
but the one with the Wolfhounds returning for their captives.

I almost felt sorry for them; they had no idea what hit them.

⁎⁎⁎

I cleaned my sword with torn cloth from one of the Wolfhounds as the others readied their horses, taking a moment to

look at the pile of corpses we had just created, feeling a look of satisfaction etch its way onto my face as I did. Do not misunderstand though; I was never pleased to kill – I loathed it in fact – but, putting a permeant end to those who would do unspeakable acts? That is something I would never be sorry for.

So it should come as no surprise that I felt no mercy for these…'*people*', especially when they have struck a place that I love, hurt people I know. And if I had my way, their leader would know the true meaning of pain; not out of vengeance mind you, but so that he might truly understand what he has inflicted upon others.

We had kept a few alive at first, taking them away from each other so that they wouldn't hear the others being interrogated, so that we might check for discrepancies in what they – and the previous Wolfhounds – told us about their group.

Samu was dragging the bodies of the Wolfhounds to their prison cart and loading them in as Zaxx, Bough and Monro carefully and respectfully gathered the bodies of the fallen villagers, lining them up in the chapel, making sure known family members were kept together. We used what linens we found to cover them, and I felt a heavy weight upon me as I looked upon them, whether I recognised them or not.

Once they had finished, I mounted my horse, and I gave the order to begin our journey to the Great Tear.

***

We rode unceasingly until the thick of night was upon us, forcing us to make camp in a sheltered wood. Bough was fast asleep in his bedroll, giving subtle breathing sounds, whilst Zaxx lay down next to his horse, leaning on it as he drank what we thought was the last of his mead.

"What's the plan again?" he uttered, weary eyed.

"We scout out the camp" replied Samu, staring at our small fire as he spoke "see what defences they have; how many archers, weak points and so on" his voice was a heavy one, and quite gruff at that.

"Right" Zaxx slurred as he took another longing sip from the mead bottle.

Samu turned to look at him.

"Why you drink so much?" he asked bluntly.

Zaxx gave a slight shrug.

"Dunno; stuff happens, things change...mead stays the same."

"That doesn't sound healthy" added Monro, joining the conversation.

"I'm alive aren't I? Can't be that unhealthy."

"That's not what I meant."

A few moments of silence, bar the crackling of the fire, went by as we sat there.

It was at this point I joined the conversation, deciding that would be better than an awkward silence.

"The thing you should realise is we've seen things we would rather not have. I mean, Zaxx almost died not all that long ago."

"And?" asked Samu, now looking at me "We're soldiers. We do that more often than most."

"And we don't try to drink it away" added Monro.

Zaxx got to his feet.

"I don't need this" he said, in a groggier voice than normal, as he began to walk off.

The others just watched him, wondering, trying to judge what was going on in his head.

As soon as they were sure he was out of earshot they turned to me, Monro now sharpening his longsword.

"I get he's good in a fight. I really do. But how can you trust someone who's drunk all the time?" Monro asked, now looking at his blade as he felt its sharpness between strikes of his whetstone.

"Well..." I hesitated to reply, looking off into the distance as if it would hold the answer.

"What you hiding for him?" Samu asked, sensing I knew more; Orcs, clever bunch, even if they don't speak much.

Monro stopped sharpening, wanting to hear my reply.

Another brief and awkward silence passed.

"To be truthful" I began, throwing back my shoulders and looking up at the night sky "there was a time where he did not drink as much. I mean he's always been a drinker, it's what he is, but..."

"But...?" prompted Monro.

"There was a...an incident. One he would rather forget." I turned my gaze back to my comrades "But what that is his business."

Monro moved to ask again, but I cut him short.

"No. I will not tell you what it was. Why? Because he is my friend" I said, my tone a defensive one "Just understand, he's lost so much, too much. The mead either numbs the pain or makes him forget, I don't much know."-I returned my gaze to

the stars-"The point is, you don't abandon your friends, not ever."

Samu nodded, understanding what I meant; Monro not so
much, but he seemed to respect my decision.

We didn't talk for a while after that.

About half an hour later Zaxx returned, and once again a
conversation began, only this time in the form of an argument
as to whether Blackwood or Bahvil had the best hunting
grounds, and then as to which had the most beautiful lands
(and women, which I had no part of...okay, I had a bit to say,
but only in the interest of fairness).

After an hour or so we settled down for the night, rotating
every three hours for watch duty, our thoughts on the day
ahead.

***

We had set out early that morning, determined to make the
most of the daylight. We rode for hours that never seemed to
end, the sun scorching our backs, what cloud cover there was so
dispersed it offered no real respite.

As we rode towards our destination, Maralin, Yates and Kyle
were in the midst of a discussion with the Count of Blackwood,
Benadict Decon, as to the number of men he could spare.

"...So you see sir, these Wolfhounds pose a real threat to
Blackwood and its people." Yates finished, hoping he had put
across what was needed.

Decon, slouched on his throne, stroked his lightly bearded chin, thoughtfully squinting his eyes as he did.

"And what, pray tell, are their number? You said one of their group told you, but what if he lied, hmm? It could be a trap." He spoke in a dry, almost sarcastically disinterested tone "I could not lend my men to such folly."

"With all due respect sire, the new Count of Bahvil is requesting your assistance, it would be...unfitting to deny it" spoke Maralin, her melodic tone a soft, yet firm statement of her power.

"Oh really?" replied Decon, shifting himself from his slouched position, his interest peaked by Maralin "And how do you know such protocol?"

Maralin hesitated a split second, and Decon tried to capitalise on it.

"I thought so" he said smugly "You're just a commoner in fine cloths, feigning any sense of nobility. Who do you think you are to make demands of *me*?"

With that Maralin pinned him to the back of his throne, her face right against his.

"I am his mistress" She hissed "and I can make your life the embodiment of hell."

He stared back at her, wide-eyed, a tad in shock and unspeaking.

"So" she spoke calmly, yet sinisterly as she unpinned Decon, returning to her elegant posture "I trust your men will be ready by sundown?"

Count Decon just nodded, mesmerised, and possibly fearful of what Maralin could be planning behind her sweet smile.

As for Yates and Kyle, well, they just tried not to laugh.

***

Bough watched as the Wolfhound patrol made its way around the wooden fortifications. They were a mixture of logged walls and battlements, and horse-traps (sharpened spears used to stop a charge of heavy-horse). He signalled Zaxx to come over without moving his gaze.

"Don't see many archers" he whispered "any sign of those re-inforcements?"

"Not yet" Zaxx replied, shifting his footing as he did "So, few archers eh? That's good."

"I wouldn't be so sure."

Zaxx looked at him, confused.

"How so?"

"See that inner battlement? The one with the spears?"

Zaxx took a moment to find it, then nodded.

"Yeah?"

"It's situated far enough behind their gates to let two streams of men to pass through."

Zaxx realised what he was saying.

"It's a damn choke point" He cursed quietly.

"Precisely" nodded Bough "Means dealing more damage with fewer archers."

"Which is why they have archer hides inside their camp... they're clever, I'll give them that" whispered Zaxx, mainly to himself.

They continued to survey the Wolfhound camp – which was arguably in truth more like a fort – a little while longer, counting again the number of archers and patrols, making a note of what weak spots there were (though they were few), before heading back to our makeshift camp at the base of the Great Tear itself.

We were going over battle strategies when Monro announced their return, as he kept watch from up a tree.

As they strode into camp, I turned my head to greet them.

"What news my friend?" I asked, directing my question at Zaxx.

"They've got a damn choke point" cursed Bough, answering for Zaxx, adding "Sir" once he remembered who he was talking to.

I waved him off.

"No need for social protocol Captain. So, a choke point you say?"

"Aye" answered Zaxx gruffly "Got themselves a shooting gallery; one main archer hide just behind the main gate, plus two more at the sides of the camp."

"And that's not counting the wall battlements" added Bough.

"Many archers?" queried Samu.

Zaxx shook his head.

"Unless they've got some hold up somewhere, no more than twenty, twenty-five."

"That's not many" shouted Monro from his perch.

"No...but with that choke point, they wouldn't need many" I thought out loud as I assessed the situation, stroking my chin as I did.

"They seemed to have a great number of swordsmen, 'bout half have shield" Zaxx said as he washed his face in the river the Great Tear poured into.

"When you say 'a great number'...?" asked Samu.

"Put it this way" he replied as he got up from his kneeling position "we better hope Maralin got us more men."

Samu pondered that for a second, before Monro called out to us.

"They're coming! They're bloody well coming straight for us!"

As he yelled, an arrow struck the tree right next to his head, causing him to flinch and fall to the ground.

We leapt to our feet, readying our weapons as Bough rushed to Monro with his longsword in hand.

"You alright man?" he yelled at him.

Monro gave a heavy groan and a thumbs up, fumbling for his longsword as he did.

"Good man." said Bough, thrusting the handle of the longsword into Monro's hands as he did, before turning to face our oncoming, yet unseen foe as we all braced ourselves, listening for their approach.

Silence.

Our eyes studied the ridge the arrow had come from, unable to see any movement.

Suddenly we heard the clashing of swords, the ever-familiar clang of metal on metal, and stampeding forces.

Shouts and battle cries echoed from behind the ridge, the pace of impacts on flesh becoming ever more vocal.

And then silence once more; the sound of battle ceasing as quickly as it had started.

Our swords still drawn, confused as to what had just happened, we slowly paced towards the ridge.

Hearing gentle footsteps we stopped, awaiting what might come at us.

Suddenly a lone figure stood atop the ridge.

"Alright boys?" she yelled.

I'll be quite honest, I've never been so pleased to see Maralin in my life.

*

I walked down the other side of the ridge to greet the men Maralin had acquired from Count Decon. Yates was checking the few injured from the skirmish with the Wolfhounds (they were mostly flesh wounds thankfully), as Kyle approached me and Maralin, the others just behind us.

"Sire" he greeted me "we are ready for your orders."

"How many are injured?" Bough enquired, surveying the men.

"'Bout fifteen Captain" he replied, gesturing towards Yates "Yates says they're mostly flesh wounds, nothing that would prevent the men from fighting."

"Good" I nodded, before turning to Maralin "So how many men did you get us then?"

"A hundred-and-twenty."

She gave a brief pause, then a slight laugh.

"What?" I asked, puzzled.

"Well..." she began, a smug smirk across her face.

"Maralin, what did you do?"

"She told Decon she were your mistress...Sir" replied Kyle, answering for her as she let out another fit of laughter.

"What?" exclaimed Zaxx, now having caught up with us, having half-carried the still winded Monro over the ridge.

I gave Maralin a look that was a mixture of disbelief and amusement.

She gave out another giggle.

"What can I say, it got the job done."

"I just can't take you anywhere can I?"

I mean, seriously.

***

I observed the entrance to the camp from behind the dense gorse. It was no longer as quiet as when Zaxx observed; clearly they had heard the commotion at the Great Tear, or had grown suspicious of their water-party's absence. Either way we were going to have a hard fight on our hands.

I looked up to the ridge Zaxx had been spying from earlier, now occupied by Maralin and seven of the heavy archers. I could just discern her golden hair behind a wall of brambles, waiting for the signal.

I turned to look to my left; a lower ridge where another six of the heavy archers were stationed with Zaxx and eighteen guardsmen.

With me were a mixture of light archers and swordsmen arranged in a needle-point formation.

The remaining heavy archers were spilt into two groups; one positing themselves behind the fortified camp as best they could, the other stealthily scaling the trees behind us.

I could sense the anticipation amongst the men, sweat visibly dripping from some.

The weather had turned partially overcast, the Sun dipping in and out of view.

Samu and Monro made my personal guard, with Bough readying to take a small division of our group to outflank our foes once inside the camp.

I turned to Monro, giving him the nod to give the signal.

He acknowledged, reflecting the sunlight with his longsword in three bursts of two flashes.

Without hesitation, a flurry of arrows flew through the air, precisely taking out their targets atop the battlements.

The remaining Wolfhounds scuttled like a disturbed nest of ants, running to their stations.

A second wave of arrows had them duck into cover, their remaining archers now inside their hide behind their open gate.

I gave a mighty roar, leading the charge as Wolfhound soldiers hurried to try and close the gate.

A few swift arrows rush past me, striking a few of our men down, but it was not near enough to stop our advance.

Twenty of our men hammered into the near-closed gates, pushing them open, Wolfhounds attempting to push them back with a flurry of strikes.

Arrows rained down into the courtyard of the camp, impaling the bewildered foes from almost all sides.

The Wolfhounds held us at the choke point, arrows streaming from their hide as their swordsmen kept us at bay.

Learning the rhythm of their volleys, I gave the call for our swordsmen to take cover, leaving our light archers to fire a torrent of arrows into the hide's open hatches.

The men got back to their feet, proceeding to hammer into our foes once more.

Bough led his group between the horse-traps and over the hide, attempting to outflank.

Monro had made his way to the front line, despite having an arrow cut through left shoulder, his longsword hacking into a Wolfhound's spine.

Samu stood at my side as I made my way through a gap in the wolfhound ranks, his war-axes slashing the limbs of the foolhardy who attempted to take him.

I was determined to find their leader, and I had no doubt he would be hiding in the camp's barracks, possibly with a few personal guards.

As we pushed past the archer's hide I could see Bough and his men battering down its sealed door, prioritising their removal from the fight; a sound plan, as it would allow our soldiers to enter the courtyard-like area much more safely.

We had been outnumbered to be sure, but we had the greater skill and strategy; our archers had picked off all theirs that had not been in the hides, and were now selecting targets at will, prioritising the larger groups of Wolfhounds. Zaxx's group had made their way into camp, cutting down those who attempted to flee or outflank us from behind, cleaning up the few archers that had crawled out of the hide.

Maralin and her archers were still atop the ridge, covering our forces with absolute precision.

I was now in a skirmish outside the barracks, the strikes and blows between the two sides a blur of metal and red.

A number of arrows plunged into the foes in front of me, cutting down the men before me, and giving us a clear path to the barracks.

I gave a quick glance to the ridge on my right, seeing Maralin reading her bow once again, a smile just visible on her face.

With the way virtually clear I pushed forward, Samu and Monro now with me.

Kicking open the door I prepared for an immediate close-quarters fight, but was instead greeted with the sight of eight heavily armoured men – three Orcs, four Nords and one Imperial from what I could tell – four either side of a man in a blue tunic, whose armour was clad in a wolf pelt, with the wolf's head covering his helm, obscuring his face; he was clearly their leader, Wolf.

Each man had considerable weaponry; two duel-wielded war-axes, two of the Orcs had warhammers, one longsword that dwarfed any I had seen before, and three with sword and shield.

Within seconds of seeing them I knew this was a greater threat than I had anticipated.

"This conflict need not end in any more bloodshed" Wolf proclaimed, his voice a familiar one, though I could not place it.

The sounds of swords on metal echoed in from the court-yard.

"Is there not a deal to be struck?" he continued "A service I could provide maybe? In exchange for our...'trouble free' exit?"

"A deal?" I seethed, walking towards him, his men taking a step forward "You expect a deal? To just walk out of here?"

I could just make out a smile from beneath his helm.

"Of course" he gestured to his men "or else none of us will."

Samu gave me a nervous glance, Monro's steely composure starting to show cracks.

It was just the three of us here, the other's detained by the Wolfhounds outside.

I had stopped just short of their striking range, attempting to show a lack of fear.

"You massacred the people of Blackwood, slain sons, slaughtered daughters...You expect me to just let you walk away?"

Realising I would not make a deal, he signalled his men to attack.

*

The scene was that of thrashing blades and churning of hammers. They had expertly driven us from the entrance, allowing their leader and two shielded comrades to flee the building, out into the still raging battle outside.

The six remaining Wolfhounds tested our limits, their strikes unrelenting. Samu fought his counterparts, the Orc and Nord with two war-axes, ducking and parrying their strikes at speed.

Monro and I danced with the other four, attempting to put distance between us and the warhammer wielding Orcs, their lumbering swings giving us a slight, if tenuous, advantage.

Monro stood at the back of the shield carrying Nord, whom was oblivious to his existence, focused entirely on waiting for the moment to strike me down as I fought both a warhammer and the longsword.

Monro's plan worked; the Orc he was facing off against swung his warhammer with immense force, Monro ducking out of the way, leaving the Nord in its path.

The blow struck home; crushing the Nord's arm and causing a moment of hesitation in the Orc.

Seizing the moment, Monro thrust his sword into the neck of the Orc, blood spurting into his face at high pressure.

The longsword had quickly left me occupied with the other warhammer wielder, thrusting his weapon into Monro's leg, his aim ruined by the impalement of one of Samu's war-axes into his helm.

The Orc with war axes drove one into Samu's side, dropping him to his knees, but as he did Samu rent his attackers face in two, leaving his weapon imbedded in Samu as he fell.

The Nord with war-axes, now recovered from a staggering blow Samu had delivered before throwing his other war-axe at Monro's attacker, dived in, bringing his right arm down at Samu's neck.

But alas, Samu's reflexes were – despite his wound – as swift as ever; grasping the weapon of his fallen foe in his hand, he thrust it upward at the arm of the Nord, severing it at the elbow, causing the war-axe it had once grasped to swing such that the hilt struck Samu in the forehead.

As this happened, Monro had pulled the longsword out of him as he readied his dagger, and had dived on the Nord with the crushed arm, proceeding to rapidly cut at any gaps in the man's armour as fast he could find them, dirtying his blade at a terrifying rate.

As for me, I battled with the warhammer wielding Orc, grappling with him for his weapon.

He lifted me off the floor and, before I had time to let go of the warhammer, pinned me against the wall with it.

Samu's now one-armed attacker let out a flurry of strikes against him, Samu barely managing to deflect the blows, until finally one managed to cut down the side of his right arm.

Samu awaited the death blow, closing his eyes as he saw it coming.

But it did not land.

Opening his eyes, he saw Monro clinging to the back of the huge man whom would have killed him, savagely hacking at the man's neck until finally he fell like a great oak.

I had just managed to kick the monstrously sized Orc, causing me to drop to the floor with a thud as I became unpinned.

The pair of us staggered, I grabbed for my fallen sword and raged to swing it at the man's neck.

He blocked the strike with the staff of his warhammer, then brought it down between my legs, barely missing me.

I once again grasped hold of his warhammer, and as he tried to pull it from me Monro jumped on his back, with Samu bringing his strength to bear against the man's knees.

With this he relinquished his grasp on the warhammer as he yelled in pain, flailing to keep the others at bay.

I got to my feet, moving my hands to the very end of the warhammer, its weight immense.

My grip tightening, I spun on the spot, my momentum dragging the super-heavy weapon off the ground and into an unstoppable orbit, yelling at my comrades to get back as I did.

As they ducked and dived out of the way, the strike connected with the man's face, removing it from existence.

As the decapitated body slumped to the ground we fell to our knees, exhausted, wounded, and almost entirely spent.

***

Whilst this went on inside the barracks, the fight outside continued, though it slowly moved to a close as our forces skill began to overwhelm their numbers.

Up on the ridge, Maralin had been selecting priority targets, picking them off one-by-one, her heavy archer team following her lead.

As she surveyed the courtyard, she spotted Zaxx cutting down cowering foes, his men now holding the gate shut to prevent their escape, and took a moment to ponder her old friend, feeling her heart skip a beat as she did.

But before she had chance to make sense of this she spotted a group of men exiting the barracks she had seen us enter, taking note on how two of the three were using their shields to cover the third and central figure from possible arrow strikes.

She pulled an arrow from her quiver, pulling her bow to its maximum tension, one eye closed as she took measure of their distance and movement.

She took a slow, deep breath.

As she exhaled she released her grip, the arrow accelerating towards her target.

The arrow arched over the battlefield, overseeing the conflict, passing overhead of Zaxx, past the archers hide, through the tiniest gap in the men's shields, embedding itself into the man's armour.

It did not seem to faze him, and now alerted to the direction of fire his men shifted their stance to block further attack.

Maralin looked round for the other archer groups, intending to direct their fire at these armour-clad men, whom she rightly assumed were in charge.

But she did not have to; one of the heavy archers in the opposite group had spotted her attempt to strike the men down, and instinctively ordered his men to focus their fire on them.

As she found sight of the archers she saw them release a torrent of arrows at the men, bringing one of them to his knees.

The other two left him to die, the middle one, clothed in some kind of hide, wrenched the man's shield off him for himself.

They marched for the gate, ordering their remaining men to give them cover and throw themselves against Zaxx's team.

It was at that moment, just as she was about to give the order for her team to open fire on them, that she realised that her team had gone silent.

No stretching of bows.

No arrows whistling through the air from behind.

As she turned to face them her feeling of dread became real; a hunting band of Wolfhounds, seven of them; each having cut the throat of one of her archers mere moments ago.

She quickly readied another arrow, shifting her aim from one man to another.

They were in a stalemate, but not for long.

***

Zaxx had just dispatched another Wolfhound when he noticed two heavily armoured men, both with shields, making their way towards the gate.

He heard them shouting orders to the Wolfhounds, and noticed that one of the men was clad in what appeared to be wolf skin.

He turned and barked orders at his men to hold steady, knowing that these two must be the leaders, and that they were preparing for escape.

Turning back he managed to notice, then quickly dodge an oncoming sword.

Taking a few steps back he pulled his sword to a defensive stance, ready for his attacker; a short but stout man with a scarred face that disrupted his beard.

They circled one another, each anticipating the others moves.

Suddenly the short man hurled his sword at Zaxx, throwing him off balance as he deflected it with a leftward strike.

Before Zaxx could recover, the man tackled him to the ground.

They wrestled, each attempting to direct Zaxx's sword into the others throat.

Then out of nowhere, accompanied by the sound of broken flesh, the man began to spew blood.

Zaxx pushed him off, revealing an arrow entrenched in the back of the man's throat.

Zaxx got to his feet wiping blood off his face, taking a moment to survey the battlefield.

He was shocked at the progression of the shielded men; their subordinates throwing themselves against the Blackwood guardsmen at a barbaric rate.

His eyes dashed to find sight of Bough, spotting him mid-fight with the Wolfhounds defending their leader.

He began to march, then jog towards him, aiming to aid him strike down the Wolfhound leader.

As he did he noticed Yates cradling the broken body of a young man, barely into his twenties. He would have gone over to help him, had his mind not been focused on stopping the Wolfhound's leader.

His pace picked up, now a full-on sprint towards the swirling mass of men and metal.

Bough had managed to break through the Wolfhound's ranks, along with three of his men, and was engaged in combat with the leader and his bodyguard.

Zaxx ducked and hacked his way through the foes before him, his men barely holding them at bay as best they could, the occasional arrow flying overhead.

As he fought his mindless foes, he could all but helplessly watch as Bough and his men fought on.

The few blows they managed to make failed to connect with the few weak points in their adversaries' armour. The leader – Wolf – took few hits; his shield and guard taking most of the blows for him.

The guard bashed one of Bough's men with his shield, striking at another, knocking him off guard long enough for Wolf to run him through.

Bough tried to capitalise on Wolf's distraction, but had his sword deflected by his shield at the last moment.

Zaxx continued to make his way into the fray, constantly being blocked by writhing Wolfhounds desperate to keep their master safe.

This time the guard ran one of the Bough's men through, using him as a shield against Bough's last man's blows.

Bough parried Wolf's strikes, skilfully avoiding shield bashes as he attempted to return the favour.

As Zaxx finally made his way into the fight, the last of Boughs men dropping to the ground, the guard swiftly moving in on Bough.

Zaxx dashed to intercept him, but in doing so distracted Bough just enough for Wolf to knock him off his feet.

Zaxx tackled the guard to the ground, bashing the man's helm with the hilt of his sword until it caved it in.

Bough blocked a strike to his torso despite being winded and on his back. Unable to get back up due to Wolf's attacks, it was all he could do to prevent his demise.

Zaxx had rendered the guard unconscious or dead; the indented helm now piercing the brow and eyes of its occupant.

Wolf knocked Bough's sword from his hand with his shield, moving to plunge his sword towards Bough's heart, snarling as he thrusted the sword downwards with both hands.

Bough clasped the sword as best he could, the blade cutting almost to the bone. Normally he would be in screaming agony, but the adrenalin and thirst for survival had numbed the pain, even as the sword slowly cut deeper into his hands, etching closer and closer towards his heart, blood dripping down the edge of the sword.

Knowing there was no time to waste, Zaxx grabbed the guards shield, and with a great heave threw it at Wolf's head.

As it connected with his helm the impact let out a massive clang, removing the wolf's head from him, knocking him out cold, thankfully causing him to fall down to his left and not onto Bough.

Zaxx ran over to him.

"You...?" he asked, panting for air.

"Yeah" Bough nodded after a deep and sharp breath.

Zaxx turned to look at the rest of the fight; the dead littered the ground, the few Wolfhounds that remained tied up in battle.

Just as he was about to deal with Wolf, he spotted Maralin on the ridge.

And he noticed she wasn't aiming her bow at the battlefield.

He realised what was happening up there.

He felt his heart stop.

***

I stumbled out of the Barracks, taking Samu's weight as Monro and I carried him; one of his arms round each of our shoulders.

The scene that greeted us was that of a dying battle, bodies strewn across the courtyard. Though they were mostly Wolfhounds, we had suffered heavier losses than I would ever find acceptable.

As we made our way towards the gate, dark clouds gathered in from the east as I scanned what remained of the battle for signs of Wolf and his bodyguards, a fine torrent of droplets, blown sideways by the wind, fell upon us as they burst their banks. Through this the sun still shone brightly, mocking the storm with its rays and warmth.

Finally my eyes found Bough sat beside the bodies of Wolf and one of his bodyguards, his hands being bandaged by one of our men.

Leaving Samu and Monro, I jogged over to him, where upon reaching him I asked if Wolf was dead, or just unconscious.

"I think dead" breathed Bough heavily "but you can't be too careful."

Giving an agreeing nod, I looked around briefly for Zaxx, though he was nowhere to be seen.

I looked back at Bough.

"Where's Zaxx?" I asked, somewhat worried for my friend.

Bough gestured to the ridge, blood dripping from his bandaged hand as he pointed.

I looked up at the ridge, my mind taking a second to process what I was seeing; my heart nearly stopping when I did.

Without hesitation I ran to the gates, yelling at some of our men to follow me; twelve of them obliging, the others caught up with the now captive Wolfhounds.

We ran round the outside of the camp, making our way up to the ridge.

My heart raced a thousand times fast, my thoughts incomprehensible gibberish of panic and worry.

Upon making the top of the ridge I was greeted with a clearer picture than from down in the courtyard: Maralin, on one side of the Wolfhounds, attempted to keep her attackers at bay, whilst on the other Zaxx furiously cleaved at them, with a rage I had never seen before.

I made my way into the fray with haste, my men following me, determined to get to Maralin before she suffered fatigue, or ran out of arrows.

She did have a short-sword sheathed at her hip, but it was a question as to whether she would be able to draw it in time to defend herself that was of worry to me.

As we fought, I caught a glimmer in Zaxx's eyes, a spark I had not seen before; it was not the fury or rage he used against our foes, no, this was something softer, rawer, and much more powerful.

Zaxx cut one of the Wolfhound's throat open, gutting another which Maralin had staggered with an arrow in a swift turn of his blade.

As a sunbeam lit up the ridge, we made our push, ending the battle swiftly, in a hail of death throws and wailing, as our men cut down the Wolfhounds.

Or so we thought.

Another of their number emerged from the bramble behind Maralin, grabbing her by the throat.

He pulled her against him, bringing his sword up against her neck.

It was a situation all too familiar.

"Let her go savage!" Zaxx barked.

The man shook his head.

"Not 'till I see Wolf" his voice was gruff and ragged "Bring him 'ere. Then we talk."

I looked down at the courtyard of the camp, now a muddy red, looking upon Wolf's body.

In a strange way I really hoped he was alive, but knew that wouldn't guarantee Maralin's safety.

I looked back at the grubby man.

"Alright. Just give me a minute to get him."

The Wolfhound nodded.

With that I turned on my heel to march down to the courtyard, leaving the others and Zaxx to ensure he didn't make a run for it.

But as I did I heard the sound of metal impacting bone.

Fearing the worst I turned back to where the Wolfhound had Maralin, drawing my sword as I did.

But upon seeing what had happened I froze with shock, somewhat perplexed and relieved; Zaxx had thrown his sword at the Wolfhound, who was so distracted by me as to not notice the blade arcing towards him. With precision that would make an archer proud, the sword struck him point first, erupting out the other side.

As the corpse fell back Maralin yelped, the Wolfhounds sword grazing the skin on her throat with its rough edge as it fell away.

Zaxx rushed over to her swiftly, just about catching her before she fell to her knees, near-fainting with shocked relief.

I would have gone over to her straight away, but...I could see it in the way he held her, gentle and delicately – something Zaxx wasn't – and in the way she looked back at him.

I could always tell what went through her mind by looking into those emerald green eyes, and now was no exception.

I smiled to myself, before ordering my men to guard them as I went to inspect our prisoners.

And as it turns out, one wolf-skin clad individual happened to be coming around.

***

Two of our men dragged Wolf by his arms, throwing him down before me. As he clambered in the mud to his knees I entertained thoughts of vengeance, before deciding a more useful tact.

"So...Wolf" I said as I crouched in front of him "You're going to tell me, say, everything I want to know."

He looked up at me. At this distance I could see his face more clearly despite his helm – which was attached to his cuirass – such that the familiarity of his voice began to make terrifying sense.

"Tomm?" I said, questioning the sight before me.

He smiled wryly, mockingly, at the question, defiant at the position he found himself in.

"How...Why? Why have you done this?" I asked, lost in a sea of confusion as the fine rain pelted my face.

"Look."

I looked about the camp, unsure of what he was getting at.

"Look at what Tomm?"

"Look" he repeated, emitting a dark confidence filled with some as yet unknown satisfaction.

"At What?!"

"Look" he gestured down to his left with his eyes.

I saw it.

That damned symbol, branded into his neck.

I reeled back, realising, though not quite believing what I saw, staggering to my feet, turning my head away in disbelief.

He began to laugh, knowing how much this disturbed me.

There were questions that needed answering; where were the rest of the villagers, were they dead or enslaved? Were there any more Wolfhounds lurking about? Was this part of something bigger? And now, what else has *he* planned for us?

"You can't stop him" Tomm cackled.

To me, at that moment, those questions did not matter; for having seen the mark branded upon the side of his neck, I knew there was no use in asking.

Without thought or worry, my arm unsheathed my sword, and with a will of its own thrust it up through his throat and into his head.

The two men charged with guarding our captive looked on in shock, not quite believing I would dispatch such a valuable captive.

My gaze staggered, responding to my disconcertion and un-ease, as Bough ran over to me.

"What happened?!" he yelled, barely concealing his anger behind etiquette.

My eyes moved their gaze over to him, then back to the muddy battlefield, observing the dead.

"What was necessary" I answered without looking at him.

"Sir, with all due respect-"

"Bough" I interrupted "some men are better dead"-I turned to face him-"no matter how valuable they are or seem to be."

He looked at me a moment, searching my face for answers.

"But the other villagers, what of their fate?"

I walked up to him, putting a hand on his shoulder.

"Trust me Bough, they'll be okay" I was not sure I believed that.

He just looked back at me, unsure and uneasy.

"Tend to the men" I smiled "tonight we celebrate a great victory."

With that I left him to his men, making my way to Zaxx and Maralin. I needed to tell them of the mark, tell them how Falkner too had it branded upon his neck and talk with them about that which I knew in my heart was the key to how and why Tomm had become Wolf, why he would attack our village, and where the rest of the villagers would ultimately be found.

I cursed myself for not telling them of the return of that accursed symbol those years ago after the incident with Falkner, even though I had truly hoped the mark was but a coincidence I should have warned Zaxx. You see, the one behind the brand, the architect of these events and horrors, was the very same that made Zaxx the way he is, the *why* of his over the top drinking.

As I made my way up the ridge, I looked down upon the camp, seeing Yates carrying one of our fallen in his arms; it suddenly hit me as to who it was, who the broken body belonged to: Kyle.

It was odd, I had only known him a short time, and yet...and yet his death hit me like stone. I think it was the fact he was so young, least compared to the rest of us.

As I embraced my friends with a mighty hug I knew what we would have to do to stop any more deaths like Kyle, how to stop any more raids like the one on the village of Blackwood.

I whispered to my friends the knowledge I had just gained, with them replying with silent and solemn nods of understanding.

Giving the word to one of the men to carry a message to Tau in Bahvil, and another man a message for Mazog in Hamurfel, I led those well enough for travel back to Blackwood City, leaving a small detachment on the off chance of any Wolfhounds remaining in the area. Once at the city we would organise a plan to rebuild *our* Blackwood, and how to protect it in the future. But once that was in Decon's hands we would leave to meet up with Tau and Mazog.

It was time we confronted our past.

It was time for Zaxx to face his demons.

It was time I struck down the evil that had plagued my friends, and corrupted people I once knew.

Mazog and Tau, once they received the message would know precisely what was planned.

The message was a single, but powerful word.

A name.

Rothgar.

***

We had marched back to Blackwood City, our dead carried in the few prison carts the Wolfhounds had around their camp, with those that would not fit resting upon the backs of our horses. We had buried the Wolfhounds; despite their heinous and vile acts, there was something unsettling about leaving them out to be feasted upon by scavengers.

Once we had seen to it that the soldiers were being treated for their wounds, and delivered the honoured dead to the city temple, we made our way to the court of Count Decon.

"Ah, Primus, I see you have returned from your endeavour" he forced a smile as we approached his throne, the others stopping a few feet behind me.

"We must talk Decon."

"Indeed. You, on behalf of Bahvil, owe me – I mean Blackwood – a sum for the rental of our troops" his smirk made my blood boil; but alas, I had to keep some measure of calm.

"Decon, we saved your people, people you abandoned! Don't you dare try to worm your way out of responsibility" Maralin interjected.

He looked at her disdainfully.

"Does your wife know of your mistress here?" Decon asked smugly, continuing to evade the real discussion.

"Yes Decon, she is very well aware of the arrangement" I spat, signalling to Maralin to let me handle it.

"Whatever do you see in such a common wench?"

"Stop being an ignorant dolt. You abandoned your people; why?"

"As I said before, the men couldn't be spared. We needed them here in case of attack."

"You have over five-hundred guardsmen alone!"

Decon fidgeted in his throne with annoyance.

"And you have come into my domain unasked, had that *woman* assault me in order to lend you our men, and now dare to belittle me in my own court?" he scolded "It is only due to you being married to the Countess that I have not had you put in chains!"

"Perhaps you should be more worried that one of your villages was sacked and raided by-"

"My men. Couldn't. Be. Spared." He seethed "Of course I could hardly refuse once you had begged for our support..." the sarcasm oozed through his voice.

"You contemptuous fool!"-it was hard for me to keep myself from saying something rather less diplomatic-"Rothgar was behind it; he is back and he won't stop until he's got the vengeance he craves!"

Decon looked at me, disbelieving.

"That's not possible" he looked mildly worried, his brow furrowed and eyes widening slightly "You're lying."

"Their leader carried Rothgar's crest" I beckoned Zaxx to my side "Show him Zaxx."

Zaxx untied a leather satchel, emptying its contents onto the floor before Decon.

"Is that...?" he began as he looked at the small square of skin, branded with the black sickle, a feeling of revulsion coming over him "Take it away!"

Zaxx picked it back up with the satchel.

"Do you see now? Do you see why we cannot stand by and let you play your stupid political games?!"

"You could have easily faked that, that grotesque display" he sneered.

"You remember the disappearances a few years back? The ones you told Leonard Diamando to cover up?"

"I have no idea–"

"The men who abducted them wore the same tunics as Tomm – the Wolfhound leader – had, and Falkner had the same goddamned crest branded into his neck as he did."

We looked uneasily at each other in the awkward stillness of the hall, neither of our people knowing quite where to look.

"What are you saying?" Decon asked finally.

"Rothgar has been planning this for a long time, and he's been slowly making moves against us; he's already reduced our village to ruin, he engineered events to have me killed by one of *your* captains"-I took a deep breath-"So what I'm saying is you need to watch your back, and look out for those he would strike down."

"Why should I be worried? It was the previous Count that was involved, not I."

"You are his nephew, which will be close enough for him."

Count Decon lost his characteristic smarminess, a wash of apprehension going through him.

"How do we stop him?" he asked after a moment of thought.

I hesitated a moment.

"We need to draw him out. Up until now he's sent others to do his work; we need him to come after us in person."

"Or we track him down" Decon added.

"Right" I nodded "We must depart for Bahvil, and ready it for whatever evil he plans for us; I leave you one of my best guardsmen, Samu, to act as my envoy as you make plans to re-build Blackwood Village, and keep an eye out for any more Wolfhounds."

"I do not need to be watched like a wee bairn, least of all by an injured orc."

"No, but having the ear of a diplomat, whilst bolstering your personal guard, is never unwise."

"Quite" he said dryly.

As we turned to leave, Decon called to me.

"Prime" he said "Next time you intrude upon Blackwood matters, I will not be so lenient."

By the divines that man liked to posture.

I kept on walking away, knowing words would be wasted on his pettiness. It's not like there was anything he could say to stop me from aiding the people of Blackwood; they are *my* people.

Mine.

***

We were halfway back to Bahvil, and had settled for the night in a breezeless, rocky cove, sat around the campfire, my thoughts on our old home, a near eerie silence drifting between us as we ate our meal of bread and broth. Zaxx sat cross-legged on the floor next to Marlin's chair, whilst I gazed emptily into the fire. As much as they knew it to be, they did not want my conclusion about Rothgar to be true; not that I could blame them for that.

Amongst our number were Bough, Monro and Yates, who had sworn a vendetta against Rothgar for the death of Kyle.

"You sure it was Rothgar's doing?" Zaxx spoke dryly, the question more of a plea than of doubt "You're absolutely sure?"

"Yes" I nodded "You saw the brand on Tomm's neck."

"The black sickle" Zaxx muttered quietly "I just...I just don't want to believe it."

"Why didn't you mention Falkner having the brand?" Maralin asked, both curious and doubtful "Why wait? Why not tell us?"

"I...I didn't want to believe it, much like how Zaxx is now" I shrugged apologetically "But I couldn't be sure then."

"You should have said something" Zaxx added, his voice scarily sober "You damn well know it too."

Monro, having kept quiet until this moment, spoke with slight hesitance, wary of how sensitive a matter this was.

"Sir" he began, leaning forward as he cupped his bowl "just *who* is this Rothgar? I have not heard his name mentioned in any report or-"

I cut him off, raising my hand to silence him.

"He is too slippery and devious to get a mention in any military reports."

"And too clever to do any of his own damned dirty work" gritted Zaxx.

Monro nodded. I could see he was using his military mind, trying to get an image of his enemy.

"So…" Bough began "just how do we draw out such a man, or find him for that matter? From what you say the man is like a shadow, and as easy to hold down as one."

"Either we get one of his men to talk, or offer ourselves on a silver platter" Maralin sighed with a heavy heart.

The mood was sombre; our last meeting with Rothgar was one we would all rather have left in the past. Maralin had not been part of that old conflict, but she knew of it, and what it had done to us, what it had cost us…what it had cost Zaxx.

"I'm just glad Mazog was in Hamurfel when the attack happened" Zaxx spoke uncharacteristically softly "I dread to think what would have become of him had they…well, you know."

"At least he'll be with us soon enough" Bough said "I sent the fastest courier I could find to the address he had left you Maralin."

She gave him a silent smile as she tore off a chunk of bread from her roll. I must confess, I would rather had her stay in Bahvil with Carmel and Joahana once it came time to confront Rothgar; there she could be could be kept safe with them, not that they couldn't handle themselves, but I could not help but want them as far away from this as possible.

It was at this point that Yates spoke up.

"If you don't mind my asking, what exactly are we up against?" he queried "It's just, by the way you speak of him, it's as if he's something supernatural."

I let out a slight laugh.

"Nothing supernatural about him Yates. He's just smart, real smart – arrogant to be sure – but smart."

"Perhaps we could use that to our advantage?"

We mulled that over a moment.

"Not sure there's a way to do that without putting ourselves in mortal danger" Zaxx replied, saying what we all knew and thought.

"Once we get back to Bahvil, then we make our plan" I said as I threw a few dry twigs onto the fire "Once all of us are there."

"How long should it take for Mazog to get there?"

"Assuming he gets the message in two or three days, I'd say about a week" Maralin replied, chewing on her bread thoughtfully.

"That's a long time to wait to make a plan" Bough commented nervously.

"We can make plans whilst we wait, but we won't decide on one until Mazog is by our side" I said firmly, Maralin giving me a little smile.

We sat quietly eating what was left of our supper, listening to the crackling of the campfire, watching its little sparks float off into the sky.

"I'm so sick of fighting" I mumbled to myself, absently thinking out loud as I put my head in my hand.

The others seemed too tired to notice, bar Maralin, who walked over and sat next to me; Zaxx having fallen asleep where he sat.

"You alright?" she whispered, putting an arm around me.

"Yes...no...I don't know" I replied, exhausted "I just don't want to...I'm tired of all the death and hurt."

She leant her head on my shoulder.

"I understand" she sighed "It's like how Mazog felt after Falkner."

"Is that why he rarely sees us now?"

She paused a moment.

"I suppose it is, but it won't always be that way, he'll be fine"-she looked up at me-"But it's okay to not want to fight, it's okay to choose not to fight."

I looked at her longingly.

"But...what if there isn't a choice? Like with Rothgar, I know, as much as I don't want it to be, that he'll only be stopped one way."

"That's different Sylon. Fighting because you have to, because it is the right thing to do, is nothing to feel ashamed of. That doesn't make it any less terrible or haunting I know, but it is different. Just so long as you fight for what is right, for the right reasons, that's what matters." She gave a comforting smile, and a small kiss to my cheek.

"You called me by my first name" I smiled back "Things must be serious."

"What can I say, someone has to mother you."

"...Thanks Maralin, really."

"Don't get all soft on me in front of the lads" she chimed, quietly teasing.

I leaned back against the smooth rock behind me, gazing up at the glittering stars with Maralin as the others wrapped themselves into their bedrolls as they bid us goodnight.

"I still can't believe you told the Count of Blackwood you're my mistress."

"Decon was being difficult."

I let out a muffled laugh.

"And that's the first thing you thought of?"

"A mistress is a terribly powerful thing to be."

"Oh?"

She raised her eyebrow questioningly.

"You doubt me?"

"Well, no, it's just, how would you know?"

"Clearly you've never been on my bad side."

"Ah."

"Yes, 'ah' indeed."

***

We had returned to pandemonium.

A barbaric army was laying siege to Bahvil, though they had not yet breached the white stone walls; the Great Gate holding mockingly against their onslaught.

Bahvil archers were laying down clouds of arrows upon them, but they would not yield, many holding their shields above the heads of their comrades, taking the brunt of the volleys.

We were stuck outside the walls, and Bahvil could not be risked by opening the gates for us without intense support from our archers and guardsmen, not whilst so many stood before it.

Unsurprisingly, as we tried to signal our men atop the battlements, we were forced to fight those barbarians that noticed us. We were out of reach of our archers, our personal skirmishes going on for much of an hour, until I noticed something that caused me to freeze: two siege towers being pulled upright by a team of sickleback, whom then started to drag them towards the walls. What turned this threat into a dreaded terror, however, was the banner each held at its front; the Black Sickle, Rothgar's house banner.

We decided we had to battle to the gates; if Rothgar was involved our only hope would be found inside Bahvil, and by using overwhelming force.

As we drew close I could see Tau atop the battements, working the men hard to keep a steady supply of arrows to the archers.

Bough blew a signal horn he carried with him, usually to call for backup within the city, hoping that Tau would hear it above the clatter of battle.

Tau looked down, spotting us, quickly ordering our archers to give us covering fire. As we got within sprinting distance of the gates they began to open, Tau cleaving his way to us with his mighty warhammer, thirty of the castle's heavy guard pouring out behind him, holding back the barbarians as we made our way through.

As we entered they withdrew with us, the gates closing behind them, crushing two barbarians that tried to enter the city.

I gave Yates and Monro orders to carry to the men, Tau racing up to the battlements with Zaxx, the pair attempting to ready the catapults to fire flaming balls of heated tar at the siege towers.

I ran to castle Bahvil, my only thought that of Carmel and to get her and Ana ready to flee Bahvil with Maralin if the worst were to befall us.

As I ran, I thought of how Rothgar had played us, played me, using the attack on Blackwood as a distraction.

*

The castle guard had already began fortifying the battlements and entrances when I arrived.

I found Carmel and Ana with Belothor – Furgus helping out with the citizens at this time – in the War Room , a map of the city and its defences hastily strewn across the dark oak table at its centre, the Captains of the Guard carefully planning their defensive strategies with them.

"Sir" they saluted as I entered with Bough and Maralin.

"They have bloody siege towers" I shouted, ignoring polite protocol.

Their eyes widened at that news.

Carmel threw her arms around me, silently whispering 'I missed you' in my ear.

"Tau is readying the catapults" I said to the Captains over her shoulder, as she relinquished her grip on me "those towers have to be our priority."

They nodded in agreement.

"Sir, what if they make it to our walls" one of them asked.

I gave Carmel a quick glance, who gave a silent nod in agreement, before looking back at him, square in the eye.

"We set the walls on fire."

*

Furgus and the city guard had rounded most of the citizens into the castle keep, with the rest hiding in either the Temple crypt or the vaults of Furgus's smithies; all the freely available guards either working on defences or the catapults.

Carmel and Ana were with Maralin and an escort of twenty guards, readying an escape, should the worst befall us and the city; no one would want to be captured by Rothgar's men.

The siege towers had come within thirty yards of the walls by the time I made it back to the battlements, though one was almost crippled.

Tau fought against the onslaught of arrows coming from Rothgar's men atop the siege towers to fire the central catapult, its fiery ball of death leaping through the air, striking the left siege tower a mortal blow to its centre.

As the fire burnt out its core, the molten tar burned away at the barbarian soldiers as the tower collapsed, crushing and impaling those who had escaped the flames.

The second siege tower remained, and was now within ten yards, too close for our catapults to hit.

I met Yates as I dashed across the battlements, just in time to see the remaining siege tower come within leaping distance of the wall.

"Tau!" I shouted with ferocity "clear the area!"

He nodded, ordering the men to do so.

"We really doing this?" Yates trembled.

"Yes" I said sternly, turning to help the men with the cauldrons of tar as the siege tower hit the wall.

As our archers stemmed the tide of barbarians spilling onto the battlements, the few of us not locked in combat began emptying the thick tar across the battlement walkway as enemy arrows hit the stone around us, as many of our men retreating as was possible.

Rothgar's savages trudged through the tar, attempting to stop us from igniting it.

Eight of our men held them in place, taking blows and arrows as they shouted at us to light them up, knowing that they would burn with the enemy.

We poured superheated coals onto the tar, igniting a torrent of flame that engulfed them all in a miniature firestorm, whose flames began to spread to the siege tower in a few tens of seconds.

Making a mental note to honour and avenge those eight brave guardsmen, I turned my gaze to the barbarians below, still trying to breach the gates.

As I watched Rothgar's banner burn, I knew that whilst their strength would wane now they had lost their greatest assets, this would be just the beginning for Rothgar.

He had been planning his vengeance for years, and now he was coming for us, mind, body and soul.

***

The siege had taken three more days to end, as one by one Rothgar's men were killed or simply fled, presumably back to their master (or as far away as they could, if they were smart; Rothgar doesn't take kindly to failure). We had sent out a detachment, led by Monro, after a group of those that fled in the hopes of catching them for interrogation.

Mazog had returned to us but a day after, in the evening, walking through the arrow scarred fields beyond the walls – there was too much debris for a horse and cart to get across safely – having to knock on the gate to be let in. First thing he did was hug Maralin, before seeing how Zaxx was coping.

We had a long and difficult discussion as to how we would approach the dire threat we faced, and it wasn't without its arguments and raised voices; Mazog kept a cool head throughout as usual though.

Having bid the others goodnight at some ungodly hour, I retreated to our private chamber with Carmel, where we lay upon our bed in our comfy nightwear, holding one another as we kissed.

I loved these moments.

There was a specialty to them, something precious and without equal; I felt mild shame that I had only recently begun truly appreciating just how special they were.

Her soft lips upon mine made me feel so...complete. The feeling of bliss in that moment was so total and complete that time seemed to stop, if only for a moment.

"I'm only happy when you're around you know" she spoke softly, having pulled away from our embrace.

"Likewise" I smiled.

I stared into those green-tinted blue eyes with joy and wonder.

"Promise me..." she began, placing her left hand upon my face as she spoke "Promise me you'll come back."

"I promise" I replied, pulling her close "and I promise, when this is done, I will never leave your side again."

She smiled, planting a kiss upon my lips once more.

"Good" she whispered, a single tear rolling down her cheek; I wiped it away gently.

"Carm" I whispered "I love you like jam and scones."

She gave a tired, soft giggle as she snuggled up against me.

"When you come back, and this is behind us, do..."-she yawned-"do you want to...to..."

"Carm?"

"Sorry, just so tired. And comfy" she sighed, her head nestled against mine.

I closed my eyes, my arm caressing her gently yet firmly, the each of us feeling the other's heartbeat.

We lay there, holding one another, enjoying the moment of peace till we drifted off to sleep.

***

The wind blew against us as we travelled to our destination.

Mazog's cowl blew wildly, mimicking his mind-set.

Monro and his men had captured and interrogated many of Rothgar's savages – thankfully they were not as loyal or brainwashed as Tomm or Falkner; a rare but important slipup on

Rothgar's part – until we found out where he was holed up; we were confident as most of the men's stories matched.

Zaxx rode next to Maralin, whom insisted on aiding on our mission, despite her brother's protests.

Yates and Monro rode behind us with an ensemble of men, some honour bound guards of Bahvil, others Blackwood soldiers with a vendetta against Rothgar. Bough had remained behind in case of further attack on Bahvil.

In all there were forty-six of us, small enough to travel undetected, large enough to storm a small keep with the right strategy.

Speaking of which, I should mention the significance of his chosen hideout; it was an old Blackwood fort by the name of Stronghold, near the Blackwood-Hamurfel border.

Once it had been the home of a great nobleman and his family, until it was decommissioned by order of the Count of Blackwood, Stanlius Obsidian (the current Count's uncle). The son of the nobleman did not take this kindly, and mustered men to lay waste to the villages of Blackwood as a matter of vendetta. The friends of this man tried to talk sense into him, but he refused to listen to reason and so turned on them, targeting their home, the original township of Blackwood; my home.

That man was Rothgar, and Zaxx and I were his friends.

And he had entrusted us with his plans, thinking we would aid him; it stands to reason that we would not, the lives of the innocent were worth more than our friendship by any measure.

Due to this Rothgar saw us as betrayers, especially Zaxx, whom had been the one to inform Stanlius about Rothgar's plans, and why he seeks not only our demise, but our suffering; to see us suffer true pain and loss.

But...if truth be told, that is not all there is to this story.

You see, the last time we had seen him was two days after Stanlius had his father arrested.

It was only meant to be a bargaining tool, that's all...

What follows is a hard tale to tell, but for you to understand...to understand *why* we must end Rothgar...and why it is Zaxx drinks the way he does.

* * * *

Six years prior to meeting Carmel

It was just before noon, and a band of guards surveyed the scene before us.

Red shone brightly in the sun, a deep contrast to the sandstone road. The man's eyes gazed outward, shocked, as if unaware of their owner's demise.

We had been careless.

And now a good man lay dead.

It would have been sad if it had been any other person, but with it being him it was far, far worse.

His name was Eizekiel; he was Rothgar's father.

The guards in the area – the village of Blackwood – were in a state of anxiousness, their fighting arms never too far away from their short-swords.

They had been placed on high alert by new orders concerning an impending attack, and the vagary of just *who* was going to attack had left the men unsettled.

There had been five of us (me, Eizekiel and three of the Count's men), all dressed in plain clothes as to make us less noticeable should we cross one of Rothgar's spies.

These two things, in of themselves, were harmless enough, but as we approached this patrol of four guards we failed to account for their nervousness, and as such their readiness to attack at even the tiniest hint of danger.

As we got within striking distance, one of the Count's men reached for his hipflask tucked under his sackcloth shirt.

One of the guards saw this, misjudging it as a man going for his weapon, and unsheathed his sword, swiping it at the man in one swift motion.

He ducked backward, the blade barely missing his chest, but cruel fate allowed the blade to carry on in its momentum in an upward arc, striking the man next to him in the throat; Eizekiel.

To say I was in a state of despair would not do my emotion, or the state of things then, any justice.

But this moment, no matter how tragic, would soon be eclipsed.

The sun had but an hour before it set, a soft and calming breeze drifted in from the west, the odd tuft of cloud following it.

To most, it was a pleasant, almost magical end to a sunny summer's day, but this picturesque evening was largely unnoticed by Zaxx.

He paced the livingroom floor, nervously rubbing his right wrist, his left thumb clasped tightly in his other hand; a nervous tick, one that helped him think in tense situations.

His brother came in from the back room, a jug of warmed, spiced milk in his hands.

"You'll wear out the floor pacing like that" he chuckled.

Zaxx just shot him a weary glance.

"Come on, I made you some spiced milk" he smiled, extending the drink towards him.

Zaxx released the grasp on his thumb and took the jug from his brother.

"Thanks" he said briefly, taking a moment to sip the slightly frothed liquid and savour its creamy-sweet taste.

Seb, Zaxx's younger brother, being a gentle soul, was more at home in the kitchen than the battlefield, and had an admiration for his older brother; and a good measure of how to calm him down.

Likewise, Zaxx knew how to wind him up, though if anyone else tried to do so he would intervene without a second thought.

"You need to talk?" he spoke calmly, in that 'it's okay if you don't' kind of voice.

Zaxx lowered the jug from his lips, shaking his head slightly as he wiped the cream from his top lip.

"No, no...I'm sure it'll be fine"-he hesitated a moment before continuing, mulling over a thought as he did-"perhaps...perhaps you should travel to Norain, see cousin Judith and Uncle Siegfried."

Seb cocked his head.

"Should I be worried?"

"No...just cautious" Zaxx did not like his brother worrying.

"Then perhaps you should come with me."

Zaxx nodded agreeingly; what better way to see him safely away from here and Rothgar.

"I guess I'll go pack then" Seb smiled.

With that he went upstairs, sensing that sooner would be better than later.

Zaxx turned to look out of the small diamond shaped window on the side of the house, once again bringing the jug to his lips.

As he sipped the tasty drink, he allowed himself a pleasant thought.

"Perhaps this ends well; Rothgar may well hand himself in now...maybe things will go back to the way they were..."

With that the front door burst open, the wood splintering apart where the lock had been.

Zaxx turned on the spot, spilling the milk as he did.

Before him were two strangers, whom rushed at him, a familiar face standing behind them in his blue tunic, hood down, the black sickle proudly embossed upon its shoulder.

It was Rothgar.

Before Zaxx had a chance to react, the two men had pinned him against the wall.

Rothgar paced calmly towards him.

"You" he pointed at Zaxx with his engraved sword, his eyes filled with menace and unfathomable rage, his anger made all the more terrifying by his calm complexion.

Zaxx's words failed to form, the suddenness and shock silencing him.

"Did you hear?"-he pressed the sword against Zaxx's neck-"someone informed old Obsidian of my plan."

Zaxx gazed back, searching his mind for something, anything, which could deescalate the situation.

Rothgar leaned closer, his face almost against Zaxx's.

"And our mate Prime" he spat "he gone got my dad killed."

"I...I'm-" Zaxx stumbled.

"Sorry?" Rothgar interrupted, leaning back, taking his sword down from Zaxx's neck "Sorry" he repeated, wiping his free hand down his face.

Zaxx just nodded.

"Sorry don't cut it Zaxx"-he shook his head-"I mean, dad had nothing to do with this, you know? Just me an' Obsidian. But nooo"-he turned his attention back to Zaxx-"you went and told him, got my dad arrested."

"I didn't suggest-"

"I know!" Rothgar screeched "I know. But if you hadn't betrayed me-"

"You were going to kill innocent people" Zaxx protested "friends, neighbours...what did you expect me to do?"

"You were my friend! You're meant to have my back!"

"Stopping you was having your back! You're better than this Rothgar...aren't you?"

They stared into each other's eyes a moment, each reading their once-friend's thoughts.

"Just get it over with Rothgar" Zaxx spoke calmly, almost with a sigh, defiant to his inner fear and realising his friend was beyond help.

Rothgar nodded, walking back up to him.

"I guess I owe you a quick one, ay?" he half-mocked as he pulled the sword back up to Zaxx's throat.

But before he could exact his revenge, a voice issued him a challenge.

"Let him go Rothgar."

He turned to see Seb, holding his brother's short-sword in both hands, slowly advancing from the base of the stairs.

Rothgar withdrew his sword once again from Zaxx's neck, a cruel smile drawn across his face.

He turned his gaze back to Zaxx.

"Let us see how you endure such pain, old friend."

Zaxx went to respond but was muffled by the hand of one of the mercenaries.

Rothgar turned back to Seb, raising his sword as he spoke.

"You better know how to use that Seb."

"You can just let us go Rothgar."

"Oh, if only I could, but no, I can't"-he took a swing at Seb, who barely deflected it-"you see, I've lost my home"-he took another half-hearted swing at him-"I've lost my father"-this time Seb threw an attack, Rothgar blocking it easily-"All because of your dear brother"-they both swung at each other-"couldn't keep his mouth shut!"

With that he hefted a two-handed strike against Seb, who, despite blocking it, was knocked back, losing his balance and falling onto his back.

Rothgar kicked him in the ribs, waiting a moment before doing so again.

Zaxx's muffled screams matched Seb's, their anguish giving Rothgar a sick pleasure.

Rothgar picked up Zaxx's sword.

"Not nice"-he put his foot on seb's back, holding him still-"when someone takes those you love from you."

"P-please..." Seb croaked through his bloodied mouth

"I've always liked you Seb" Rothgar sighed "Shame."

With that he plunged Zaxx's sword into his brother's back.

Zaxx's scream echoed as a flood of bitter tears poured off his face.

Rothgar gave a nod to the two mercenaries, who proceeded to beat Zaxx viciously, before leaving with their master, unfazed by the brutality they had just witnessed.

Zaxx crawled over to his brother, cradling him in his arms as he wept.

*   *   *   *

Five days of near nonstop riding had left us weary, and our horses on the point of exhaustion, but still we continued. Over this time our dread had transformed, shifting to become something new, like a fuel for the fire in our hearts, bringing to us an unwavering determination to see this crusade of ours through to its final, violent confrontation.

This shift in our emotions was highly noticeable; where once there was anxiousness there was now determination, where fear once grew steadfast bravery blossomed.

We were nearing Stronghold Keep, the sun having arced passed noon by an hour or so. The environment changed rapidly from lightly wooded fields to a near barren landscape, mutilated trees – some with cages holding the dead hanging from them – dominated the landscape alongside clumps of dying gorse; all clearly a warning to those who would wish Rothgar harm.

Our gallop had become a deceivingly gentle trot; there was a chance our forty-six strong band would attract more attention if we were charging at the keep from here on.

As we passed by some of the trees housing the dead which marked the path, Maralin could not help but look up at them, morbid curiosity taking over here senses.

"T'is an awful way to go" Monro muttered, noticing this.

She nodded silently, a grave look upon her; the realisation of how barbaric Rothgar was dawning on her, as it did for some of our men.

We passed desiccated farmers as we drew closer to the keep, whom looked more at home in a crypt than in the fields, their skin seemingly draped over their bones.

Women were nowhere to be seen, nor girls or young children. There was the odd lad, thin and pale, but nothing more.

"This is sickening" Mazog whispered as he watched for any potential ambush.

"Where are the women, the children?" Yates thought out loud.

"Best we don't think about that Yates" Monro said dryly, keenly aware of the situation.

Zaxx drew up beside me.

"You notice the lack of guards?"

"Aye" I replied, starting to wonder whether some of the poor souls were the kidnapped members of Blackwood; even if they were, they would be hard to recognise in their malnourished state.

"So what's keeping them in line? They could just run, go looking for help. Something ain't right."

I stayed silent a moment, surveying the field surrounding us as inconspicuously as possible, my eyes suddenly widening with a dawning realisation.

"Zaxx" I whispered "we're surrounded."

He looked at me puzzled, slowly turning his head to look for soldiers, but seeing only farmers.

"I don't see any-"

"Think about it" I interrupted "anything seem out of place?"

His brow dipped into a deep frown as he gave that some thought.

Tau had been silently listening to our conversation.

"The farmers" he spoke softly, quite different from his usual booming tone.

Zaxx turned to look at him, still not quite understanding.

"They have swords" he continued with a whisper.

Zaxx gave a quick, darting look at the farmers, scanning them for signs of weaponry.

"I don't see – oh" he saw them, tucked purposefully into sacks of gathered food, hidden cleverly beneath tattered clothes and amongst farming tools.

"Why...What is this?"

"I suspect Rothgar has made these men...obedient, desperate; no doubt he's using their families as leverage."

"Which explains the lack of women and children" Tau finished my thought.

Mazog drew up alongside us once again, leaning over a little to whisper to us.

"You noticed the weapons?"

We nodded.

"Plan?" he asked.

I looked back at Tau.

"Tell the men…quietly."

He gave a nod and fell back to the others.

I returned my gaze to the path ahead and to Stronghold Keep, now less than a third of a league away.

"We keep going" I said, finally replying to Mazog's question.

"And if we raise their suspicion?"

"Well"-I turned to look at him-"we either die fighting or run like hell."

"Well that's encouraging" Zaxx groaned.

I couldn't help but give a small laugh to that.

***

We were but a hundred yards from the keep's gate, a growing unease now circulating amongst our number. The realisation of how outnumbered we were a terrifying one.

Thankfully the gates were open, farmers bringing in carts of food and leaving with empty ones. Guarding the gate were twenty or so men clad in chainmail adorned with cloth carrying Rothgar's symbol.

They had spotted us making our way towards them. One of the men – clearly the Captain – gave another an order to (presumably) inform the Keep's inhabitants, with the man then scuttling inside. The Captain then had his men ready their swords, with each half unsheathing their own. With that they blocked the entrance, barking at the farmers to get out of the way, the Captain standing in the centre of the men and a few paces in front.

We had got within fifty yards, the farmers close to the keep now beginning to leave their fields and carts, following us at a distance.

Some of our men fidgeted uneasily at the unnerving sight; Yates told them to man-up and keep calm.

I could feel the hairs on the back of my neck stand up on end as the tension in the air grew steeper with every step towards the gates.

At ten yards from them the Captain bellowed a command at us.

"Hold right there!" his voice was unnervingly calm.

We obliged, not yet wanting to start a fight.

"What business do you have here?" he questioned.

I gave a small cough to clear my throat.

"We have come to seek trade arrangements."

The Captain mulled that over for a moment.

"And what trade do you seek?"

I gestured to the fields around us.

He gave an understanding nod, then turned and whispered to one of his men before returning his attention to us.

"And *who* is it that seeks trade?" he quizzed, one eyebrow raised.

I gave an unintentional pause, perhaps for too long.

"The Count of Blackwood."

With that the guard ran into the keep, the Captain drawing his sword, though not threateningly.

"Wait there" he gestured with it.

I nodded with a smile.

Zaxx gave me an uneasy look.

"Don't fret Zaxx" I whispered "when has any of my plans gone wrong?"

Zaxx just rolled his eyes.

***

We were led through Stronghold's entrance hall by an escort of guards. The dark stone walls a filthy grey, draped with dark green banners with the black sickle upon them.

Our plan of storming the keep had, unsurprisingly, changed; instead of storming the keep, infiltration and sleight of hand was to be our method of attack. Yates and our men were being held in the courtyard, just behind the gate, Rothgar's soldiers keeping their eyes on them at all times. The rest of us were – for better or worse – on our own and being led to Rothgar's throne room.

Maralin was acting as my scribe, Tau and Monro as personal guard, with Mazog acting as diplomatic counsel.

I know what you're thinking; that there's a flaw in this plan, that Rothgar would recognise me and Zaxx. Well, that was the plan, or rather, it was the plan for him to recognise me, and as such keep him occupied, thus buying Zaxx time to complete his mission.

So where is he as we make our way to Rothgar, I hear you ask.

Allow me to explain: about half way through the keep towards Rothgar, Zaxx – acting as scribe's assistant – proclaims he has left the scribe's parchment with our men in the courtyard. With this Maralin, to her credit, displayed marvellous acting skills as she ranted at him for this error, and ordered him to go back at fetch it. To this end two of our escorts escorted Zaxx back towards the courtyard as we continued our way towards Rothgar.

As soon as we were out of sight Zaxx pulled out a concealed dagger (our weapons had been confiscated, or as the Captain put it 'willingly surrendered'), thrust it into the neck of the guard on his left, kicking the one on the right in the side as he did, then turning to knee him in the face before retrieving his dagger to finish him off. After dragging the bodies behind one of the banners hung on the walls, he silently slinked off into the shadows, dispatching any lone guard he came across.

As for us, we were waiting in the throne room, Rothgar not yet presenting himself; at least twelve men surrounded us, each clad in heavy chainmail and plate-steel armour, equipped with a short-sword and dagger.

To be honest, it was quite nerve-racking; we were surrounded, unarmed, probably – definitely – going to be recognised, and all our lives relied upon Zaxx being stealthy; which to be frank, was not his strong suit.

At this point an old and heavy door, splintered at the edges, creaked open.

Out from the void it enclosed emerged Rothgar; his hair was prematurely grey, with an odd streak of black on the right side, his eyes hate-drowned and sunken, dulled by an unkind life.

I took note of his armour, clad in blue silk robes – an attempt at 'nobility' – was made of plate-steel and backed with leather, the gauntlets spiked and discoloured from terrible actions. It was just like Rothgar to be ready for a fight at a moment's notice.

I held my breath in silence as he made his way to his false throne, wondering how he was going to react to my brazen – and seemingly foolish – attempt to get close to him.

It was only as he sat down did he finally look at us, and for a moment our eyes locked, an eerie and tortuously long silence flowing throughout the room.

"So" he began "you seek a trade arrangement?"

If he recognised me, he was keeping quiet about it; probably seeing how far I'd go, so I thought.

"Yes, trade for crops sire" I replied as I attempted to disguise my voice, barely able to stop myself from speaking with gritted teeth.

"Yes, one of my men told me. And what does your Count offer in exchange?" his tone was condescending, and most unsettling.

I took a moment to reply, my mouth having become dryer than desiccated bone.

"My lord offers ten gold per pound."

Rothgar stroked his chin thoughtfully, seemingly mulling the idea over.

"What is the best price you can offer me?" he asked dryly "I have not the time for bartering."

"Fifteen is the highest I'm authorised for sir."

He paused a moment.

"Deal. Now leave." He waved for his men to escort us away.

As the guards moved to do so, he spoke, raising his right hand in a halting gesture as he did.

"There is one more thing"-I felt my nerves shattering-"I'll be having your head Prime."

***

During this time Zaxx had made his way to the Keep's inner sanctum and dungeon, leaving a trail of hastily concealed corpses in his wake.

As he edged into the dim light of a solitary torch he could just make out the outlines of women and children behind the rusted iron bars.

Lifting the torch out of its sconce, he paced down the narrow hall, lighting the few other torches down there. With this added light, he staggered back on impulse and shock at the sight within each cell; each one cramped with skeletal women holding onto even more skeletal children, the odd baby clinging to its mother's breast, desperate for milk that would not yield.

They were silent, no doubt too weak to plea or beg for help or mercy. Clearly they had only been given just enough food for them to cling to life, and nothing more.

Zaxx knelt down near the bars of one cell, looking at what he assumed to be a teenage girl slumped on the floor, pressed against the bars for support.

"I'll get you out of here" he whispered.

Her eyes turned to him, the tiniest glint of hope the only colour in her once vibrant blue eyes.

Others in the cell turned their heads wearily, attempting to get a glimpse of the voice that offered them freedom.

Zaxx turned his head, looking from one cell to the next.

"All of you" his voice was a little louder now "I will get you all out of here."

The blue-eyed girl gave a weak, but unmistakably joyous smile.

* * * *

Zaxx stooped over the blooded body of the jailor, checking him for keys to the cells below. He had found him in the keep's kitchen – a filthy if well stocked one at that – gorging upon the spoils of the enslaved farmers' efforts. It was too much for Zaxx to bear, seeing such a portly figure consuming with so much gluttony as those innocents – especially the children – starved no more than twenty yards away. He told me how he had lost his sense of stealth and cunning, and had charged at the man, hacking at him furiously and viciously, and had not been able to stop even after it ceased to matter. It is understandable, having witnessed the state of those poor souls, the way they were kept so close to death...horrific doesn't quite cut it.

It was as he finally managed to pull the keys off the jailer's belt that he heard someone enter the kitchen, and had turned, dagger raised ready to start slashing, only to be greeted by the sight of a dishevelled man, his feet in chains and not all that better off than the farmers outside.

The man cowered on instinct.

"Pl-ple-ease don't" he stuttered fearfully.

"Calm down, it's alright" Zaxx whispered, signalling with his hands for the man to quieten down "I'm here to rescue you."

The man looked at him disbelievingly from behind his still trembling hands.

"My friends and I, we came here with forty soldiers, the ones in the courtyard."

"The-then they are as good as dead" the man sighed pitifully.

Zaxx shook his head.

"You're a prisoner here too right?"

The man nodded.

"Th-they ke-keep me here to coo-cook for th-them."

"Do they let you go outside?"

"On-only if I've ear-earnt it" the man nervously rubbed the back of his hand "Not th-that th-that happens much."

Zaxx smiled at him.

"Your fellows in the fields, they are armed to fight at Rothgar's command, right?"-the man gave a weak nod-"Then today you've earned a day out" Zaxx walked over with the ring of keys, checking which looked like the right one.

"I-is th-this a trick?" the man's eyes began to water.

"No trick friend"-Zaxx put a comforting hand upon his shoulder-"But I need you to be strong, and take a message to the farmers."

The man threw his arms around Zaxx.

"Th-th-thank y-you."

Zaxx patted him on the back.

"Just tell the farmers what I'm doing, and that I need them to storm the place so I can get their families out safely."

With that Zaxx unlocked the man's chains, before moving to free the families in the cells as the newly liberated soul moved with hopeful vigour out into the fields, the thought of retribution on his mind.

"Tell me Prime" Rothgar scathed "how did you see this going down?"

I said nothing; my arms held back by two of his men.

"You disappoint me, truly you do" he sighed "I was looking forward to one of your *'brilliant'* plans. Shame."

With that he gestured for his men to release me, and as they did, he fired a punch that toppled me to the floor, the spikes on his gauntlets cutting deep across the right side of my head.

I attempted to get back up, but he kicked me in the ribs, knocking me back down.

"Perhaps you could be so kind as to tell me where Zaxx is, hmm?" he mocked.

I stayed silent.

He kicked me again. And again. And again.

I felt one of my ribs break on the fourth kick, the fifth one causing my mouth to bleed.

The pain was excruciating.

As for my companions; Maralin had been taken to the cells with the 'others' – I had no doubt he meant the families of the farmers – whilst Tau had been escorted out towards the courtyard by three guards, with Monro and Mazog being held back and forced to watch.

"That's enough Rothgar!" Monro yelled, the two guards holding him tightening their grip as he did.

Rothgar paused his volley of blows as he looked upon him.

"Enough?" he cocked his head as he spoke, pacing towards him, stepping over my broken body as he did "Enough...no, no it is not. You see..." he paused for Monro to give his name, though he did not oblige "...Well, whoever you are, *this* cretin, this *lizard*, caused the death of my father"-he spat on the floor beside me-"and as for that betrayer Zaxx...well, that will be fun when the time comes."

"You're sick" Monro gritted.

Rothgar nodded agreeingly at that.

"Perhaps" he stroked his chin "but that's the thing when friends betray you, and cause harm to your closest; you get a little warped."

He backhanded Monro with his left hand, causing him to yelp in pain as the spikes gashed his jaw.

"You see, I needn't have done that"-he turned back to me-"Now don't think I put the blame all with you Prime"-he crouched over me, holding me by the throat to face him-"I understand. Had Zaxx not told Obsidian, none of this would have happened. So...tell me where he is, and all of this will end here. No more pain, no more fighting." He gave a grim smile.

No more fighting...

Mazog broke his silence.

"I know where he is."

Rothgar turned his head to look at him, still crouched over me.

"Go on."

"First assure me we will be allowed to leave."

Rothgar mulled that over a moment before releasing his grasp on my throat.

"Of course, although I will have to rough you up a bit; can't have people think I've gone soft, can I?" he smiled menacingly.

"Ok" Mazog nodded "You know of the gorse hills near the Great Tear?"

"Yes" he stepped a bit closer to Mazog.

"Within the Forrest of Thorns upon its western edge."

"Is that it?"

"No" Mazog paused a moment, stalling for time "You swear to let us go?"

"Of course, of course" Rothgar's voice elevated a little in frustration; in his mind he was so close to finding his prey.

"At its heart there is a cave system, obscured by shrubbery."

He paused again.

"Get on with it!" Rothgar yelled with menace.

"What will you do with him?" Mazog asked as if in ignorance.

Rothgar closed his eyes, biting his lips and gritting his teeth as he held himself back from throttling him to death.

"If you don't finish telling me"-he muttered in a forced calm voice-"then I *will* gut you like a fish."

"You'll need to take the right-hand cave, and stick to the left wall. He'll be at the end of the passage" Mazog blurted, half acting scared, half petrified.

Rothgar gave a wide smile.

"That wasn't so hard was it?" he joked mockingly as he patted Mazog's left check patronisingly, before turning his attention back to me.

"You see Prime? In the end, I always get what I want" he unsheathed his sword "Speaking of which-"

Before he could finish his taunting, one of his men came bursting into the room, bloodied and dishevelled.

"Sir, the farmers! The farmers are revolting!"

Rothgar gave a heavy sigh.

"I guess you'll have to wait Prime"-he gestured for his men to hold us here-"I want to take my time with you, you see."

He ordered three of the guards to follow him as he left, muttering "we must remind them what they stand to lose" as he did.

The guards holding Monro and Mazog threw them to the floor beside me, unsheathing their weapons as they did.

"Stay down, or we'll cut you down" one of them grunted.

Mazog knelt beside me, checking over my wounds.

"You're a bloody fool Prime...I mean sir" Monro whispered.

Mazog gave him a scathing look of 'not now'.

"I...Kinda...underestimated..." I wheezed painfully.

"Hush" Mazog interrupted "Save your strength; I feel we may need it."

I just wheezed a wry smile, knowing – hoping – that the plan was working.

* * * *

Rothgar stood atop the battlements of Stronghold's gate wall, taking a moment to survey the scene before speaking. He noticed the soldiers of Blackwood and Bahvil were aiding the farmers he had kept down for so long, that the goliath who had stood guard over Prime in the throne room had crushed many of his men beneath an oversized warhammer.

It made him suspicious.

"Listen to me you barbarous swine!" he bellowed.

Few of the withered farmers listened; those that did hurled abuse and stones back at him.

He turned to the Captain.

"Bring me one of the children" he growled.

The Captain hesitantly fumbled his words as he spoke.

"Well...you see sir, the prisoners, the families of the farmers...they've, well"-the man braced himself-"escaped."

Rothgar grabbed the man by the chestplate.

"Did you not think I would want to know this beforehand?!"

The Captain attempted to get his response out, fumbling once again as he did.

Rothgar groaned in anger, throwing the man over the edge of the wall to his death, and that of an unfortunate farmer beneath him.

He turned to the rest of his men.

"Well? Don't just stand there, Kill them...All of them!"

"But sir, we're outnumbered" one man pleaded.

"You'll have to kill more than one each then, won't you?" Rothgar scathed vengefully, shutting down another question before it could be asked "Try using your arrows you scum!"

The men quickly obliged, fearful of the man they once followed out of loyalty.

* * * *

The guards had started to become restless, and I could hear their whispers of contemplation over our execution.

Rothgar had not returned, and the sounds of the growing rebellion outside had begun to echo throughout the keep. One of the guards left the throne room to find Rothgar, the other four confident they could take the three of us should the need arise.

I had been able to gather enough strength to sit upright, Mazog's makeshift bandages tightly holding my broken rib to my chest.

"You think we can finish him, here and now?" I whispered to Mazog.

He weighed it over for a moment.

"If we are fast enough"-he glanced over at the guards-"and if we can dispatch this lot."

I nodded wearily, my mouth sore though no longer bleeding.

A new guard entered the room, his armour and helm bloodied. One of the four turned to ask what was happening.

"Rothgar wants these three in the cells" he answered, in a gruff, familiar voice.

The guards moved to march us to the dungeon.

"You heard him, on your feet!" one grunted.

We got up, Mazog supporting and steadying me.

They gestured with their swords for us to exit first, and we obliged.

As we walked back through the keep's halls I began to wonder how I thought this was a good plan, and became more concerned at the fact Mazog had agreed with me that it was.

Suddenly, a mighty set of screams came from behind us.

Monro dived to the floor on instinct, whilst I turned to face whatever was happening.

The new guard had plunged his sword into one of the other guards, following up with a dagger into the neck of another.

As the other two drew up their swords to strike, Mazog charged at them, successfully tackling one of them to the ground and began to wrestle the man for his sword.

The last guard fought his assailant viciously, the echo of clashing swords hacking at one another dominating the large hall.

By this time Monro had joined the ruckus, aiding Mazog with his fight; not that Mazog needed it.

I was determined to join the fight, despite my injuries, and so moved towards the one guard still standing, when an arrow flew through the air beside me and buried itself into the shoulder of the guard, despite his armour.

Seizing the moment, the guard with the bloodied armour who had started the assault finished the man with a single, hefty blow to the head; the guard Mazog and Monro had been wrestling with now silent and still.

"You alright?" called a female voice I was glad to hear.

"We're alright Maralin" the bloodied guard shouted back before looking back at us, removing his helm as he did "We are, aren't we?" I gave a heavy sigh of relief to see it was Zaxx.

"Yeah. We're alright" Mazog said as he passed me a sword.

"What now?" Monro asked, as Maralin quickly walked over to us.

"Now"-I spoke heavily, my free arm around my chest-"Now we finish this."

Zaxx retrieved his dagger from a fallen guard.

"If it's all the same to you, I'd like to do this...alone" he spoke with a sombre, determined tone.

We all looked at him with the same sense of concern.

"Zaxx, don't be a fool an-" Mazog began, Zaxx cutting him off.

"Look, the people from the dungeons, I promised them I would get them out, keep them safe."

"And you kept that promise" Maralin spoke softly, a hand on his right shoulder.

"They're not safe yet, even if we slaughter all of Rothgar's men"-he turned to face me, looking into my eyes as if staring directly into my soul-"Take them somewhere safe, keep them safe, and let me finish this."

"Zaxx old friend, you can't take him on by yourself" Mazog's worry was evident in his voice "He'll kill you."

"It's exactly what he wants; you and him alone" Maralin added, her eyes begging him.

"You know I must do this" he was adamant, and I knew there would be no dissuading him.

"I'll go with you"-he tried to interrupt but I continued over him-"look, the others can get the people out to safety, and if I'm with you I can keep any guards of his off your back."

"Prime-"

"You know this makes sense."

He bit his lip.

"Ok" he was reluctant but knew I was as stubborn as he was.

As we parted ways with the others, Maralin hung back to ask me something.

"You sure you're up to this?" she asked pointing to my bandages.

"Yeah, a broken rib hasn't stopped me before has it?" I smiled.

"True" she nodded, before leaning in close, her expression becoming a little more serious, showing concern through her calm demeanour "Promise me Prime..."

"I promise" I smiled again, putting my hand up to the side of her face "And in one piece."

She rolled her eyes somewhat.

"Well, see that you do."

With that we parted ways, the hunt for Rothgar now afoot. As we ran (well, I kind of just hobbled at high speed) it occurred to me how odd these events truly were; two friends, now foes, each now seeking vengeance against the other. It was almost cliché. With this I felt worry as I remembered an old saying: 'those that seek revenge shall dig two graves'.

***

As we chased down Rothgar the others were attempting to escape with the farmers families. Monro had gone atop the battlements, attempting to halt the volleys of arrows that descended upon them any time they broke cover, whilst Yates and our men fended off the ground troops.

Maralin had gathered the families, whom Zaxx had hid inside the keep's decrepit kitchen, and had readied them to run – with the aid of some of the farmers – once she gave the signal.

In the meantime Mazog had fought his way across the courtyard to Tau, who was surrounded, though not outnumbered, by those foolish enough not to be deterred by the litter of corpses he had crushed with his mighty warhammer; the newly dubbed 'End of All Things'.

"Tau!" he shouted with a sense of urgency.

Tau turned to face him, an arrow grazing just past his head.

"Clear us a path!"

Tau nodded, turning back to the fight at hand, contemplating for a split second the correct direction to clear, before then beginning to slew his way through our foes.

Mazog went back to the keep's Great Hall, shouting for Maralin to bring the families, before remembering the archers were still in play as an arrow gnashed the top of his shoulder.

"Monro! Kill those bloody archers already!" he shouted.

Up on the battlements Monro blocked incoming arrows with the body of a fallen archer.

"Not like I ain't trying" he muttered to himself.

Rallying his strength, he hefted the archer up and charged at the others with it. The nearest archer fumbled to get his short-sword unsheathed, but was too slow; Monro knocking him to the ground, before quickly kneeing him in the throat.

The other archers, however, had now drawn their swords and readied themselves for his attacks.

Monro rushed at them, deflecting a blow to his left, followed swiftly by a strike with his elbow to the head of the archer on his right mid-swing. Two more archers rushed him, putting him on the back foot as they struck at him, barely avoiding a blow from the first one that cut across the top of his chainmail chest piece. By this time Maralin had brought the families to the Great Hall's doorway, supporting a blue-eyed girl with her left arm.

"Mazog!" she called out; he was back out in the courtyard.

Blood stained, he came back into the keep.

"Still waiting for Monro" he turned to look back into the on-going fight "don't think he can take them archers by himself-"

Before he could finish his thought Maralin interrupted as she passed the girl into his arms.

"Hold onto her" she said as she strode into battle.

"Maralin?!" he called after her.

Out in the light of the courtyard, light beams dotting the sky amongst threatening clouds, she took a moment to appraise the situation, moving to reclaim her bow and quiver from the now small pile of confiscated weapons.

"Eight archers, six with their sword drawn" she thought to herself "and one Monro flailing like a child."

She slung her quiver over her shoulder as she reclaimed her trusty bow, dropping the one she had pinched from Strong-hold's armoury. After a quick pull on the bowstring to check it over, she drew an arrow at lightning speed, letting loose a volley of arrows toward the archers.

Atop the battlements Monro was just about to be over-whelmed – certain his fate was sealed – when, as he held two swords back with his own and a third came towards him, in what seemed to him to be slow-motion, an arrow dug through his would-be executioner's chainmail neck guard, jolting the man's body such that he stumbled over the edge of the battle-ments. Before the other archers had time to turn, two more arrows struck down the ones on the far side. Monro hefted back with all his might, using this distraction to push the two hold-ing him back, hacking at them with avengeance as they moved to regain their footing.

Another two arrows found their targets, knocking one of them off the battlements completely.

The last archer not in direct combat with Monro had drawn his bow, unleashing a barbed arrow at Maralin. She ducked in-stinctively, only just avoiding it as the barbs ripped some of her hair out as it grazed past her neck on the right side.

"You bitch!" she yelled, enraged as she drew two arrows at once, the enemy archer readying another barbed one with her name on it. But Maralin was faster, and smiled with satisfac-tion as her arrows buried themselves into his neck and chest; not even Divines can help those that mess with her hair.

Monro staggered one of the remaining archers, seizing the opportunity to grab the other as he lunged for him, utilising the man's momentum to throw him off the battlements.

"Please-" the last archer whimpered as he realised his fate, but Monro ran him through as an arrow ruptured the man's shoulder.

"Sorry pal" he whispered into the man's ear before kicking him off his sword "but you don't get to beg."

He looked out towards the farmers and Yates, our soldiers remaining firm, noting how Tau had cleared quite a large area with that warhammer of his.

He turned back to Maralin.

"All clear!" he shouted, beckoning her and the families to make a break for it.

She gave an agreeing nod before returning to the keep's entrance, the blue-eyed girl's safety and my promise on the forefront of her mind.

*

Zaxx and I had cleared a third of the keep, and still no sign of Rothgar. I could see Zaxx was worried he had gotten away, perhaps having sneaked out of some hidden passage or another. To this end I suggested checking the dungeon for an escape root, Zaxx having given his silent approval. We check cell after cell, room by room.

Nothing.

"He doesn't get to walk away" Zaxx muttered to himself.

I stayed silent, unsure of what to say.

We made our way through the last room in the dungeon, a spiral staircase on the far side. As we got closer I could see the anger on Zaxx's face; that with each step, each room that did not yield Rothgar, the more it began to consume him, make him desperate.

I did not know what to do for the better for my friend. Before Rothgar resurfaced Zaxx could bury his emotions beneath mead and wine, but now? Now there was no hiding, no quelling the loss, the fear, the hate.

If he didn't get a resolution this day I feared what would become of him. Would he be lost entirely to drink, or worse? My thoughts turned to Maralin and the promise I had made her, and wondered how possible it was to keep.

*

Maralin was now carrying the girl in her arms, her legs having finally given out to exhaustion and famine. Our soldiers had lined the path Tau had cleared, holding what remained of Rothgar's puppets at bay as Mazog and Monro led the families away from their oppressors.

Tau continued beating back Rothgar's men, crushing all that dared to try and impede their progress, whilst Yates took up the rear, barking orders at our men and getting them to form a protective ring around the families as the farmers continued to fight valiantly to aid their loved ones' escape.

*

We had come out of the dungeon on the west side of the keep, the only sign of Rothgar being a characteristic trail of broken chairs and destroyed ornaments; although they were spaced far enough apart as to make working out his direction of travel difficult, to say the least.

I have to say, I had never seen Zaxx so focused. All that bottled emotion had become fuel for him, and he wasn't going to stop till he found Rothgar, and put an end to him.

We worked our way down a once ornate hallway, now dishevelled and deteriorating. I remembered this hall, how it used to be bright, yellow artwork embossed and encased by vibrant lines of red marble; now it was but a dusty and fractured mosaic, stained by mould growth. There was the odd sign of objects broken in anger – some seemed recent – which we followed, swords drawn, in the direction we thought they led.

"Prime" Zaxx spoke in a whisper without shifting his gaze.

"Yeah?"

"When we find him...I – we – need to finish this."

"Agreed."

"But..."-I turned to look at him, sensing he was conflicted about something-"those families, that girl, don't they need to *see* justice delivered?"

'What girl?' I thought to myself, though shrugging it off as I answered his question.

"The thing is, we can't risk him getting away."

"Right."

"Don't get me wrong, if we could, I would have him tried and hanged. I know that would give a better sense of closure."

He stayed silent a while as we moved further into the keep, clearly mulling it over.

We had moved out of the hallway and into the last corner of the keep when he finally spoke again.

"I...I don't want to be like him."

I gave him a questioning look.

"If we kill him, it'll be because we have to"-I could see the broiling mass of conflicting emotion inside him had focused itself into something more...controlled-"I don't want to kill him because I *want* to kill him."

I said nothing in reply, merely nodding in understanding. I could see what he was saying, and pondered whether I could be so controlled, but realised quickly that I couldn't; after all, history shows that I put such people down with little hesitation.

Perhaps this makes Zaxx a better man then me. Perhaps.

The trail of broken objects had run cold, though we made a point of checking the last few rooms. I was thankful that all of Rothgar's men had been wrapped up in the conflict outside, and so allowing our uninterrupted search. The thing was, I had no intention of getting Rothgar to stand trial; I was going to end him at the earliest opportunity. It would upset Zaxx sure, perhaps raise the question of how I was any better than Rothgar even, but it would ensure he would be dead, gone, and no longer able to hurt anyone. And that's what was important, stopping him for good; putting an end to the fighting.

*

The farmers, whilst weak from their coerced labour, continued to fight and hold back Rothgar's remaining men with their sheer number, and were appearing to start to overwhelm them.

The families were now clear of the fighting, though incredibly weak, many of them struggling to walk even at the slowest pace. To this end our remaining men carried the weakest and the children, our horses loaded with all the people they could carry; a handful of farmers having joined us to aid their escape.

There had been many casualties, much more than what I had anticipated or could accept. Twelve of our men – good men – and at least twenty of the farmers, although it was likely many more. Despite this there was a confidence that Rothgar's men would, if not yield, eventually flee the fight due to the sheer number of foes coming down upon them.

Maralin carried the blue-eyed girl in her arms, Mazog not too far behind her as he helped a mother and her new-born. She had managed to learn the girl's name, Rose, and had said what a pretty name it was. There was something about this Rose that stirred emotion in Maralin, a love of sorts, perhaps born from a desire to protect one so helpless, though she could not place it.

Yates and Monro scouted ahead – weapons drawn – at just under a hundred yards in front; although she could still hear Yates every now and then.

'That man sure is loud' she thought to herself.

"Should I go back for them?" she heard Tau ask Mazog.

"Not sure..."-she could tell her brother was conflicted by his tone-"they can handle themselves, and we could need that hammer of yours if we're ambushed."

"But..?" Tau asked, sensing his hesitation.

Mazog looked at him.

"If they find Rothgar, it couldn't hurt to have you break his legs."

Tau smiled and nodded.

"Just...be careful, okay?"

Tau laughed reassuringly before turning around and making his way back towards Stronghold.

Maralin returned her attention to Rose.

"So, how old are you?" she asked, expecting an answer in the mid-teens.

Rose looked back at her with her now bright blue eyes, hope and freedom having returned to her.

"Twenty-two" she replied softly, her mouth audibly dry.

'Twenty-two?!' Maralin thought to herself 'she weighs nothing', before then chastising herself for forgetting the girl was severely malnourished 'of course she weighs nothing, they barely gave her enough food to survive, poor thing'.

The group walked in a sort of silence, footsteps and hooves lightly trotting being the ambient sound, the odd exchange from mother to child, and the lucky husband and wife fluttering in now and then.

The fighting was still going on in the distance behind them, although it seemed to be smaller, shrinking even, and Maralin hoped it wasn't just an illusion of distance.

"Maralin?" Rose asked gently.

"Hmm?" Maralin replied as she snapped out of her thoughts.

"I...I think I love you."

Maralin blushed, taken aback by this declaration, and gave a caring but quizzical look.

"You've known me less than three hours" she chuckled.

Rose closed her eyes, resting her head on Maralin's shoulder.

"You did just rescue me from a castle" she whispered "and you seem so nice, and you're better than any boy I've seen with a bow...and you're quite pretty too."

"Thanks" Maralin blushed with a smile, not sure what else to say.

As they walked onwards to Blackwood City, Maralin could not help but feel happy, smiling like an idiot as she put it; she had finally placed the emotion she felt, and understood it, and it felt good.

*

We were now making our way out of Stronghold, not one room yielding Rothgar. I could not tell if it was determination or denial that kept Zaxx going at this point, but in either case he refused to give up the search.

"There's no way he got out" he muttered angrily to himself "There ain't no way out but the front!"-I contemplated telling him to relax, but felt it would come off as patronising and make it worse-"So where is he?"

"He's a clever man" I shrugged.

"Huh, coward more like."

"Oh really?" came a voice from behind us.

We turned as fast we could but it wasn't quite quick enough.

"Argh!" an arrow cut into Zaxx's armour, pinning his pauldron to his left shoulder.

Rothgar stood before us, about twenty feet away, and had already readied another arrow.

I shoved Zaxx to the side as he released it, stumbling to the floor as the arrow passed overhead.

Scrambling to my feet I rushed at him as he drew another arrow.

As he fired I managed to raise my sword just in time to cut it in half; the half with the arrowhead just grazing the side of my head.

Throwing his bow to the ground he drew his sword and strode towards me, readying himself for my attack as Zaxx, having got back on his feet, ran to join us.

*

Tau had made it back to stronghold and past the last bit of resistance from Rothgar's men. He had told a group of farmers to spread the word of their loved ones' safety, and where to find them, knowing that they would be desperate to reunite with them as soon as it were possible.

As he made his way across the courtyard he could hear the faint sound of swords clashing coming from inside. Realising it to be his friends he picked up the pace, striding forward with purpose, warhammer readied, towards the sound's origin.

*

Rothgar held us at bay with ease. Between Zaxx's injury, my broken rib and Rothgar's skill we were barely able to keep up with his attacks.

We tried to strike at the same time, Zaxx going for his left side as I went for the right; but it was of no use, as he deflected Zaxx's swing he ducked under mine, finishing the one swift movement with a punch to Zaxx's face.

Zaxx staggered back, knocked off guard, as I threw several more blows at Rothgar, each more vicious then the last.

He blocked and deflected them with artful ease, and countered with hateful, hacking moves that I could barely block in time, before swinging his engraved blade at Zaxx – who had just regained his footing – with such speed and force to send his sword flying from his hands as he tried strike back with his full might.

I rushed in for another attack as I thrust my sword at him; Rothgar blocked it, locking my sword in place with the hilt of his, ramming me to the floor as he hammered into me with his shoulder.

With that he turned back to Zaxx, now having picked up his sword, unleashing a frenzy of brutal swings at him, each going for the other's head.

Rothgar's strike had left me winded, having hit me in my broken rib; as I struggled to get back up I was certain of our fate.

Then, out of nowhere, Rothgar let out a bloodcurdling scream.

I turned around as I finally pushed myself off the ground and onto my knees, and saw Tau standing tall, holding his war-hammer in a post-swing stance; he had shattered both of Rothgar's knees in a single blow, his legs now crumpled in an unholy and sickening position.

I gave a sigh of relief as Zaxx helped me to my feet.

I walked up to Rothgar, and pulled up my sword.

"You will hurt no one else" I spoke callously.

"Prime?!" Zaxx yelled, sensing my motives.

I went to thrust my sword into him, but Zaxx pulled me back.

"Seriously? After all I said?!" he barked, upset and offended by my attempted action.

"Don't you see?"-I pointed at Rothgar, still wailing over his destroyed legs-"We can't risk his escape."

"His legs are broken!" he pointed to the misshapen things.

"He's devious, who knows what trick he could pull."

Zaxx bit his lip, frustrated.

"The people, those farmers and their families, they need to see *justice*, not some act of revenge."

"And you?"

He paused a moment.

"Would his death not be enough?" I asked.

"I – they – need to see him tried for his crimes."

"They'll hang him anyway, what difference does it make if we kill him here?"

"It'll make us no better than him!"

"Is Carmel no better than Balford then?" I seethed.

"That's not what I-"

"It sure sounds a lot like it" I interrupted "or at least that's where your logic goes."

"You're twisting my words."

"Am I?!"

We stood in silence for only a short moment, though as we looked each other in the eye it felt like an eternity.

"Yes" Zaxx said, calming down as he broke the silence "You know I understand what she did. Anyone would."

"Then what's so different about-"

I stopped, my attention grabbed by a sudden, yet subtle sound of cracking bone, a slight echo reverberating through the keep.

In unison Zaxx and I turned our heads and our gaze towards Rothgar, seeing his limp body held off the floor by the neck by Tau, whom then gently lowered him to the ground.

"We should wrap the body up in some of these banners" he spoke softly "the Count of Blackwood will need proof of his death."

Zaxx and I exchanged a silent glance, both shocked and stunned by our friend's chosen action.

I wondered whether he had done it to spare us – and our friendship – from the burden and potential rift it could cause, or if it had simply seemed the least bothersome option.

An odd silence hung in the air around us as we ripped the banners from the wall and wrapped the body in them. Neither I nor Zaxx got what we wanted, not the public justice or personal vengeance, but...somehow, somehow it felt right.

I think it was because, regardless of how it was achieved, we did not need to be afraid anymore.

There was no longer a need to fight.

***

Zaxx had been quiet on our journey back to Bahvil, ever since we had delivered Rothgar's remains to Blackwood officials; Count Decon having publicly praised us for our work ending this horror, although he still had to make a remark about me being an 'interfering lizard' under his breath; I'll let it slide this time.

The once captive farmers and their families – which included those kidnaped Blackwood villagers who had been left unaccounted for after the events with the Wolfhounds – had been delivered to the city, where the priests and physicians of the Temple gave them food, shelter and treatments for their wounds and aliments. It would take them time to heal mentally in any real measure, but with the kindness of the people of Blackwood I have no doubt they will find happiness and contentment once more.

As we arrived back in Bahvil Carmel had a welcoming party ready for us, Furgus standing by her side as always.

It was glorious to see her again, and as we embraced each other lovingly, I whispered into her ear.

"I love you so, so much...and I'm never leaving your side again."

With that she gave me a soft kiss, and all felt right in the world.

It was on the night that Zaxx opened up and spoke what was on his mind. We were in one of Bahvil Castle's smaller lounges, curtains drawn to keep in the heat of the large, roaring fire. Carmel had told us she had had the furniture reconditioned with new, softer fabrics; it sure made the place more comfy I must say. Zaxx was sitting in front of the fire thinking, and did so for some time before finally talking his mind.

"How do you get over loss, when it is someone you could not live without, who you loved more than the world?" he seemed to be asking himself more than us.

"When I lost Rejik" Belothor replied "I felt my world shatter"- Zaxx looked up from the fire-"I know it is not quite the same as a brother, but it is love all the same, no matter the form it takes"-he wiped a tear from his eyes casually as he spoke; he was not one to cry openly-"I wanted Balford dead, I wanted justice for his crimes and vengeance for loss I suffered. But here's the thing: when they're dead – those that take our loved ones from us – you are still left with a...a void, an emptiness that cannot be filled"-Zaxx stared at him, a hint of desperate hope that Belothor would say something that would magic away the pain-"So what do we do? Do we lose ourselves to hating the dead? Or hide from reality, numbing ourselves with drink or drug?"-he gave a small shrug-"Truth is Zaxx, I'm not sure. But I know that, for me, never forgetting the good times helps. The wound never does heal right, like a scar it sticks around to remind you...but, it's not a bad thing; use it to remember the good"-he put a hand upon Zaxx's shoulder-"Truth is, only you and time can work out how you come to terms with it."

He patted him on the shoulder comfortingly, then made his goodnights as he left for bed.

As the next couple of hours passed we talked and laughed as one by one we left for bed, until Zaxx sat alone.

In front of the fire, a bottle of strong mead to his right, his hand clasped strongly around its neck as he frowned in deep thought.

He pulled the bottle to his lips and went to down the lot, throwing his head back as he tilted the bottle, but stopped himself, the mead sloshing against his closed lips.

He took it away from his mouth, looking at it for a moment before setting it down on the table beside him.

He held his head in his hands, taking several deep breaths, and, for the first time in years, permitted himself to cry without restraint.

When his tears had finally stopped he made his way back to his room, though his rough skin was still damp from their trails. As he undressed he felt somewhat unburdened, as if his mind had gotten lighter somehow.

For the first time since the loss of his brother, Zaxx slept soundly, the glimmer of a smile upon his face.

CHAPTER SEVEN

886, 3RD Era

Furgus is dead.

I...Carmel is distraught beyond words, inconsolable. My heart bleeds for her, as I'm sure hers does for him. And Agatha, poor Agatha, she was the one who found him; he was in the Forge – his smithy in the Temple District – in his workshop, and she had thought him asleep until she brought him his morning tea to his workbench...what a terrible thing.

He was like a father to them both, and a good friend. We shall miss him terribly, to be sure. Now they have to make the funeral arrangements, and I'm not sure how to help – if I can help.

Carmel sobbed herself to sleep an hour or so ago, exhausted from today's trauma; I...I just don't know. I've been doing some official paperwork, waiting to think of some ingenious plan to bring a smile to her face and lift her from this sadness, but alas, only time can do that I'm afraid.

I'm...I'm going to go lie next to her now, hold her close, keep her warm; now is not the time to be writing.

* * *

Furgus's funeral was beautiful, if such things can be. The ceremony – service? – was held in the city Temple, which Carmel had had decorated with white roses and the pews covered in a cloth of his signature dark turquoise-blue. It wasn't a grand affair – that wouldn't have been his style – but it still had an air of respect and scale normally reserved for great noblemen; not surprising given how respected, renown and trusted he was throughout Bahvil and its outskirts. He was a good man. And a loving father to Agatha and Carmel, if I might say.

Carmel had managed to hold herself together as she said a few words before those gathered, taking a moment here and there to pause and take a deep breath to hold herself back from crying. Agatha spoke too, telling of his skill as a blacksmith, his legendary steel and gentle heart. He was a strong man – a real man – and I do not think there is a person who has met him, who had known him, that will not miss him, and that all feel hurt at his passing; something reinforced by the filled Temple hall and near overflowing pews.

Furgus had always said he would be buried under a yew tree – just like his mother and father before him – in the centre of the Forge's courtyard, and so he was, the yew planted over him grown from a cutting of the one above his parents' burial site, which seemed fitting.

We held a small wake in the castle's Dance Hall, where the servants had laid out a small buffet for us all – I asked those of them that had known Furgus personally to join us – where we shared stories of Furgus, reflecting on the paths he had helped us forge for ourselves, how had shaped the steel of our lives and the empty space left by his passing.

Apologies for the blacksmith metaphors, it's just...I mean...funerals, they have a funny effect on me – on everyone really, don't they? – let's leave it at that.

Carmel is sitting in bed at the moment, looking at the wedding amulet he had made her for our wedding and that dagger – *that* dagger – he had helped her forge. It must be a strange feeling, remembering those happy times through the lens of loss and sadness that currently flowed through her. I do what I can but...it is all I can do to simply be there for her, to offer a shoulder to cry on when she needs it, a hand to hold, arms to be held by and a voice when hers falters. She is strong – stronger than I could ever hope to be – but she is mortal, like the rest of us; she just needs time, and love.

Agatha seems to be holding steadfast, though I'm unsure how much of that is for show. During the wake she mentioned that the last thing he had done – the last bit of metalwork he had finished before the end – was fix Agatha's little copper kettle with twin spouts that made it spin like a child's spinning top. I could see the sentimentality of that, how much it had meant to her, and how much more it meant as his last piece of metalwork, his last act. It is sad that he'll never see the look of joy on her face when she'd realised what he had done, nor that sincere look of missing him and his laughter.

I find myself feeling oddly mortal now – the loss of a loved one, someone close, does that to you – but so long as I can stay strong for Carm, and our friends continue to see us from time to time, we'll get there. I just hope Agatha will be able to ask for help, should she ever need it.

Time for bed; I think I shall give Carm a backrub to calm her before sleep, and failing that, hold her close 'til she falls asleep.

...Just one final thing before I put my quill down for the night: take the ones you love – be it romantically, friend or family – and hold them tight; you never know how long you'll have them, so let them know you love them.

CHAPTER EIGHT

887, 3RD Era

I gazed at the statue of eight men holding back barbarians, and thought on how long ago that felt, and yet still as if only a few days had passed. It was a small thing, as far as statues go, but stood pride-of-place in the main square of the market district; a good way to gently remind people of their bravery I thought.

I was in the district to visit one of Belothor's merchant houses about a special willow-thread bracelet set I had ordered in from Hamurfel's southern province, a place well renowned for its woodwork. They were to be a wedding present to Maralin and Rose, and I had had them engraved with their initials encircled by Blackwood tulips; Maralin's favourite flower (apart from Rose of course).

As I began my walk back to the castle – taking the longer, more scenic route through the Rose Garden – I could not help but laugh at myself; how I had mistaken the brother-sister type love between Zaxx and Maralin for something more I don't know, but it kinda made me smile. Heck, it actually makes me weirdly happy, to know even I cannot predict love and its mysterious twists and turns. Although it did give me a sombre moment as I mused on how Zaxx's brotherly love towards Maralin was influenced by the loss of his brother.

I knelt down to smell a white rose in the area of the garden Carmel and I had had our wedding ceremony, closing my eyes as the soft sweet scent enveloped my senses. The Rose Garden always uplifted my mood, bringing back sweet memories with its aromas.

There was a minstrel playing the requests of those roaming the gardens, whom I gave a generous amount of silver to play an old song.

As the fun melody played I reflected upon the past a while, the times of violence the thorns to the roses of kinder times.

I gave a silent chuckle, remembering Mazog's awkward reaction to Maralin's engagement. Poor fellow, despite all that wisdom in that head of his he could not string a sentence together, trying to congratulate her whilst trying to not get emotional over the idea of his little sister finally getting her big day; Maralin found it quite endearing, and hilarious.

Funny thing about Orcs – or rather their cultural history – back in the Second Era there had been a war between the Orc Isles and Hamurfel over some disputed lands, during which the leader of the Orc's High Council (Mazog could probably tell you his name – and recount the story better for that matter) had, for reasons all but forgotten to history, tried to stamp out love like that between Maralin and Rose. Despite his efforts, the people stayed steadfast in their morality, ultimately allowing a great noblewoman to rally them against him, bringing about a cultural change that cemented freedom for love, no matter its form. Due to this there was something of an Orcish tradition of celebrating the marriage of two women a little differently, often involving the lighting of ceremonial lanterns – adorned with the etchings of the Hamurfel crest entwined with that of the Orc Isles – which would be released to float into the night sky and join the stars above.

A cool breeze softly swayed the blossom trees as the sun began its slow decent during the early afternoon, the odd silky cloud drifting in from the coast. I was at the other end of the gardens now, the minstrel's amusing melodies still faintly audible above the quiet surroundings, my thoughts drifting from current matters to memories, sometimes to non-thought. I liked days like this; calm and gentle, the only threat that of an unexpected rain coming in from the sea.

As I exited the gardens into the Castle District my thoughts turned to Tau, now with his third child (a second boy, much to Ana's dismay) and how he had settled into family life, taking the safer, steadier hunting jobs that never took him to far away. I understood of course, but...I don't know, something about such a giant of a man – who I know loves the tougher kind of work – living a quiet life seemed not quite right. Having said that, there's nothing more important to him than family, and I can understand that; perhaps more than most.

I gave a quiet sigh as I walked up the steps to the castle gate, an odd tinge of numb pain in my left hand, most likely from the cold breeze that had just picked up behind me. Truth was, what really bothered me was that time was moving on, and all we seemed to do was get older. Don't get me wrong, I wouldn't have things any other way, it's just...well, it sometimes feels as if our adventures, or at least the best of them, were long behind us.

'Still'-I thought to myself-'shouldn't complain, I've got the love of my life, my friends, and we still have our health.'

It made me laugh a little as I thought on how the nostalgia for the past often forgets the more distressing bits, before thinking about how Belothor had been saying how he had started to really feel his old age catching up to him.

As I made my way through the entrance hall Bough came up to me.

"Sire, Countess Carmel is waiting for you in the North Wing lounge."

"Thank you Bough" I replied with a tired and sincere smile.

He gave a brief nod then carried on his way to whatever business needed attending to.

As I walked up the stone steps, smoothed by countless years of use and footsteps, I felt the day catching up to me, thinking of how good it will feel to get off my feet.

As I opened the door to the large, comfy lounge where we spent our quiet time relaxing, I was greeted by the sight of my most treasured and truest loves. They stood there in their off-white ribboned dresses, Carmel beaming a grand, warm smile behind them.

"Daddy!" they called in unison as they ran over to me "look at the dresses Momma made us!"

"Aunt Maralin helped" Carmel smiled.

"Now don't you two look beautiful!" I grinned as I embraced the twins in a big, all-encompassing hug.

Natilily and Nicole; my whole world, my whole life was them and Carmel. I remember holding them when they were new-born, so small I could hold both in one arm. That feeling you have, when they are born healthy and happy – well, as happy as new-borns can be – and when they first feed, it is the most marvellous thing; so overwhelmed by this loveliness was I that I didn't write in my journal for a whole month. Motherhood came naturally to Carmel, and one could see it on her face and in her spirit; she loved it almost as much as she loved them, and it made me love her even more than I already did.

I remember our excitement when we first realised she was pregnant, and that moment Carmel first felt them kick, my constant worrying and mothering of Carmel – oh how I got on her nerves sometimes – and how much love and kinship I felt for all people throughout that time. If I was to sum it up – and do know that these words are inadequate to do it any justice – I would say it was like finding that something you've known in your heart you needed, and that you were made and destined for, but which you did not know what it was before you found it, which shows you what true love really is, and that all that came before was but a mere drop, a tiny taste of what could be or was to come.

They had just turned four this past week, and were still en-
ergetic over this new number.

I gave Carmel a kiss.

"Sorry I've been gone all day, I-"

"Shh" she gently put a finger to my lips "You're here now, so
let's enjoy it" she spoke softly, her voice soothing as always.

"Okay" I replied, a dumb grin upon my face.

"Daddy" Nicole said, pulling on my jacket "I'm gonna to beat
you at chess now."

"Are you?" I chuckled.

"Me too!" said Natilily, eager to play.

I gave a fatherly laugh at the challenge.

The night came fast as we played chess and read stories, letting the twins beat me in our last game. After tucking them into
bed, Carmel and I lay on the large lounger beside the open fire,
her head resting upon my shoulder.

"Carmel?"

"Yeah?"

"Do we work too much?"

She looked up at me.

"What do you mean?"

"Well, it's just...I mean, sometimes I think-"

"You wish we could both be with them all the time?" she interrupted.

"Yeah. I know we can't, but still..."

"At least we can switch between which of us is with them for
the day" she said tiredly as she repositioned herself to get more
comfy.

"True."

We spent a while listening to the flickering embers and sparks as the fire began to die down, the dense wood fuelling it turning to ash as the orange glow dimmed like a setting sun.

"Here's a question" she said, her eyes closed "what if one of the girls turns out like Maralin?"

I gave a light shrug.

"Same as if she doesn't I suppose."

Carmel gave a smile.

"What?" I chuckled quizzically.

"Oh, just thinking how excited you'd be having an extra excuse to go dress shopping...haha" she chuckled.

I frowned for a moment before laughing.

"Yeah, that does sound like something I'd do."

CHAPTER NINE

890, 3ᴿᴰ Era

Bahvil in the winter is something to behold. It may not have the grand majesty of Blackwood and its roaring hills and woodlands that become hauntingly beautiful beneath a blanket of snow, but there is a certain something about the way the unusually large, fluffy snowflakes fall upon the streets and buildings, and get caught upon shrubs and evergreens dotted amongst the city streets, and transform the castle into a giant snowfort of sorts. There is also a calm that comes to the city, something about the reflective white on the still sunny days paired with a cold that is not quite bitter.

The twins love it of course, revelling in the chance to build snowmen and launch snowball fights with the other children – and adults – of Bahvil; Carmel was a dab hand at it too, avoiding being struck more often than not, and always getting me when I least expected it. I do love how she looks with flakes of snow caught in her thick mahogany hair, the glistening white entrapped by her luscious curls...how could one so beautiful get more beautiful with time? How did she fall in love with me? By the divines I'm so lucky to have her by my side.

The Rose Gardens were a perfect place for such fun things, and was the favourite place for families and children to have such fun, not that there was much else to do in such snowy weather. There was almost no time of day one could go there without seeing a family of snowmen, or a volley of snowballs hurtling through the air in all directions, or a fort being built or collapsed by a group of friends; what a blissful time the winter was in Bahvil.

Thankfully our food stores were as full as ever from the autumn harvest – dried fruits and grains being something of a staple of our winter diet – with fresh eggs still coming in from the farms; their hens were kept in massive wood and stone barns of sorts over winter – to keep them safe from the cold and predators – filled with straw bedding and every comfort a hen could ask for, to the point that they made some homes look drab and uncomfortable by comparison. Yet another reason why I love Bahvil (almost) as much as Blackwood; its people treat their animals with loving care, dignity and respect.

There was one issue we needed be concerned of over winter in any real sense, and that was if we get the strong winds come in from the south, up from Bahvil's docks and ultimately coming from the sea beyond, as they would almost universally bring blizzards, or failing that choke the docks with ice too thick to break and thus halt our intake of supplies we cannot otherwise obtain for ourselves; of which the latter of the two is starting to occur.

Tau had organised a team of icebreakers to let the last of the supply ships in and out of the docks last week – whilst the ice was still thin enough to do so – and since then the ice has spread out a good hundred yards or so. At its thickest it is like granite, or hardened steel, and as such Bahvil's fleet now sits marooned in the docks, coated white and unnervingly still even in the wind; it looks particularly eerie when the moonlight shines behind them, like something from a ghost story.

I must say I am most grateful for the bloomin' large fireplace in our main sitting room – where we would often cosy around in the evenings beneath thick woolly blankets, the twins wedged between Carmel and I as we read them stories or told them of our more fun past adventures – and for Carmel's loyal servants and cook, who makes the most warming soups and broth east of Hamurfel.

Speaking of Carmel, she has organised a group of our – her – guardsmen to patrol, twice a day, throughout the city and its outskirts to check in on the populous, making sure everyone has enough food, water and warmth; and should they need it, that a physician able to get to them readily. She is such a kind soul, and the people's loyalty and respect for her is well earned; I'm still amazed that she and I are married to this day, and most thankful for that.

The new year approaches quickly, and with it a grand feast to celebrate it, as is Bahvil tradition, which will be held in the castles Dance hall. Carmel tells me that she has ordered in something special – not that she'll tell me what – to make it feel more homely for me this year, and that her and Ana have organised the musical ensemble that will fuel the celebrations dancing; I must say it has me quite excited for the new year's celebration for once. Not sure what we're doing with the twins, but if Tau's kids come with him and Ana it could be fun for them, but we'll see.

Until then, I've got to read a story to the family; I think it'll be the one about the Agrian and the Dragon.

CHAPTER TEN

891, 3RD Era

As the new year chimed in at the midnight hour the entire Dance Hall burst into celebration and dance. The minstrels played upbeat tunes as the other musicians set the pace of the melodies and the dancing that accompanied them; Carmel would end up playing her harp once things had begun to calm down and the people began to need something softer at such a late hour – and she was magical as always, enchanting the entire hall with her delicate touch and seamless movements. Of my friends only Tau was there, accompanied by Ana, the pair of them dancing an unfamiliar jig, his lumbering mass somehow moving rhythmically to the strumming of musical strings. Bough was there too, and though he and I are not as close as my friends from Blackwood, it was nice to have him around; an honest man if ever there were one.

Carmel led me to the dancing space with a wide smile, the two of us dancing without care, ultimately joining Tau and Ana; at one point we all linked arms and kicked our feet high in unison, much to the amusement and humorous joy of the other guests.

Eventually needing a break from all the dancing and to quench a well-earned thirst (if I do say so myself) I took a seat on the far side of the hall, having grabbed a large tankard of Blackwood mead Carmel had had brought in specially (have I said how much I love that girl?) – which was sweet and light – which Tau also found to be quite marvellous in flavour. As I sat there I watched servants, cooks, guardsmen and their Captains (including Bough) and nobles celebrate as equals, sharing laughs, drinks and stories and dances as the merriment continued. It was most fitting, especially for a city like Bahvil, who's people had open hearts almost as big as their Rose Gardens; it made me happy to see them like this, to see others happy and content, having good, honest fun, even more so on a night as dark and cold as that had been. It made me think, how would we all look to the sands of time, if it could see? I'm most certain it couldn't tell us apart; it made me think how different it would have been had Balford not met his end when he did.

"Alright Prime?" Tau asked as he took a seat beside me.

"Aye" I smiled "The girls still dancing together?"

"Aye, the two were having a slow dance other side of that lot when I came over" he gestured with his tankard of mead "It's nice to celebrate like this."

"Agreed; as much as I love Blackwood, there never was anything like this at new years" I mused as I took a sip of mead
"still, even this can only be improved by Blackwood mead."

Tau gave dry laugh to that.

"Aye; Zaxx'll be fuming that he missed it."

"He still off the drink?" I asked, curious about my friend.

"For the most part; he'll have a tankard here and there, but
nothing like he use to" he replied as he took a deep swig of his
tankard "Last letter I got from him said he was wrapped up in
something up in Norain, a family matter – or was it a friend of
the family? – either way, he's stuck up there for the foreseeable."

"Right" I nodded, absently thinking on what adventures he
might have been having without us.

We sat and chatted for a little while, Natilily and Tau's sons –
Siran and Zayx – coming up to us to ask if they could have Mon-
roe show them the armoury and its many suits of armour, the
pair of us telling them to ask their mothers, as Nicole taught
little Annie – Tau and Ana's daughter – how to dance a slow
dance; her impression of what a waltz should be, so Carmel tells
me.

Finally the night drew to a close, Carmel still playing her
harp for the mostly seated crowd, the twins asleep next to me,
leaning against one another, with Tau's children asleep on and
against him, his eyes also shut – much to Ana's amusement. I
had got up and danced several more times before this moment,
but alas the late hour had me rooted to my seat, my head leant
against my hand, my arm leant upon an oak table as I watched
my beautiful wife entwine me with her musical snare, happily
lost in the moment.

It was a good night, and I'd say the best start to a new year in a long time.

***

Not three days later, there was a commotion as Carmel's winter patrol led a sobbing woman through the Great Hall and toward her throne; the poor lass's daughter had gone missing the night before, having gone out with a group of friends.

"Whatever is the matter?" I remember Carmel asking as she got up from her throne, putting an arm around the woman as she retold her story to her, one of the patrols guardsmen having stayed at her home on the off chance her daughter returned of her own accord.

"So her friends say they got separated as they got caught up in a blizzard?" Carmel asked gently as the woman dabbed the tears from her eyes with a small handkerchief.

"Indeed m'lady, they say they last saw her out by the farms near the docks."

"Whatever were they doing out there at such a late hour?" I asked as softly as I could.

"Adolescents, who knows why they do what they do" she said weakly "She's so bold and adventurous she fails to think of the dangers..."

"It'll be okay; we'll find her" Carmel smiled as she tried to comfort her.

"Indeed, I myself shall help the search" I said, placing a gently hand upon the woman's other shoulder.

"You...you would do so for my daughter? But we are but textile makers, we sew dresses, you are-"

"I am a father" I cut her off, politely of course "and as such I know the fear that is all too real for you now; you have my word, we will bring her back safe."

"Th-thank you" she cried, Carmel rubbing her shoulders instinctively.

"What is your daughter's name miss? So we can call out to her" one of the patrolmen asked.

"Lidia. Her name's Lidia."

"Right; Bough, Tau you two are with me. Patrolmen, gather our spare guardsmen and fan out across the area she was last seen before the blizzard." I said as one of the servants brought me my coat "and bring a spare coat or two, she'll probably need it."

As the other search parties fanned out across the farms, asking the farmworkers as they came across them for any sign of her – I should note that they joined the search too; honourable lot those Bahvil farmers – as Tau, Bough and I headed through the docks with a few of our guardsmen.

We had to be careful with our footing, as fallen snow had turned to ice most slippery, crates and ropes made harder than stone by its cold embrace. The blizzard had been especially strong, and as such gave us reason to worry for Lidia's safety, and to hope she had made it to some kind of shelter before...well, I shouldn't need to say it.

"This could be useful" Tau said as he wrenched an axe out of its partially entombed placement next to one of the dock's storehouses "Should we check in here?"

"Aye" I replied, looking around its padlocked doors "Bough check around the back, see if she could have broken in any place."

He gave a brief nod before swiftly moving off round the side of the building.

"Lidia!" I called, hands cupped around my mouth "Lidia!" but there came no reply.

"Prime, you don't think she could have fallen through the ice?" Tau asked, looking back at the ships, now glacial in appearance "Suppose she tried to get on board and slipped off on a piece of ice?"

I looked at him silently a moment, then back the way he was looking.

"I sure hope not...but check, just to be sure" I said sombrely.

"Aye; hopefully it's not the case, as you say" he remarked as he strode off, axe in hand.

"Be careful, that ice is still-" I called out.

"I know, I know" he replied, cutting me off.

I turned back to the storehouse just as Bough came back around.

"No sign of entry; she definitely didn't get in here" he said with a sigh "Where's Tau?"

"Checking she hasn't fallen onto the lake, or worse."

"Oh...right, yes, best to be sure" he replied, obviously not wanting to think of that possibility.

With that we began making our way through the docks, checking each ship we passed, calling out to Lidia as Bough and I looked over the decks and cabins that were accessible as Tau checked the lake below.

"How goes it?" Tau asked as he made his way up the gangplank up to the fourth ship we were checking – the other guardsmen with us checking the ships further down the dock – having finished his search of the ice below.

"Nothing yet" Bough shivered "Nothing down there?"

"No; thankfully the ice and snowfall show nothing of her."

"Thank the divines" I let out a heavy breath as I spoke, relieved for that small mercy.

"Any sign of her here?" Tau asked as he joined us on the ship's deck.

"Truth be told we've only just started on this one; the damned ice from the blizzard has made it impossible to know if we've missed any sign of her though" Bough said as he pulled on the main cabin doors, though they did not give.

"Locked or frozen?" I asked.

"A bit of both I think."

"Lidia?!" Tau boomed, the three of us pausing our conversation as we waited for a reply "Lidia?!"

"She's not here" Bough signed.

"Call her again Tau" I ordered as I moved quietly over to another part of the ship.

"Lidia!!"

Still silence came the reply, only the sound of the faint wind through the ice clad masts filling the quiet between us.

"I think we should-" Bough began, before Tau hastily shushed us, holding a finger to his lips as he listened intently; as we all did, realising he had heard something.

"Lidia!" he boomed once more.

There was a muffled sound, a voice, weak form cold, coming from somewhere on the ship. We spread out, calling to her to let her know we were still there and could hear her, as we tried to pinpoint the direction of her voice.

Tau stopped atop a mound of ice, lowing himself towards it; she was below deck. In a swift movement he raised himself up and smashed at the ice mound with the axe's hammer side, revealing it to be the trapdoor to the lower decks.

The metal frame of the trapdoor had frozen together tightly, and it took Tau a considerable effort to pry it open even a little, but as he did Bough and I managed to hold it in that position long enough for him to wedge the axe into the small gap and lever it open. As the ice cracked off it and the metal hinges creaked loudly as it fell back the other way, I looked down the hatchway and in the dulling light saw Lidia huddled beneath what cloth and fabric she had managed to find in the ship's cabins, and immediately descended the steps to her.

"Lidia?" I asked as I knelt before her.

"Y-y-yes" she shivered, weak and not really able to say much else.

"Can you move at all?" she shook her head as I asked, and so I took the gathered cloths off her and lifted her up into my arms, as Bough tucked one of the fur coats we had brought around her before we made our way back out into the chilled air outside.

In retrospect it would have been better – and easier on my back – if I had had Tau carry her, especially in that cold, but it was just the instinctual thing to do. We stopped halfway out of the docks to wrap the other fur coat around her as it became apparent just how cold she was; the poor lass was as pale as the ice coating the walkway. We came across one of the search parties, and sent them off to spread the word that we had found her – and that she was alive – sending one of them ahead of us to both calm her mother and summon the castle physician, as we walked with great speed, unable to have a carriage come to us in the icy conditions.

It was now late afternoon, and Lidia was being treated by the castle physician, her mother by her side. I cannot begin to explain the joy I felt, nor the look of relief upon her face as I brought Lidia back to her; as a father I could only imagine what it must have been like for her, waiting, not knowing what had become of her daughter.

"Poor thing, she must have been so frightened" Carmel mused as she looked over some new dresses for the twins Maralin had sent from Norain "Do we know if she will be alright?"

"Not sure" I answered as I rubbed my left arm as I felt the muscles twinge; probably from carrying Lidia for so long in the cold weather so I thought "But the physician seems hopeful; say's it is mostly a case of keeping her warm and well fed."

"Hmm" she thought out loud as she folded the dresses "We should have Cook make her some of her signature soup, that'd do her the world of good."

"Aye" I said as I moved up behind her, and wrapped my arms around her waist, lightly leaning my head upon her shoulder "have I told you how much I love you and the girls lately?"

She gave me a funny look of affection, before returning her attention to the dresses.

"I'll have to write Maralin a 'thank you' letter for these; they must have cost her a fair bit of coin" she looked back at me "And yes; you tell us each and every day – sometimes more"-I planted a kiss on her cheek-"You getting all emotional because of Lidia and her mother?"

"Aye" I sighed "I just...I couldn't bear it if something happened to you or the girls..."-I relinquished my hold on her as I moved to the side, studying the dresses-"Maralin sure has an eye for what looks good on people, doesn't she?" I smiled "These'll look perfect on the twins."

Carmel took my hand in hers, looking deep into my soul with those sapphire rich, green-tinted eyes I could just dive into, smiling at me.

"See, this is why I love you" she said.

"...My taste in dresses?"

"No" she laughed "Because deep down, you're the softest, most loving person I know"-she pulled me close-"And you care, with all your great big heart you care about everyone; you never stop trying to do the right thing."

"But...what of Falkner, and Rothgar?" I looked down at our entwined hands "I tried to do the right thing...but it...it went so wrong."

She lifted my head up with her right hand, gently holding the side of my face.

"I love you Sylon, so know I tell you the truth here: they are not your fault. Understand? They done what they did in spite of you, not because of you."

I looked longingly at her, before embracing her in a strong hug that made me feel safe.

"What would I do without you Carm?"

"I dunno, probably be looking for someone to share jam and scones with?" she smiled wryly.

"...And now I'm hungry" I laughed.

"But seriously though" she said as she pulled me to follow her "There's no one I'd rather share them with."

CHAPTER ELEVEN

892, 3RD Era

I looked upon the metal contraption as it spun, two streams of steam emitting from the two curved pipes on its side, and I pondered its usefulness.

"What function does this have Agatha?" I asked.

"Oh it's nothing more than a novelty, not unlike a toy" she sighed "But it is most fun to watch...it was the last thing Furgus finished before..."

"I remember" I said sympathetically "Carmel still isn't used to him not being around either; I couldn't even bring myself to put it in my journal, least not in any meaningful way..."

She looked at me and gave a little smile, comforted by the knowledge she wasn't alone in missing him.

"How heavy a thing can it push?" I asked, curious about the copper thing, and eager to change the topic.

"Only light things such as its copper frame" she mused "although the I see no reason a stronger jet or greater amount of steam couldn't push something...heavier..." she trailed off as a thought came to her as she looked upon her rotating kettle.

"Agatha?" I cajoled her gently.

"Oh my...by the divines! How has no one worked this out before!" she exclaimed as she moved to her workbench, pulling out a blank roll of parchment and a stick of charcoal.

I stood silently as I watched her sketch plans for some mechanical thing I could not understand, until finally she beckoned me over to look at them.

"You seem excited by this" I said as I leant over the sketch.

"Damn right I am Prime, this...this could – or should – change the world"-she pointed back at the still spinning copper pot-"See that? If I scale that up, put it on its side and use a strong enough pressure valve, some levers...maybe a gear or two-"

"You're going to attach it to a wheel..." I interrupted as I began to comprehend her design "Attach to a wheel...my word! Agatha, this would change mill work forever; how much faster we could mill grains!"

"Oh, that's just the beginning my friend" she grinned triumphantly "if I can work out the...the...the power ratio of the thrust of the steam to how much it can push, I could use it to move coaches without the need of horses."

I stood up straight, pacing up and down at the prospect of such a wonder.

"Horseless coaches...you sure such a thing is possible?"

"Not a hundred percent, no; I fear such a device would become too heavy to be practical or safe, but I am confident in the principle."

I gazed at the copper pot, still gently spinning like a child's spinning top, captivated by how such a simple, unassuming thing could change everything.

"So what will you need?"

"To build which?"

"The one for the mill, what do you need?"

She looked back at her plans, biting her lip as she thought on it.

"Quite a few labourers with deft hands for metalwork that's for sure."-She turned back to look at me-"I'll need time to work out the specifics, and how best to protect the piping from rust and corrosion, but...are you commissioning me to build this?"

"Yes Agatha, I am. I can see it in your eyes – and in your plans there – that this can work. Furgus would be so proud."

She gave a sombre smile at that.

"Aye, I think he would"-she turned back to her designs-"Would you like me to present my plans at the castle Prime, get all the bureaucracy and formalities out of the way? Once I've calculated the cost and materials of course."

"Yes, yes that would be easier; send a note ahead of when you're coming so I can gather the advisers. In the meantime, I'll be having a word with the treasurer to start setting aside funds; would you be doing the recruiting or...?"

"I have a few good smiths working at the smithies, but I cannot spare all of them, so perhaps putting up some advertisements would be best."

"Of course" I agreed, putting my scarf and jacket back on "I shall be on my way now Agatha; Carmel will be most joyous at this news."

"Indeed she will" She replied as she walked me to the door "Just...keep her expectations low, this steam...engine, will be the first of its kind; odds are something will go wrong."

"Have more faith in yourself Agatha, I know I do" I smiled as I waved goodbye, and began the reasonably long walk home in the windy night.

As I strode up the cobbled streets of the Temple District, now empty of all bar the night-watchmen and the faded light of streetlight candles, I could see my breath in the cool evening air, and gazed upward at the stars.

I contemplated them in a new light now, pondering what mysteries and new frontiers could be opened up by Agatha's 'steam engine', and how they might be used to make life better for us and our people; and more importantly to me, how it could give my daughters a better and brighter future than the one I was born into.

I laughed to myself as a grabbed hold of a railing that ran alongside a set of stairs as a means of steading myself. It was the most peculiar thing when you think about it, that a simple copper kettle made to spin by its own steam could suddenly change how one viewed the world, and perhaps how the world viewed itself.

As I came to the great white gates of the castle estate I felt a heaviness about me, something I wrote off as being overtired and a little too excited by the day's sudden turn of events. The guards on watch greeted me, with one of them accompanying me to the locked oak doors of the main entrance, which he unlocked and opened for me. I bid him good night and made my way to our sleeping quarters, looking forward to telling Carmel of Agatha's plans.

***

Agatha walked briskly through the Grand hall and up into the old Court room, now fitted out as a Council Chamber, many scrolls of design and detail tucked under her arm.

"Greetings m'Lord" she called as she entered, then looking at the council of advisers around me "Councillors."

"Good day my friend, are those the plans we spoke of?" I replied with a confident and hearty smile.

"Aye, that they are" she untucked them, gently placing them leaning against the dark mahogany table we were stood around (bar Carmel, who's turn it was to be with the twins), a lone hint of nervous energy about her "May I begin?"

"Of course" I gestured with my hands.

With that she began to unfurl one of the scrolls as she placed it upon the table, my advisers leaning over in intrigue.

"As you can see ladies and gents, I have here designs for what I have taken to calling a 'steam engine'" she began "To put it simply, it works by using steam to push a given structure in a particular direction; in this case thin sheets of fabric around a pivot."

"Like a windmill?" John, the Castle bursar, asked.

"Yes, it works very much like that; though this will be far more reliable and efficient."-she drew her finger to a pulley system of sorts-"Now these plans here are for a prototype; a cheap test build to see if there are any flaws we might have missed."

"Flaws?" asked Bough, whom alongside Joahana was my adviser on labour (Tau was away on business in Blackwood, I should note).

"Yes, as this is the first device of its kind it is sensible to expect, or make allowances for, something to go wrong" Agatha said convincingly.

"So, tell us where this will lead us Agatha; to what ends does this steam engine take us?" I encouraged.

"Well"-she unrolled another scroll-"once we've worked out the kinks, we move on to the main build I'm proposing today."

We all gasped at the magnitude of the plans before us.

"My word Agatha, is that what I think that is?" Bough asked, near dumbstruck.

"This here will transform Bahvil into the most advanced city in all the land; mills that can run at all hours and at thrice the speed and half the manpower, water pumps that can bring multitudes more water to us at just the turn of a tap, to all parts of a building, all across the city, and that is just-"

"How much would this cost?" John interrupted "And how long would it take to build?"

Agatha stumbled with her words a little, taken off-guard.

"I...I have some projections..." she quickly looked through her scrolls "Here we are" she laid them over the other scrolls.

"By the Divines!" exclaimed Bough at the sight of the figure.

"That is...rather a lot" said Joahana, agreeing.

John looked at me, stern and disbelieving.

"Sire, with all due respect, you said this to be a fruitful endeavour, but instead we have...*this*" he pointed at the offending number.

"Calm yourself John; that is merely the total cost when all is said and done, right Agatha?" I had faith in Agatha, and wasn't going to let John get silly with his tight-fisted nature, however well-meaning it was.

"Indeed it is" she seemed a bit more relaxed knowing I was still on her side "The figure we should be taking view of is this one over here, 'cost per engine', which I have split into a column for materials and a column for labour"

"What sum have you used for the labour?" Joahana asked as she read through the table of figures.

"Going off the typical rates for blacksmiths, I've used apprentice appropriate sums for most of the labourers, and expert ones for the foremen."

"We might need to alter some of these once we write out the specifics for recruitment, but your figure seems reasonable to me Agatha, what do you think Bough?" Joahana asked.

"I think I'll need a deeper explanation of the work they'll be doing, but yes, I agree that it sounds about right."

"This is still a great cost" John muttered "Are all these materials necessary? We'd have to import some of these..."

"John, I'm sure Agatha wouldn't have included anything that wasn't necessary" I smiled.

"Right."

There were a few moments of near silence as we looked through the plans before us, John counting the cost over and over again, Agatha offering brief explanations when one of us had a question.

"So what's in those other two scrolls then?" Bough asked after a few minutes of discussion.

"Ah, now these are something else" she replied as she rolled up the other plans to stand to one side "These two are not what I'm proposing today, and will most likely take years to design right – especially if my time is taken up overseeing the plans I've just shown you – but they are, well, it's best seen."

She unfolded the scrolls before us, and we each took a moment to look them over, not quite understanding what we were looking at.

"What...what are these Agatha?" Bough asked, scratching his head in confusion.

"Is this the horseless carriage you told me about?" I asked, my hand on my chin.

"Horseless carriage?" John asked, disbelieving.

"Yes and no" Agatha replied coyly "After I calculated the size of the engine, it seemed too unstable for a simple coach, but if I made the design longer and a bit bigger, add some guide railing..."

"This...this is too much" John threw his hands in the air.

"Yeah, I'm struggling with this too Prime" Bough agreed.

Agatha looked at me expectantly.

"Well, as Agatha said, this is a much longer term plan; what we are here to discus and potentially approve is the steam engine mill and water pump system, with prototypes of course."

"Right" Joahana said, looking relieved she didn't have to spend more time on the horseless coach design "Well, I see no reason not to approve."

"Are we all agreed?" I asked.

They all nodded in agreement, bar John.

"Whilst I would advise caution, I too agree; on the proviso that the prototype be shown to work fully before going forward on the main project" he said finally.

"Congratulations Agatha" I smiled as I shook her hand "You've just got yourself a commission."

"Thank you Prime" she whispered with an excited smile "now if you'll excuse me, I have some preparations to make."

As she left we discussed as to where the appropriate site for construction would be for the Prototype, given Agatha's specifications, and how best to organise the funding.

Just as we were about to depart from the chamber Joahana stopped me.

"Prime, are you okay?"

"Why do you ask?" I asked, puzzled by her question.

"Your hand" she pointed to my left side.

As I looked down I saw my hand shaking, almost in a twitching motion. It unnerved me, however slight the shaking was.

"Yes...yes I'm fine Ana; just haven't eaten yet today" I grinned.

"Oh, okay; best you get the cooks to whip something up for you then" she smiled back before leaving to go about her business.

Once I was alone I took my shaking hand in the other, gently rubbing it as I tried to keep it still, until finally it relented.

I could feel myself fill with worry; needless to say, I had just lied to Joahana, and was rather disconcerted by this sudden, unexplained symptom.

***

A month later and construction of the prototype was under-way, with news of this strange new mechanism causing quite the bout of excitement amongst the folk of Bahvil, although some worried it would render them obsolete; I had to send out reassurances that those who would be replaced by the steam engine would not be abandoned, and would be trained to help maintain them, with those surplus being compensated and aid-ed with finding alternate work.

John was keeping a close eye on the cost, whilst Agatha over-saw construction, directing her blacksmiths and the carpenters that built the supports with great easy.

Carmel was planning on taking the twins to see it once it was finally ready to start working, and had wrote letters to Ma-zog and Maralin to come visit and see the 'new marvel', as she put it. Tau had returned and was helping bring Agatha's dream to fruition as he oversaw the offloading of copper ingots off the trade ships.

I had sent Zaxx a letter a week and a half prior, but had yet to hear back from him.

I was in my private study when there came a knocking at my chamber door.

"You in here Prime?" called Tau, his voice as mild and quiet as ever.

"Aye." I answered, carefully putting the Bahvil seal upon an official document.

Tau entered, ducking under the doorframe as he did.

"What can I do you for my friend?" I smiled as I turned to him.

"Just a chat" he said as he sat delicately down on an old oak chair that he barely fit in "If you have the time that is."

"I always have time for my friends"-I grabbed the medium sized teapot on the left of my desk-"Would you like some tea? A glass of honey-mead perhaps?"

"Tea, thank you"-I poured some out into a small cup and handed it to him-"Long gone are the days of barrels of mead down the old tavern, ay?"

"Don't I know it" I chuckled, taking my seat and resting my elbow upon my desk "So how are the children? Can't say I've seen them this last month."

"Two months" Tau corrected.

"Has it really been that long?" I shook my head "Where does the time go?"

"Indeed"-Tau took a sip from his cup, which looked comically small in his big hands-"But at least they get to see the twins on the odd weekends. They do enjoy that."

"That they do" I agreed "I would have them mingle with more of the children from Bahvil, but I just have to keep them in arms reach, you know?"

"Aye."

A few moments past as we sipped our tea, the vapours warming our lungs.

"Agatha's prototype seems to be coming along well"-I put my cup back on its saucer-"Biscuit?"

"No, thank you."-he held his cup in his lap-"She says within a week or two it'll be ready to demonstrate, so she said this morning."

"Excellent" I beamed "Not much longer then."

I looked at Tau, weighing him up for a moment.

"Tau, I can tell you didn't come see me for idle chatter, what's on your mind?"

"I...we lost a child." He hung his head low.

"Oh...oh Tau, I am so very sorry" I got up and walked over to him, putting an arm around his mighty shoulders.

"We...we didn't even know she were...I don't know how to feel" his voice was still quiet, his hands still clasping the teacup in his lap.

"I imagine it was quite the shock"-I rubbed his shoulders-"Is this why I haven't seen Ana about the last few days?"

"Aye."

"I'll get you more tea" I said, gently taking his teacup back to my desk "Has she seen the castle physician? Or any doctor in Bahvil for that matter?"

"Aye" he let out a deep, bellowing sigh "Said it were natural, that there was nothing to be done or that could have been done. But still it hurts."

"Aye, loss is loss, whether expected or not" I said as I handed him back his now replenished tea.

He blew on it a little before taking a sip, and letting out another deep sigh that raised his shoulders.

"Is there anything we can do?" I asked, pondering how to ease his – and Joahana's – burden.

"No, I fear not. But talk is good; although I may not be much good at it, talk is good."

"Has Ana someone to talk to about this?"

"Her Ma and Da, but I have but you."

"And Carmel" I added.

"True, but you and I are oldest of friends."

I gave him a smile.

"That we are" I warmed my fingers on the warm cup as I covered a slight tremble in my left hand.

"Perhaps you both would like some time away from work, with the boys and little Annie?" I asked as the thought came to me.

Tau nodded silently, eyes glistening to tearful thoughts unexpressed. To see such a mammoth of a man so deeply hurt, after all the war-wounds and battle scars of our past endeavours, is a humbling experience; one that gives great context to one's own trials and tribulations.

We sat there a while as he drank his tea, until at last he sobbed, and I wrapped my arms around him, patting him on the back as friends do, encouraging him to let it out.

"Come on" I said once he had wiped his eyes clear of tears with his off-white handkerchief "I shall get cook to make you and Ana the heartiest pasties south of Blackwood" I smiled, grabbing the document from before "I just have to hand this to Bough on our way."

"Thank you, Prime" Tau whispered as he walked next to me.

"If ever you need a shoulder, I'm here" I replied, nudging him gently in the arm.

The night came in unusually cool as a chilled wind came from the southwest, and so I lit a hearty and glowing fire in the main sitting room.

Natilily and Nicole sat upon large cushions either side of a short end-table, playing a game of chess, whilst Carmel lay co-sied up beneath a fluffy brown blanket upon the chaise longue reading 'An account of the Forrest City: Furnhaven, the Nordic Crown'.

I was toasting some bread on the open flame of the fire, a slab of soft butter waiting on the table behind me.

"Have you talked to Ana lately?" I asked as casually as I could.

"Joahana? No, I haven't seen her for the last few days. Why'd you ask?"

"Oh, it's nothing that can't wait 'till later" I smiled, switching the hand holding the poker with the toasting bread "Now who want's the first piece?"

Nicole and Natilily stared each other down for a moment.

"Perhaps we cut it in half and share?" Nicole proposed thoughtfully.

"...That sounds good to me" Natilily chimed as she moved her rook across the chessboard "Check."

"That's what I get for being fair" Nicole sighed, looking about her pieces for any means of escape.

Carmel chuckled quietly at our little girl's tone.

I pulled the piping hot toast off the poker, bringing it to the table and slathering it with the butter, the crunch as I sliced it in half sounding very tasty indeed.

"Here you are" I smiled as I gave the two halves to the girls.

"Thank you" Nicole smiled as she took her half, Natilily having already shoved half of hers into her mouth, mumbling the same.

"Dibs on the next one" Carmel chimed without shifting her gaze from her book.

I pulled up a chair to sit on as I toasted the newly speared slice of bread, staring largely into the smouldering logs beneath the flames. There is something magical about fire, like one is seeing raw primal energy when you witness it. There's also a sense of safety about fire – something to do with the warmth I think – when it is under control, like how it is confined in the fireplace, trapped in place by stone and metal, and how it draws you close with its warmth as its heat keeps you back. But no matter how great the flame, all fires come to the same end.

"Dad!" Nicole shouted, snapping me out of my thoughts.

"Hmm?" I looked at the now burnt toast, blackened and smoking.

I quickly pulled it off the poker and threw it into the fire.

"Well, I guess I won't be having the next one then" Carmel laughed.

"How didn't you see it was burning?" Nicole asked as she brought me a fresh slice to toast.

"I got lost in my thoughts Nico" I sighed "Promise I'll pay attention to this one though."

She pulled up a footrest beside me to sit on, watching the fire as I did.

The pair of us sat there as Natilily played solitaire, trying her best to beat my quickest time.

"Dad" Nicole asked "Is it true you once slew a dragon?"

"Whoever told you that?" I replied, eyebrow raised and quite amused, as I turned the toast around to its undone side.

"Zaxx said last time he was here, but I didn't believe him."

"Then why ask?"

"On the off chance he wasn't being silly" she rested her head against me.

"I see."-I pulled the toast off and handed it to her-"Well I've done no dragon slaying I'm afraid."

She seemed a little saddened by that, blowing on the toast to cool it a little before taking a bite.

"I rode a mammoth once though" I said casually, putting my right arm around her as I put the poker down.

She looked up at me expectantly, mouth too full to ask.

"Okay then" I began, lifting her up onto my lap "I was eighteen at the time, and me and Mazog were off gathering pine nuts to store for the winter, when we came across a mighty mammoth, sleeping beneath an equally mighty pine tree."

"All on its own?"

"Aye, all by its lonesome. It was a young bull – a boy mammoth – that had yet to find a heard of its own you see. So, being the young fool, I wagered Mazog I could get atop the great beast without it noticing."

"What did you wager?" she asked, nibbling at another corner of toast.

"That I'd get to ask Maralin out to the harvest dance."

"Aunt Maralin?" Natilily asked, somewhat horrified at the thought, now sitting on the chairs armrest and eager to hear my story "Didn't you know she liked girls?"

"Not then I didn't" I laughed "And it was years before I met or even knew of your mother. So, I strolled on over to it, over-confident and cocky, and began to climb up its think pelt."

"What did it feel like?" Nicole asked, wiping away the crumbs from the corners of her mouth.

"Well"-I thought for a moment-"It was thick and coarse like hundreds of little ropes that made a dense coat not unlike a matted woollen rug."

"Sounds comfy" she mused.

"Anyhow, so I climbed atop the slumbering mammoth, and being oh-so-pleased with myself, called back to Mazog triumphantly; needless to say, the mammoth did not take too kindly to being so rudely awoken by my shouting, much less by little old me being upon its back. In a flash it was on its feet, Mazog laughing as I clung on for dear life as it sped off through the trees."-I leaned my head back-"I had to wait for it to tire out before I could get off the darn thing."

"But how did you get off?"

"I had to jump onto a tree branch, which broke off as I landed on it, dropping me in a river that was thankfully quite deep; got completely soaked, and had a few hours walk back to town."

"So, does that mean you won or lost the bet?" Nicole asked, eyebrow raised.

"Lost I'm afraid" I chuckled "had to do Mazog's chores for a whole month."

The girls returned their gaze to the fire as it spat out a few sparks.

"Dad?" Natilily asked.

"Yes?"

"Annie and Siran were saying that Ana had been crying a lot lately."

Carmel looked over her book at me.

"Well, they've had some bad news my dear; nothing for you to worry about though" I smiled comfortingly.

"Should we make them something?" Nicole asked "Zayx said they shouldn't have told us but, now that we know…"

"A gift to make them feel better you mean? That would be most kind of you my loves" Carmel replied as she came up beside us, before taking a seat beside me, Natilily then sitting upon her lap.

We sat there a while, looking at the fire, feeling its warmth as its flames flickered like elegant, glowing dancers, each of us rather content just being in each other's company.

***

I looked upon the prototype machine, thinking upon the great promise of its design. It would be far less useful than its fully realised counterpart, but certainly good enough to disprove any doubts anyone had.

"Alright lads, let's get that steam going!" Agatha called to the fire stokers, whose sole job was to keep the fire going inside the cast iron furnace that made the belly of the beast. Together a team of four men fanned the flames with large bellows and added its charcoal fuel.

Agatha herself was looking over the whole of the engine, from furnace to wooden grindstone that stood in for a stone one.

John tapped his foot impatiently, thoughts of the cost of failure – and that of success – troubling his mind, although I knew he truly wanted it to work, even if it meant more work for him in the long run. Other advisers – with the exception of Joahana – were gathered too, eager to see if my judgment was still as good as when I first came to Bahvil, and if Carmel's faith in Agatha was as well founded as she said it was. Carmel stood beside me, along with the twins, whom marvelled at the size of the thing.

Steam had begun to rise from the flume atop the boiler that would focus it into a jet, though not yet enough to push the fans of the windmill-like part.

Bough came trotting up to us.

"Has it started yet?" he asked as he came to a stop.

"Not yet" Carmel chimed sweetly "But soon by the looks of things."

We stood in near silence, bar Agatha and her team, as we waited with bated breath. You could almost taste the anticipation.

Slowly, more and more steam came from the focused jet, and the fans began to turn.

"It moved!" exclaimed Natilily as the fan jutted upwards.

"More air lads!" Agatha shouted at the stokers, visibly excited at seeing that which had only been on paper become reality.

And then the jet of steam caught the next fan, moving it upward, and then the next.

We all looked at the grindstone, which was now not just turning, but picking up speed.

I began to laugh in excitement as Agatha fist-pumped the air in victory, Carmel leading in a round of applause that came from the gathered crowd; even John smiled.

"My oh my" Bough said, turning to me "Looks like we may have entered a new age, if I may dare to say."

"Aye, and it is Bahvil that shall lead that new age" Carmel smiled "Satisfied John?"

"Indeed I am Countess Carmel, as are the other advisers" he nodded courteously "I shall begin making funds available for Agatha's full design right away."

"So, this will take the place of a mill worker?" Nicole asked as she watched the fans spin.

"Not just one" Carmel answered "with this a whole set of mills would only need a handful of people. And it would get so much more work done too."

"But...I get that is amazing and it is rather fascinating to watch, but what will happen to the workers? Are we to let them go poor?" her voice was the most sincere thing I had ever heard.

"Oh Nico, you have such an old and caring head upon those shoulders" Carmel put an arm around her lovingly "Do not worry my dear, we've made plans to train as many of them as is needed to carry out the new tasks."

"And those who aren't needed?" she looked up at me.

"Everyone is needed dear girl" called Agatha as she strolled up to us, a firm grin etched unwaveringly upon her face "Your father and mother have planned ahead; they're going to help the good folks find alternate work."

"Aye, we are" I smiled.

"Oh that's good" Nicole sighed in relief.

"Agatha?" Natilily asked, her tone earnest and full of hopefulness "How many of those engines are we going to have? And can I watch you build them, maybe even help out?"

"Well that depends on how many we need" Agatha knelt down to be at her eye level "See, the next test is to see how many grindstones we can get spinning off one engine, so I'm not too sure of the number we'll end up with; but we'll have more than anyplace else, even after they try to copy us."

"And you can watch" added Carmel "so long as you keep your distance, and are with either me or your father."

"But Agatha would be there!" she protested.

"Agatha will be too busy to keep an eye on you."

"T'is true lass, I've these metalworkers to keep in line; they're not as well behaved as you are, you see" Agatha backed up Carmel "But I promise to tell you what we're doing, and invite you when something real interesting is about to happen."

"Okay" Natilily pouted, yearning to help with the metalwork; not unlike her mother in her youth.

"Don't be down Nat" Nicole smiled, putting an arm around her "You'd only end up in the furnace anyway."

"Hey!" Natilily pushed her off.

"Don't start you two" I warned, in that parental menacing-calm, before turning my attention back to Agatha "So how long until we get to work on the fully-functional thing?"

"Let's say another fortnight to see how many grindstones per engine; after that, about two months, everything going smoothly" she said as she stood back up, arms folded in thought.

"Two months? Isn't that a little too ambitious?" Carmel asked, a tinge sceptical and worried "I mean, all the metal you need to forge and treat alone, plus the construction."

"Carmel my dear, I have the two best forges south of Norain, the aid of the lesser blacksmiths of Bahvil, apprentices by the bucketful and enough masons to make a cathedral; it will be fine."-she gave a wry smile-"It's not like I have a choice; if I fail, Furgus would come back from the grave to strip me of the title of Master Blacksmith himself!" she laughed heartily, Carmel joining her.

"Oh, how I wish he could have seen this, he would be just like you two girls; bright eyed and full of excitement."

"Aye, that he would"-she turned back to her creation-"And he would have loved teaching your girls too" I got the sense she was stifling a tear or two.

"Perhaps you could tell us about him sometime" Nicole said thoughtfully.

"Right ladies" I clasped my hands together "I think it best we get ready for tea, fancy joining us Agatha?"

"I would love to Prime, but this"-she gestured at the engine-"will keep me occupied for quite a few hours."

"Another time then, tomorrow perhaps?"

"Aye, tomorrow sounds good" she beamed.

***

"So this is what a working steam engine is like" Monro said, looking at the prototype, now with an extra two grindstones attached "It seems kind of underwhelming, given the flurry of excitement it's causing."

"Well it is just a prototype" I replied "and there is an issue of maintaining the turning power across multiple grindstones."

"A big problem or?"

"Just an issue of distance and gears, at the right ratio, as Agatha says."

"Right."

"You know why it is this doesn't seem a big deal to you?"

"I bet you're going to tell me."

"You look at it and see milled wheat, or barley and what have you, and perhaps that it is done better and faster, but you don't *see* the engine."

"What do you mean?" he asked, eyebrow raised.

"The engine. You don't see what else it could do. You don't see a means to pump vast amounts of water without manual labour, you don't see a horseless cart or some kind of automated loom...wait, that's a good idea; remind me to tell Agatha."

He looked at the steam pushing the fans as he thought on that a moment.

"I see what you mean, I do, but there's something about this that has me hesitant to celebrate it."

"Oh?"

"So, the mill workers here in Bahvil will be looked after by you until they can find new employment, but what of everywhere else? What happens to people when all manner of goods are made by the power of steam?"

"Not everything can be made by a turning wheel" I interjected with a laugh, a little defensive.

"Look"-he folded his arms reflexively-"the point is, people will be replaced by these things, not just here but across all the cities, maybe even the towns, and not everyone is governed by people as good as you and Countess Carmel."

I turned my gaze away from him and back to the steam engine. We stood there a few minutes listening to the rumble of its furnace and the turning of its mechanisms.

"Most people are good Monro."

"But not all of them sir, not all of them."

"Then we had best be careful as to whom we share the technology with" I sighed, accepting he was right "You know Monro, for a guy with little imagination, you sure do imagine the worst in people."

He gave a laugh.

"Not the worst in people Prime, just the *worst* people; it is my job after all."

"True" I chuckled, beginning to walk off before quickly falling over.

"You alright?" Monro offered a hand.

"Yes, just tripped over my own feet then" I said as he helped me to my feet "I tell you, getting older, it does nothing for your sense of co-ordination."

"Too true sir, too true."

＊

It was now midsummer, and construction of the fleet of steam engines was well underway, the first one being fully built, including the millhouse itself. Agatha was overseeing the metalwork mainly – having assigned her most trusted apprentices to be foremen for each construction site – even going so far as to do some of the work herself; particularly when it came to treating the metal, as to make it resistant to corrosion and rust. And I have to say, it was all paying off; the first automated mill was producing a bounty of finely milled grain (though obviously not enough by itself) and was a perfect training ground for the mill workers who were to keep their jobs once all the engines were complete. As for those who would lose their jobs, I had had Tau begin making enquiries about alternate employment (he could do it mostly through writing letters – with a little help from Joahana – from home; they were not yet over their loss and I felt this was a way to keep them feeling useful without putting undue strain upon them), and kept them in good spirits as best I could; from what I could tell, they seemed to trust me, and I was not going to let them down.

As for my personal life, it was nearing the anniversary of the day Carmel and I met, or at least had our first dance. As such I had been pondering as to what to do to celebrate, something small? Something large? It was a hard decision, but at least not as hard as coming up with another grand gesture as I had done for our wedding anniversary.

Ultimately I decided it was best to just ask Carmel what she thought we should do, concluding that a surprise isn't always the best kind of gift.

"How about a walk?" she said softly.

"A walk?"

She put down her quill, taking the cup of spiced tea I handed her.

"Like the ones we use to go on before we got so busy"-she took a small sip-"I'd like that, a nice walk through the Rose Gardens."

"I can't remember the last time we did that" I mumbled, looking off into the distance as I leaned on one arm.

Carmel began proof reading what she had written as she warmed her fingers on her cup.

"How is it my fingers get so cold, even when it is so warm?" she asked absently.

"I think we might be getting old."

"How dare you"-she playfully threw a ball of paper at me that she had scrunched up a while ago-"I'm still young."

"My apologies; I forgot you never age in any way" I mocked cheekily.

"Oh you" she stuck her tongue out at me "be thankful I still love you, you absolute berk."

"Oh I am" I leant over the table, kissing her forehead "Each and every day."

She gave a glowing smile as she got back to writing.

"Are the girls eating with us tonight?" she asked, the thought just popping into her head.

"Yes, I think so. Diana hasn't told me otherwise."

"Good." She dibbed her quill in the inkpot "I think I'll have Cook put on a full roast."

"With sausages?"

"With sausages."

"I really do love you."

"You love that I let you eat things you shouldn't."

"And the difference is?"

"...just for that, I'm having your batter puddings."

"Well...damn."

***

We walked through the Rose Garden, the day just like the first time we had done so, hand in hand, and still as in love as we were then.

"You still think we can eat as many scones and cream as we use to?" I smiled.

"And Jam" Carmel chimed "One cannot forget the jam; but yes, I dare say we could."

She rested her head on my shoulder as we stopped to look at the flower arch we had gotten married under.

"Perhaps we should find a minstrel to play us music whilst we dance" she mused.

"I like the sound of that" I whispered as old memories flowed through me, my free hand beginning to twitch a little.

As we began to walk off, Carmel spotted a white rose not unlike the ones she'd always use to weave into her hair, and leant down to pick it.

"Look Sylon, it's just like – Sylon!" she turned around fast as she could, hearing me hit the ground hard "Sylon! Oh Divines no..."

It was all she could do to watch, shouting for help as I shook uncontrollably on the ground, fully conscious, but unable to do a thing.

It was terrifying for me, but my mind was more concerned with the horror Carmel was experiencing; she felt so helpless and afraid as she stood there.

Eventually the shaking subsided, and I was finally able to mutter a few words to Carmel as she held me in her arms.

"I...I lo...love you Carm..."

As she talked I drifted out into unconsciousness.

* * *

I awoke three days later, feeling parched and filled with hunger pains, to the sight of Carmel asleep in the chair next to me, holding my hand. With all the strength I could muster I hefted myself up into a sitting position, causing Carmel to stir a little but not wake. It was late, or very early, in the day; a lone candelabra lighting the room from its left side.

I rubbed the right side of my temple as I tried to recall what had happened, a strange sense of disembodied nausea about me. It took me a few minutes to recall falling to the floor, and the horrifying experience of losing control of one's functions; it made me shudder in fear of such a thing happening again.

"Prime...?" Carmel said as she began to wake; due to all my fidgeting no doubt.

She gently put her arms around me, resting her head upon my left shoulder.

"I thought I was going to lose you" she whispered.

"Aye, I thought I was about to leave too"-I held her tightly-
"But thankfully we were both wrong."

She gave me a light kiss then leant back.

"The doctors and physicians...they did not know what was
happening to you; I had them scour every medicine book, every
anatomy text..."-she looked into my eyes with both deep affection and fear-"All we could do was restrain you and wait for the
shaking to stop."

"...Is there nothing...nothing they can do to stop this from
happening again?"

She looked down at our embraced hands, gently rubbing the
backs of mine with her thumbs.

"They said that one book mentioned shakes like yours, but it
was an account from Hamurfel."

"It did not end well?"

She shook her head, unable to say the words.

I took a deep breath, trying not to think about it.

"We sent the castle physician's understudy to Hamurfel,
with an envoy on our behalf, to see if their records have something ours do not, but..." her voice trailed off as a few tears tried
to break free.

"Hush now my love" I said as I caressed the side of her face "I
am awake now, and our sadness can wait; perhaps we can have
a family day all to ourselves? Go down to the Rose Gardens for
scones and cream?" I smiled.

"The doctors said you should rest in bed for as long as possible"-she held my hand as I let out a deep and disappointed sigh-
"But, I'll see if I can get the cook to make some scones for us,

and get the jam delivered?" she smiled back "You'll have to wait a few hours though, the girls will still be asleep."

"Ah, so it's early then; been trying to work that out for a while."

She gave a little laugh.

"Oh Prime, don't you ever change" she said as she got off the bed "Now I'll just see if there's some leftovers you can have for breakfast."

"What kind of leftovers?"

"Roasted vegetables with turkey and mashed potatoes" she chimed as she got to the door.

"Lovely" I replied as I rubbed my hands together, my mouth filling with saliva in anticipation.

"Just don't go running about before I get back, okay?"

"Oh, very funny."

*

As I finished the last bit of mashed potato, using it to mop up the last dregs of gravy off my plate, Carmel beaming at me, so very pleased to see me eating, Natilily and Nicole came bursting through the door, accompanied by their nanny and tutor, Diana Dienic.

"Daddy!" they shouted as they threw themselves around me.

"Girls, be careful!" Carmel cautioned them "Your father is most delicate at the moment."

"Sorry daddy" they apologised sweetly.

"No harm done my loves" I chuckled "How have you been anyway, what have you been up to?" I looked up at Diana "I hope they haven't been too much of a handful Di."

"Oh no, they've been as good as gold" she smiled "just eager to see you is all."

"We've been making you a gift" Natilily chimed.

"Oh?"

"Yes, a get-well present" Nicole smiled "may we give it to him now momma?" she asked Carmel expectantly.

Carmel gave a little nod as she smiled, leaning over to whisper into my ear.

"They had a little help from Agatha."

Natilily jumped off the bed and walked up to Diana, whom handed her a little box she had been hiding behind her back.

"It took us all day to make" Nicole hummed.

"Quiet Nico" Natilily scolded as she got back on the bed "You might let slip what it is."

Nicole rolled her eyes comically, as Natilily handed me the box.

I fumbled a little as I tried to get the lid off, until I finally undone its clasp and opened it slowly.

I let out a little 'aww' as I lifted the delicate looking necklace from its padded container, resting it in my hand as I looked it over. It was made of a thin silver chain, which glistened like fine snow, with a pendant of sorts, made of a dusk-brown enamel flower around a polished orb of red tiger-eye gemstone.

"You two made this?" I asked.

"Do you like it?" Nicole asked in return, somewhat hesitant.

"It is the second most beautiful thing I have ever seen" I smiled.

"Second?" Natilily asked, sounding hurt.

I gave them a big grin.

"Well you two are joint first, you see."

The two of them grinned triumphantly at that.

"Charming" Carmel chuckled.

* * *

Four days passed, albeit slowly, as I sat in bed, venturing off only to do that most private of business. The girls kept me company for the most part, Carmel joining us whenever she wasn't occupied by the duties of a Countess – and trying ever so hard to not strangle John whenever he queried every detail in the steam engine plan over and over again. We'd often play several games of cards, chess and dominoes (and they were increasingly beating me without my letting them), and they'd tell me about what they were being tutored on; Nicole usually claiming she somehow had superiority in the subject, save for needlework; she hated needlework (I think she fears pointy things).

It was on this forth day, in the late afternoon, the sky a light amber, that Maralin and Mazog arrived. They had obviously not heard of my condition, as they were on their journey here when it happened, but Carmel informed them as soon as they arrived.

I was sitting up in bed, a freshly puffed pillow behind my back, playing a game of solitaire (the girls had gone down to the kitchens to ask Cook for an early tea), somehow with a handful of odd reds, when Maralin entered the room in what I can only call a hesitant haste.

"Hello Maralin" I smiled, pleased to see my old friend.

"Oh Prime!" she sighed, throwing her arms around me "I'm so sorry."

"It's alright" I said, rubbing her back affectionately "I've survived worse."

As we withdrew from our embrace she held my hand, not unlike Carmel did.

"That's not the point" she smiled.

"That green suites you" I nodded at her latest dress, gold trimmed at the sleeves "and the silk, so smooth."

She tilted her head, shaking it knowingly.

"Thank you, but stop trying to change the subject."

"Can't a man talk about dresses with his best friend?" I asked, mock serious.

"Not when he's put the fear of life in his wife he can't."

I let out a telling sigh.

"Where's Mazog then?" I asked.

"Down in the Market District; our coach dropped him off there before we got to the castle. Poor berk will have a right fright when they tell him"-she gave out a little chuckle-"Sorry, it's not funny I know, but the thought of him rushing up to the castle in his finery..." she let out another little sighing laugh.

"I take it Carmel has gone to fetch him?"

"She was going to go herself yes, but someone named John came up to her, said 'Agatha needs authorisation' or something, so she sent Bough instead."

"Ah" I nodded "Agatha has probably been shouting at him again."

"That about this miraculous 'steam engine' Carmel wrote about?"

"Aye. I tell you now, that thing will change how the world works."

"I'm sure it will, and I look forward to seeing it"-she looked off into the distance unsure of what to say for a moment-"I take it Tau has been to see you? I know he's still in Bahvil."

I bit my lip.

"He...he hasn't actually" I said quietly, as if to make her not notice I'd said it.

"What?!" she fumed, getting to her feet instinctively "He does know doesn't he? What in the...I'm gonna give him a right piece of my mind!"

"Maralin, calm down" I said, patting the side of the bed "sit next to me a while."

"But he-"

"Tau can deal with wounds, scars, lost limbs and blood; it's the things he can't see that terrify him."

Maralin calmed a little, but was still agitated, her hands on her hips.

"Has Ana seen you at least?"

"Yes, yes she came by two days ago" I answered, neglecting to tell her how brief the visit was "Now will you please keep me company?"

"Fine" She rolled her eyes in a half-serious, exasperated way "But I'm still telling him off."

"I wouldn't dare stand in your way" I laughed.

"Too right" she smirked as she sat next to me, our shoulders touching.

"But go gently on him, please; he has been through...he's delicate as of late" I added as I held her hand, though she just rolled her eyes once again and nodded.

We sat in silence for a bit, listening out for the echo of a running Mazog amongst the castle sounds.

"Have you seen the girls yet?" I asked finally.

"No; when Carmel told me about your...about what happened, I came right to your room; after giving Carm a great big hug of course. Where are they anyway?"

"Well, when they left they were going down into the kitchens to ask Cook for an earlier dinner, so odds are high she's spoiling them something rotten."

"You have such caring people work for you, you know" she rested her head against mine "However do you find them?"

I gave a small shrug.

"Not sure really, I guess I just treat people as nice and as thoughtfully as I can; that or Carmel's near divinity draws them in. Not sure which."

She turned her head to look at me.

"Prime?"

"Hm?"

"Are you scared?"

We looked into each other's eyes, and I felt as if I were diving into those emerald edged pupils of hers.

She rested her head back on my shoulder, knowing my answer without having to hear it.

"You should talk to Carmel about it. You'll feel better."

"Perhaps" I answered, her hand grasping mine tightly, but comfortingly.

"Do you...do you ever wonder how things would have turned out, had we never come to Bahvil when we did?" she asked thoughtfully.

"What do you mean?"

"Like, if you'd never met Carmel, I'd never have met Rose, and so on."

"Can't say that I have, not in any real sense at least" I pondered a moment "Though I would have definitely made a move on you at some point."

"Or I you. I think we would have ended up married you know" she gave a wishful sigh.

"Are things not well between you and Rose?" I asked, genuinely concerned.

"No, we're fine, really"-she straightened herself up a little-"It's...it's just difficult."

"Is it about children again?"

She put her head in her hand.

"I'm sorry Prime, here I am trying to make you feel better, and now I'm putting more worry on you."

"Hey, it'd be a sad day when I'm too delicate to listen to you; so go on, tell me."

She took a deep, slow breath.

"Right" she began, regaining her composure "So, if I'd married you, I would...having children would come easy – for both the obvious reason and that they would be *ours*, and I love you."

"And I you...but wait, don't you love Rose?"

"I do, but…I cannot share her Prime, even for this, and the only man I'd make a child with is you."

"Oh. I see" I felt rather awkward at that moment, understandably so, I dare say.

"Relax; I'd never ask such a thing of you or Carmel"-she got up off the bed, pacing over to a nightstand, fumbling with the ornaments upon it-"I just do not know how to proceed."

"Maralin, have you–"

"Yes, we've tried talking it out" she muttered loudly.

There was an awkward silence between us for a moment or two.

"Well, have you tried falling over and shaking a bunch? I find it's the best way to get everyone doting on you."

She began laughing at that quite hard.

"Oh Prime, you always know just what to say."

*

An hour later and Carmel was with us, joined by a most frantic looking Mazog; he had – as we predicted – ran all the way from the Market District in his finery, and most assuredly would have looked quite the fool doing so; but I am so very glad to have a friend care so much and so deeply about my wellbeing.

Once the three of us had calmed him down, and he relaxed a little, we got to talking of his latest endeavours, news from Blackwood, and the steam engine – of which he was most intrigued.

"...and so it should make getting good, clean water much easier too" Carmel finished, having been saying what Agatha's latest plans were.

"Well blow me down" Mazog said, raising his cup of tea to his mouth.

"Aye, and then there's that horseless cart of hers" I added, causing Mazog to almost spit out his tea.

"Horseless cart?" he asked, confused despite his sharp mind.

"Prime told me earlier" Maralin jumped in to answer "Said it was a few years away, right?"

"Yes, Carmel gets it more than I do, but the gist of the thing is that she'd use the same principle as the ones used in the mills and water pumps she's working on, only instead of millstones being turned it'd be cartwheels."

"Won't the darn thing be too big and heavy, not to mention the risk of fire?" Mazog asked.

"She says she has a few ideas" Carmel answered, dunking a biscuit into her tea "but as she has her hands full with the engines she's building, it'll be a fair few years as you said Maralin. Still, she showed me a few designs, and they looked good to me; huge things, but good – damn it" the dunked half of her biscuit fell into her cup.

"I hate it when that happens" Maralin laughed.

"So how is Nicole and Natilily then?" Mazog asked as Carmel fished the soggy remains out of her cup.

"They're doing well" she said "They were a bit shook up when he was unconscious, but you know kids, they bounce back quickly."

"They've been keeping me company the last few days too" I added "which has been nice; I always feel like I could be spending more time with them."

"I can understand that" Mazog nodded "Do they get to play with other kids much? Tau's for example?"

"Every weekend or so, unless our schedules line up just right in the week."

"Do they not have the same tutor?" Maralin asked.

"They do, but she prefers to teach them separately, says she can focus on each of them better that way" Carmel answered, braving another dunk of a biscuit.

"I see."

"Have you heard from Zaxx at all?" Carmel asked the pair of them "Only we've sent numerous letters now, and have yet to get a reply."

"Can't say I have" Maralin said plainly "He's been rather distant since giving up the mead, hasn't he?"

"Last I heard from him he mentioned traveling to the Nordic coast; not sure as to the why though." Mazog added.

"When was this?" I asked, inquisitive of this news.

"Gosh, it was, what, five months ago now?"-he leant back in his chair-"Or was it six?"

"Why didn't you say something?" Maralin scolded.

"I didn't think...I thought he would have sent you all a letter; he figured he'd be back before the fall anyhow."

"So he might just be getting our letters" Carmel said mostly to herself, taking a bite of a well dunked biscuit, before offering Maralin another one.

"Scones!" I said all of a sudden, our small gathering looking at me perplexed "That's what we should have for breakfast, lovely warm scones, with thick whipped cream and blueberry jam…"

"Don't mind him; he's still upset he never got to have any on our walk" she gave a teary little laugh.

"Oh Carm" Maralin cooed gently as she got from her seat and gave her a warm hug.

Mazog didn't know what to do with himself, giving me that look of 'do I stay seated, or give a hug?'; I gave him a subtle hint he need not worry.

"I'm sorry, I…it's just, being there, remembering what he went through…"

I outstretched my hand, gently taking hold of hers.

"It's understandable to feel…overcome in these situations." Mazog reassured her "When my Ma was ill, I felt powerless, and at times I found myself crying, overcome at the strangest times. We pull through – we always hurt, but we pull through."

Whilst not reassured by that, she did feel better for Mazog's sincerity, and gave him a small smile.

"Right" I said, clapping my hands together "I think it best we get Diana to find the girls and bring them here to say hello to you two; and for a game of cards of course" I gave a wry smile.

"Sounds like fun to me" Mazog smiled, his large canines showing in his wide grin "I'm going to try and win; ain't gonna lose for nobody" he laughed.

"Just you try, they're actually pretty good."

"Oh yeah?"

"No, really; I've had to work blooming hard to beat them the few times that I have these last few days."

Maralin gave a little giggle at that.

"Right, let's see where they've got to, shall we?" Carmel smiled as she crossed the room to talk to the maid waiting outside.

Mazog walked over to me as I pulled the deck of cards from behind me.

"The old pack from Blackwood?" he asked upon seeing the tattered box the cards were in.

"Aye; got to have a bit of home with me" I smiled as I began to shuffle the cards.

Mazog put a hand upon my shoulder.

"I'm here for you Sylon" his voice was full of checked emotion.

"Using my first name? Must be serious" I joked.

"I mean it old friend; you are family, and I'll be at your side, no matter which path this takes you down."

I turned my head, looking him in the eyes. We shared emotions without words, that sense of *knowing* each other's thoughts by just the expression of our eyes. He was my brother, and I his; not by blood, but by bond, and that was all that mattered.

"Right" I said, rubbing the hint of tears from my eye "Who wants to get a practice in before my two heathens fleece us?"

***

The next day Carmel took Mazog and Maralin down to see the steam engine, the twins in tow, as I sat in bed, still forbidden to leave by the plethora of doctors and physicians that I was lucky enough to have around me (however annoying they could be).

As the maid that brought me lunch left, I sat there listening to the distant sounds coming in through my window, left slightly ajar so that I might get some fresh air, as I allowed my vegetable broth to cool.

It was a funny thing to listen to, and yet so captivating, this background noise often ignored and left unheard. There was the murmurings of many voices, interspersed with the sound of hooves and bleating of sheep brought in for sale, the odd, occasional echo of hammers working at a forge. And then there was the new sounds, the ones of metal and steam, as I could hear what could only be Agatha testing some component or demonstrating some feature of her engines or their construction.

The loudest noise, however, wavered between the songbirds that roosted upon the castle roof, and the mild wind that carried the noise up from the city proper.

As I listened I ripped one of my bread rolls in half, and slathered it in rich, creamy butter, the poppy seeds that adorned its crust scattering across the food tray on my lap.

I dipped it gently into the broth, steam rising enticingly as it wafted delicious smells up to me as I took a moment to blow on it as I held it before my watering mouth. As I took the first bite I felt the crunch of the seeded crust, the smooth slathering of butter melting, and the warm cauldron of favour that was the broth mush effortlessly as I chewed. It was strangely the most pleasurable meal I'd ever had.

I watched the clouds waft by as I ate, counting how many cottony shapes I saw as their wispy ends melded seamlessly with the bright blue background of the sky.

I felt rather at peace in that quite moment, despite a dribble of broth rolling down my chin.

Simple things, all of them. Yet they become a dynamic orchestra of sensation when experienced together.

As I finished my broth, having licked the bowl clean, I let out a little sigh of contentment, feeling full and warm. I gave my legs a little stretch as I sat there, pre-emptively stopping them from feeling stiff (well, stiffer than they were), and took off the necklace the twins had made me, turning it over in my hands, gently running my thumb across its surface, feeling the polish of the tiger-eye and enamel rose. It was arguably the most precious thing I had, bar perhaps my wedding band.

A lone tear rolled down my face; although more would have come had I not came over so tired all of a sudden.

I grasped it firmly but gently, as I readjusted my pillow as to allow me to lie back a bit, though not full down.

I lay there, hands resting over my chest, necklace cupped between my hands, a slight twitch in my left one, and thought deeply on where I was headed in my life now.

I pondered on the events that led here, on the possible futures made possible by Agatha's innovations and inventions, and all that wondrous potential.

I was in a happy sad mood – or was it sad happy? – as I thought of one place I would like to see, before it was all said and done.

And so I fell asleep, a smile upon my face at such a possibility.

CHAPTER TWELVE

892, 3RD Era
three weeks after
diagnosis

"You promised me you would never leave my side again" she accused, teary eyed and hurt "You swore to me."

"Carm, if I stay until the end, what will be left will not be *me*" I held her hands gently "You heard the physicians as well as I. And this...this will spare you and the girls the pain of having to watch me deteriorate; I do not want you or them to remember me like that."

"But...you can't leave, you just...you just can't."

"It would be selfish of me to stay."

"Then be selfish."

"Carm..."

"..."

"...I love you with everything I have."

"I love you too."

We held each other as we cried upon each other's shoulders, cherishing the feel of one another in our arms.

CHAPTER THIRTEEN

892, 3RD Era seven weeks after diagnosis

I sat at the old oak table, listening to the heavy pattering of rain against the glass of the window before me and the castle stone beyond as I ate a light meal. It was quiet, in a funny way, and most reassuringly calm. I spooned the porridge out of a ceramic bowl I've had so long I no longer remember whence it came. The texture of the crushed oats was soothing when paired with its warmth and the smooth taste of heather-honey which I had mixed into it, the combined flavour raising it from a satisfactory meal to an inspiring sensation. All the while I stared out at the exotic dwarf acre trees and miniature pines and pine flowers that had been planted in the miniature garden not far from the castle walls. Despite the raindrops being large and heavy, they seemed delicate, bouncing and bending leaves lightly as they came against them, the echo of them crashing against the weathered stone a dull, sleepy note that played in rhythmic harmony with itself; it was beautiful.

Carmel put her arm around my shoulders, having crept silently up to me, greeting me with a smile as I turned to see who it was. I smiled back, as best I could with a mouth still full of porridge and honey, before returning my gaze to the living picture beyond the window.

"Nothing quite as soothing is there?" she whispered lightly as she too looked upon the rainfall and listening to its music.

"Nothing but you" I sighed lovingly, having finished my mouthful of loveliness.

She gave a wry smile, amused by my unshaking admiration for her. We gazed out in silence for a few minutes, content to watch and listen to it all as I quietly ate, until Carmel asked a question she felt compelled to ask.

"There's nothing I can say to change your mind, is there?" she asked softly, her eyes drawn to a sheltering robin hiding itself from the rain beneath the tree's miniature canopy.

I looked up at her, a faint smile upon my face, gently rubbing the back of the hand she had placed upon my shoulder.

"My love, you know I would not leave you by choice. This is the only way my parting both brings you the least amount of pain, and is on my own terms."

"Are you so sure?" she asked, pulling up a chair beside me.

I spooned another mouthful of sweet porridge, thinking on her question as I chewed.

"No" I replied at last as I finished my mouthful "But it is the best plan I've got; I need you to remember me as I am, not what this illness will make of me."

She leaned her head upon my shoulder, her arm wrapped around mine. We sat there a while, looking out at the world as raindrops filled the silence with a new rhythm as a wind came through from the east, our hands as entwined as our hearts.

****

The waxy leaf, rimmed by a deep and bright yellow, felt smooth and artificial beneath my hand. I had taken it from a shrub that lined this part of the city, where many vines climbed the stone walls, some nearly disappearing up the protective heights of Bahvil's Great Wall – an unusual sight for a city that prides itself on its order and control over nature. I could hear nesting birds chirp and call as I walked the paths and roads of the oldest district of the city – the Old Town as it was commonly called – the weather warm but not unbearably so.

It is funny, for I was about to write how quiet it was, but there was so much noise, from the background hum of city life – the chirping of birds – the sound of old wood and stone creaking in the heat and shade, and the tumbles of wind that drew over and down from the tall expanse above; all this and more I could hear, but quiet was the sound that I heard.

Still living and breathing, as all things do, was the leaf as I twirled it between the fingers on my right hand as I strolled down the ancient paved walkway, worn flat and smooth by centuries of footsteps, unaware it had been plucked away from itself.

It was not a place I had visited much – if I could be said to have visited at all – and as such it held my interest much more than the other districts, or the castle I had come to call home.

I let out a sigh, heavy and cooling, as I stopped beneath an ancient oak of immense girth and size, its vast branches offering bountiful shade. As I stand there I watch the people, each going about their business as they had done so the day before, and the day before that. Some of the oldest families of Bahvil – most of them, truth be told – lived here in their ancestral homes, all considered noble or at least of high standing. Despite this, they offered cheerful smiles freely as and when I caught their eye, and I could see they were not false ones either; a pleasant reminder that not all nobles are like those of Blackwood. I regard them all with a thoughtful gaze, pondering upon their motives for staying in this place; did they stay because it had always been their families' home, or was it that the newer stone housing of the Plaza district seemed improper and less dignified? Perhaps it was the history of the Old Town that kept them here, and that the Plaza district lacked that for them.

According to one of the tales told to the children of Bahvil, this oldest part of their home allows the growth of vines in a tradition of honouring the first Countess, retaining a hint of the natural disorder of the surrounding wilds that was as near to her heart as her own children.

I am unsure if this is the true reason, but it is a pleasant one to be sure.

Carmel is with the twins and Agatha, who now teaches them metallurgy – and the importance of the blacksmith's trade to Bahvil's wellbeing – as well as offering Carmel that sisterhood that runs deep between them.

Some would question why I am not with them on such a day as this, why it is I have chosen to walk the backstreets of the city instead of being with friends and family; such questions miss the point.

An older lady – perhaps maybe in her early sixties – drops her basket of apples, their bright red skins shimmering almost as they roll away from her grasp. Without thought I help her gather them back into her basket, and she thanks me with a smile that I return, gifting me with one of the apples in gratitude which I accept, taking care to thank her back.

As I begin my walk back I bite into the fist sized fruit, its pink flesh juicy and ripe, the sweet taste tingling my tongue with excitement.

I feel my heart drop a little, sadness at the coming time when I cannot even miss such things briefly coming to the front of my mind.

I now stand in something of a peculiarity; a small garden of wildflowers dancing in a rainbow of colour, intersected by sandstone paths leading to well protected beehives. I watch the bees visit flowers as beekeepers gather honey, and marvel at the golden glory as they sample some and conclude it is delicious.

I take leave of this place, carrying on with my journey back, until I find a seat upon a short stone wall that ran along the side of a square of eateries; a place well frequented by the labourers and skilled hands of the city.

I waited there for what felt like an hour – though I doubt it was that long – taking note of how each interacted with the other, and the group as a whole, making a game of guessing who was friends with who.

I do love to go on walks, to stretch my legs and watch the world – one can learn so much doing so. As I get back to my feet I feel confident in my adopted people, for having watched them I can see the good about them, and it brings a smile to my face. As I walked back to the castle – this time with no stops – my thoughts turned to my friends, whom would be arriving at the castle that evening. They were to stay with us for the next few weeks or so, where we will spend much time together; though that time feels most short. Carmel and I have made arrangements for the running of the city over this period so our time together might not be interrupted, and a generous sum of coin put aside to be gifted to our friends as a way of saying thanks for being our friends, and for putting up with me all these years.

I find myself in a strange state, both happy and sad; though I shall gladly spend these last weeks with my chosen family.

* * *

My friends arrived a few days ago, and alas I had not been able to bring myself to write these last few nights, opting instead to dwell amongst my family and listen to their tales.

There came a moment when it was just Rose and I, standing by bush sized roses as the others played with the twins and Tau's children upon the lawn of the Rose Garden eatery. We made small talk a while, until she spoke of what was on her mind.

"I feel Maralin still feels for you" she whispered, almost accusing but not quite "In the way I feel for her."

I said nothing for a moment, watching Natilily laugh as Zaxx tickled her, before himself getting tickled by Nicole.

"I suppose you feel Carmel has the same fear" I said, smiling to myself as Zaxx was toppled by the combined might of the children and mercilessly tickled in retribution "But she does not."

"No?"

"She understands – as you will in time – that Maralin and I share more than just history, that we have something of a unique relationship, one that is deep and connecting"-I turn to look at her fully-"So I understand how it can seem, but I assure you she only cares about you in *that* way, far more than was ever between us."

She turned back to the others as they joyously frolicked in the sunlight.

"They seem so happy" she said after a moment "But I know how distraught Maralin is, how much she hurts over you – and how your children will hurt when...and I wonder how they can laugh knowing what is to come."

"It is their way" I shrugged "There is no point in spending this time locked in sorrow."

"But you mean so much to them."

"...I hope so."

She glanced at me from the side, silently thinking.

"I must ask, before I do not have the chance, why it is you have done the things you have done?"

"What do you mean?"

"All those investigations, standing against dark figures like Balford and Rothgar; why not live the quiet life?"

I take a moment to answer, looking fondly at Carmel as she giggles heartily at some joke Mazog has told.

"Honestly Rose, I could not say; I'm just compelled to do...what is right."

Moments pass, the children now seeing how many of them Tau can hold on one arm, before she then puts a hand upon my shoulder.

"I've never said this, for I never wanted to remember those times, but...thank you Prime, for saving me from that dark place."

"I did not do so alone; Zaxx and Maralin-"

"I have time enough to thank them for their part" she interrupted "and without you there would have been no rescue."

I give a smile, thinking upon how true or not that statement was.

"Might I ask a favour of you Rose?"

"Of course."

"When all is done and I am no longer...keep a watchful eye upon Maralin and Mazog...be gentle and kind with them" I asked her.

"You have my word" she replied solemnly.

"It has been an honour knowing you Rose" I smiled, looking at my family as a waitress from the eatery brings a tray of scones and jam towards them, my tone changing to a more cheerful one "Now I think we should re-join them; I can see those lovely scones of mine."

She gave a light laugh, the two of us making our way over to them, joining in on a feast of pure sweetness, Carmel once again getting a blot of cream on her nose, my heart melting in response.

CHAPTER FOURTEEN

892, 3ᴿᴰ Era twelve weeks after diagnosis

Carmel stood, hands firmly clasped around those of our daughters, as she looked at me teary eyed outside the city walls.

"I would rather you stayed. We all would" she said softly, the girls silent.

"I know…I would too"-I embraced the three of them in an all-encompassing hug-"But you heard what the physicians said, how this will end for me. I will not put you through that." I reminded her as I relinquished my grasp on them, taking a deep breath to steady myself as I did "Mazog will drive me to Norain, and from there to the base of Mount Evera-"

"He will watch you as you begin your climb?" Carmel interrupted.

"Yes, yes he will. Then he'll return to you, and tell you all of my triumphant climb to its summit" I forced a laugh as I looked about at my friends and loved ones "I have said my goodbyes to you all, so let this parting memory be a glorious one, a happy one."

"Daddy… we don't want you to go, we don't care how bad it gets so long as you're here with us" Nicole cried.

"Oh Nico"-I wrapped my arms around her, kneeling, Natilily joining her beneath my arms as her tears left her without a voice-"Nati…my beautiful girls…you are both more than I could have ever wished for or deserved. But do not fret my lovelies, I shall carry a piece of you both with me"-I held out the necklace they had made me-"and I shall forever be in here"-I pointed at my head-"and here"-I pointed at my heart-"and there'll be no getting rid of me, even if you want to" I smiled, getting back to my feet.

Maralin wiped tears away from her eyes, Rose holding her close, Zaxx putting an arm around them both as he gave me a comforting smile. Agatha stood stoic next to Bough, Tau and Ana; all of them with eyes that glistened with tears waiting to come forth. Mazog sat up on the coach, looking outward, refusing to look back; he knew if he did his emotions would overcome him.

As I began to walk away, and climb up on the coach, stopping to look back at them all, I gave them the largest smile I could.

"Do not think of me as gone, think of me as being very far away."

With that I clambered atop the coach.

"Drive as fast as you can Mazog" I whispered to him "I don't know how long any of us can hold back our tears."

He gave a silent, reserved nod as he flicked the horses' reigns.

*

Carmel let out a small tear as she looked upon her love as she waved him off, bidding him a silent farewell, knowing that if she spoke she would not be able to stop herself from falling to her knees and cry until there were no tears left; and she did not want that to be his last memory of her.

*

We had reached the base of Mount Evera, the winter snow still dominating the landscape. Our journey had been a mixture of silence and laughter, and Mazog had done his best to stay positive; he was a true friend, and I loved him like a brother, but the man needed to be more open about his sadness, for his sake. As we sat in the lodge at the base of the mountain, around an obsidian fire pit, the bitter cold of dusk having set outside with a thick frost, we talked about all sorts of things, from Agatha and her engines to old tales and our past adventures.

"-and who would have thought that it would lead to Maralin finding Rose" I half laughed as I sipped some warmed spiced milk.

"Aye; but I am most glad it did. Despite their recent disagreements, the two love each other dearly, and that's all I can ask for my dear sister"-he pulled the furred fleece around his shoulders a bit tighter together-"You know, I was surprised the two of you never got together."

"Yeah, she said the same thing to me a while back"-I rubbed my thumb around the warm mug in my hands-"But I met Carmel before...well, *before*."

"I hear you."

"Do you think...do you think I've done enough?" I asked him, my eyes not quite teary, but a gentle seriousness in their expression.

He looked at me a moment, silently weighing his answer to the question.

"Depends how you define 'enough', doesn't it?"

"True."-I took another sip of my milk-"But you know what I mean; for my girls, for the people...the world at large" I gave a little laugh "Do you think it has all been enough?"

He shuffled over and put an arm around me.

"Prime – Sylon – my dearest friend, I doubt you, or anyone else, could have done more with what you've had."

"Really?"

"Really."-He turned his gaze to the fire-"I'm not saying there weren't times you were a fool or just plain wrong, but your heart, that great big heart of yours that you often try to keep hidden, has always been doing the right thing, and that's what counts."

"I'm not sure that it does."

"Think about it Prime, what have we been talking about?"-he began to gesticulate with his hands-"We've solved mysteries, gone on adventures. You've fought fiends – rescued Carmel from that monstrous Balford – pushed for the betterment of a people that weren't even yours – a people who were prone to disliking you due to nothing but you skin – and made them better, made behave and act better too. You freed them, you believed in Agatha, and now the whole world is changing under the weight of your actions."-He looked back at me-"Why can't you see that?"

I mulled it over a few short moments.

"Because I can only see my regrets" I sighed "Just the way my mind works I guess."

Mazog sighed at that too.

"Well, there is one thing I can think of, that even you can't be a downer on."

"Oh?"

"Natilily and Nicole" he smiled "You helped make them."

I paused as I lifted my mug up to my mouth, before smiling the widest grin.

"Now see, *that* is what has made all else worth it."

*****

We stood embraced in a long hug at the base of Mount Evera, the lodge a few hundred yards or so behind us, at the beginning of the roughest looking climbing track I had ever seen.

"Now don't you go giving up halfway" he said as we released each other from our arms "Even if the track has long since passed."

"No worries there old friend; I shall climb to the top before you start your travel back to Bahvil" I smiled soberly.

He looked up at the gargantuan feat I would try to accomplish.

"Few have ever tried such a thing Prime; no one has ever made it more than a third of the way up."

"You doubt me?" I laughed.

"No, no. Just thinking how typical of you to try and do the impossible, even at the end."

"Aye" I turned my head to look at the great spire of rock and ice, its pinnacle well beyond the cloudline.

"So, the path ends a little under a third of the way up?"

"So they say."

I looked back at him.

"I shall miss you my brother."

"And I you."

We stood in silence a moment as I checked my rucksack, making a last-minute check I had all my supplies. As I was about to close it, Mazog handed me something from his satchel.

"What's this?" I asked as I took it from him.

"A little something to make you think of home." He smiled "But don't open it until...well, you know."

"Aye" I nodded "Thank you Mazog; please look after everyone for me, and make sure my girls don't forget me."

"I don't think they ever could. But yes, I give you my pledged word on that Prime."

"...How should we do this?"

"Do what?"

"Say goodbye?"

He rubbed his chin in thought before grinning as he came up with something.

"So, you'll be very far away then?" he asked, and I immediately knew what he was doing.

"Aye" I replied "So very far; might take me decades to come back you know."

"Perhaps longer."

"Aye. Maybe you all could come see me – pay me a visit and all that – at some distant moment in time?"

"Sounds like a plan, and do make sure to have the finest tea and mead ready for us; perhaps a scone or two too?"

"I'll try my best there" I laughed as I turned and began to walk away "Just be sure to take your time, I'll need all the time I can get to be ready for guests."

"Shall we be fashionably late then?" he shouted heartily as I made my way up the path, turning my head for one last look back.

"Better late than early." I shouted, waving at him one last and final time, before disappearing up the snow trodden path.

*

Mazog watched his friend walk up the path until he disappeared from view, not quite hearing his final words. He stood there a while longer, stuck in a dream of him running back down, and miraculously healed. How long did he stand there? One hour, two? He finally turned and walked slowly back to the lodge as the cold began to make his fingers stiff and pain-ful, a deep sigh releasing itself as the weight of never again seeing or hearing his chosen brother fell upon him. And for once, despite the freezing cold, he let out a little cry.

*

I had walked up the path to its termination, and had begun to climb the rocky, ice-covered slopes and climbs that had claimed the lives of many adventurers. It goes without saying, that there was no going back, and knowing that I was going to end regardless made me a bit more fearless than was advisable. I am unsure as to how long I had climbed as I took my first real rest, nestled into a small but stable outcrop of rock that gave me some small shelter, the sun looking a little over halfway through the sky.

I ate some dense fruit-loaf, taking sips of sweetened milk from a sealed flask to aid it going down. Tasty sure, but it was a chore to eat; nothing more packed with energy to climb with though. I was leant against my rucksack, having turned it somewhat to the side so I could access its top, looking out at the vast scenery before me. I was most surprised the weather had stayed clear enough for such a view to be possible, but most glad; I could see the Forrest City – Furnhaven – its vastness and monolithic size now but a small meadow of colour against the mountains and valleys, the streams and lakes and forests that dominated the landscape. As I put the remainder of the fruit-loaf back into the rucksack, I pulled out Mazog's parting gift. I looked it over, its wrapping clearly concealing a box of...something, and pondered whether to open it now or later, worried by the possibility of there not being a later. I looked back up at the sun, guessing roughly how long I would have sunlight, and how far up I could make it before being forced to stop.

I returned the gift to the rucksack, and after getting to my feet and hefting it back onto my back, returned to my climbing.

*

I had been fortunate enough to have found a near flat place to settle down for the night as dusk began to settle in, barely able to make a fire in the small shelter I had made for it out of loose rock. I snuggled into the thick and heavy bedroll that had been strung to the back of my rucksack, my fur hat tightly tied around my head. I had rested myself against a corner of rock where the snow had not fallen, likely due to the odd angle and shape of the mountainside, though it was still as cold as the ice around it. The fire was not large or strong, but its light and the little warmth it brought was most comforting as I drifted into a deep sleep.

I awoke in a shiver, a patch of snow having landed on my head from the rocks above. Thankfully it was morning, the sun about a sixth of the way through its rise. I had a breakfast of fruit-loaf and the last of my sweetened milk, and a smoked sausage that had that nice charcoal flavour that I had cooked before leaving for my climb. I looked at the gift once more as I returned the last third of the loaf to its spot in the rucksack, and

resolved to open it once I was at least half way; not that I would
be all that sure when that would be.

*

It was around mid-afternoon, on the third day, and I had
stopped for the sixth time over the last few hours. The shaking
had started to get worse, be it due to the exertion or cold – or
just the progression of my condition – I could not guess.

I sat in a seat of wrappings from the food I had eaten, which
slightly softened the feel of the ice beneath me. I held in my
hands the gift, and had slowly began unwrapping it, trying
quite hard not to drop it. It was a little wooden box, made of a
light mahogany, the crest of Blackwood etched into its front. I
fiddled with the gold coloured metal clasp on its side a moment, before finally opening it. Inside was crystal-glass bottle
of mead – the same kind we use to drink in Blackwood, made
with the thickest and sweetest honey – which had been brewed
specially for my birthday; the one that I would miss.

It made me smile I must say.

Beneath it was an etching of all of us, carved into slate, our
old Blackwood home etched on the reverse – Tau's handiwork,
if I'm not mistaken – that made me shed a tear or two.

I looked up at what remained to be climbed, then back down
to the bottle.

I wasn't sure how much longer I would be around, but now
that I was over halfway up, I decide I would enjoy this one last
drink once I had conquered this beast of a mountain.

*

I think I'm almost there now.

The view I had as I climbed above the thin layer of clouds was truly mesmerizing, the sight of cloud tops and the world beneath something only birds have ever seen, and I dare say most would be jealous of such a sight. My supplies are low, my bedroll and Mazog's gift being the heaviest things left. My food was all but gone, only the jam preserves remaining, my water had – has – frozen, but I can see the peak. It does not seem like one could stand or sit up there. I might settle here for a while; I'll see how I feel in an hour or so.

*

I sit on a plateau of sorts, not twenty yards down from the peak from what I can tell, small but more than roomy enough to not worry about being blown off the side. There is a sort of cave, if it can be called that, hollowed into the side of the spire of ice-covered rock behind me by years of weathering and wind, where I think I'll sit if or when the weather turns bad. But for now I shall sit here upon my rucksack, gazing out at the world beneath, and think upon my loves as I drink this fine honey-mead gift.

I think this might be where I stop; but I'll see if I can at least make it up there, seeing as I'm so close.

*

It is getting hard to write anymore, my hands are numb with the pain of the cold, and holding back my tremors is getting almost impossible. I made it up as far as possible, the true peak being a slippery pillar of ice-covered rock; ultimately I returned to the small plateau, and now sit upon my rucksack and bedroll in the little alcove I mentioned before. I can see the faint mists of rain shimmering in the distance as I look out beyond the mountain, deep clouds rolling over the land far from this sunny place, and as I watch I wonder whether they will roll over Blackwood.

I think this will be my last entry, and these my last few words; though I wish that I had something wise or noble to say, but alas I cannot think of anything bar Carmel, the twins and my friends.

So I think I shall end my story thusly:

Carmel, my dearest and brightest star, you were the one to show me what life is meant to be. How your beauty was not confined to your looks, but ran through your heart and mind, and your intelligence put me to shame more times than I could count. I love you my Bahvil rose, and without you my life would have felt empty, despite my friends.

Nicole and Natilily, lights of my life, you are my everything, the why of both my and your mother's lives. I can see you both have your mother's heart, her kindness and wit; never forget that you can be as much or as little as you want to be, and that when you love, you love with all you can give, but never for those that want you to be who you are not. I shall carry you with me always, and shall always, always be your guiding star in the night sky.

Mazog, Maralin, Rose, Zaxx, Tau, Ana and Agatha, and Bough too, you are not just friends, you are family to me. My brothers and sisters. I cannot put into words the thanks I owe you for standing with me through the dark times, or the joy of having you laugh alongside me during the good, but I can say this: I love you one and all, and hope your lives are as long and glorious as they deserve to be.

I have loved every moment, and every breath.

But I loved the ones where I met you Carmel, and you my beautiful daughters, most of all.

And now it is time for me to rest.

I am Sylon Primus "Prime" Blackwood, Count of Bahvil, and this is where my story ends.

A figure, cloaked in S͟h͟a͟d͟o͟w and D͟a͟r͟k stood looking over him, yet its feet were not touching the ground. It regarded him silently for a moment – or was it an eon? – before finally speaking its few words.

"You were wrong"

It stared down, expecting an answer from that which cannot talk.

"Your story doesn't end here"

H. Sulfwin grew up admiring the heathered hills and rolling mountains of Scotland, often going on long walks and hikes and getting lost (not literally, thankfully) in the green forests and woodland, and the great rocky boundaries between lochs, waterfalls and the peaks of mountains, admiring the castles and villages as they were passed. This, combined with a love of storytelling that started from a young age and a passion for medieval knights and dragons, led ol' Sulfwin down the path of becoming an author.

www.ingramcontent.com/pod-product-compliance
Lightning Source LLC
Chambersburg PA
CBHW050903130726
47900CB00015B/1899